To Tevi -
Thank you

KJK PUBLISHING

PRESENTS
THE
HORROR
COLLECTION

LGBTQIA+ EDITION

The Horror Collection

LGBTQIA+ Edition

The Horror Collection: LGBTQIA+ Edition © 2023
Kevin J. Kennedy

Edited by Ann Keeran & Kevin J. Kennedy

Cover design by Michael Bray

All rights reserved. No part of this publication may be reproduced, distributed, or transmitted in any form or by any means, including photocopying, recording, or other electronic or mechanical methods, without the prior written permission of the publisher, except in the case of brief quotations embodied in critical reviews and certain other non-commercial uses permitted by copyright law.

First Printing, 2023

Other Books by KJK Publishing

Collections

Dark Thoughts

Vampiro and Other Strange Tales of the Macabre

Merry Fuckin' Christmas and Other Yuletide Shit!

The A to Z of Horror

Anthologies

Collected Christmas Horror Shorts

Collected Easter Horror Shorts

Collected Halloween Horror Shorts

Collected Christmas Horror Shorts 2

The Horror Collection: Gold Edition

The Horror Collection: Black Edition

The Horror Collection: Purple Edition

The Horror Collection: White Edition

The Horror Collection: Silver Edition

The Horror Collection: Pink Edition

The Horror Collection: Emerald Edition

The Horror Collection: Pumpkin Edition

The Horror Collection: Yellow Edition

The Horror Collection: Ruby Edition

The Horror Collection: Extreme Edition

The Horror Collection: Nightmare Edition

The Horror Collection: Sapphire Edition

The Horror Collection: The Lost Edition

100 Word Horrors

100 Word Horrors 2

100 Word Horrors 3

100 Word Horrors 4

Carnival of Horror

Novels and Novellas

Pandemonium by J.C. Michael

You Only Get One Shot by Kevin J. Kennedy & J.C. Michael

Screechers by Kevin J. Kennedy & Christina Bergling

Stitches by Steven Stacy & Kevin J. Kennedy

Halloween Land by Kevin J. Kennedy

Dedication

I'd like to dedicate this book to my step daughter,
Rachel & her fiancé, Emma.

Foreword

I've been putting books together for a good few years now and I often work with the same authors more than once. I had a conversation with Mark Allan Gunnells where he told me he felt queer authors were underrepresented in horror fiction. As we chatted, he felt he had come up against prejudice in the industry and although he struggled on and managed to get a solid body of work out there, ut hadn't been easy. He also felt there weren't enough LGBT characters in horror fiction as well.

While I didn't think I could change the industry, I knew I could put a damn fine horror book together. I knew I could invite only authors who identify as LGBTQIA+, and I knew I could offer them the opportunity to write stories with characters that identified as such. That wasn't mandatory to the story, but it was an option.

It occurred to me upon setting out to do the book, I had no idea what most people identified as. I knew a load of authors, but I didn't know how they identified. I asked Mark for a few author suggestions. I posted info about the book in some LGBT groups and some horror book groups. I rarely do this as my anthologies are invite only but as the author list grew, mor recommendations came to me.

The book you hold in your hands is a compilation of my favourite stories that were sent in. That's what the entire Horror Collection is comprised of. You will know some of the names in this book and others may be new to you, but I can guarantee one thing. Each of them is overflowing with talent.

I never thought this series would see 15 books, but you are holding the 15th right now. It's a testament to the quality of the authors who send me their work and it has only continued thanks to the readers. As long as people keep following the series, I will keep it going. Books 16 & 17 are underway.

I've probably said enough. As always, I hope you love this edition of the collection. Happy reading.

Kevin J. Kennedy

Table of Contents

X-Treme
Callum Pearce

Husk
James Bennett

Toy Box
Mark Young

My Cin
Maxwell I. Gold

The Ride
Brandon Ford

Drop. Rock. Death.
James Lefebure

Effigy
Mark Allan Gunnells

Like Peonies
Caitlin Marceau

Wolves Within,
Zachary Rosenberg

The Loss
Michael R. Collins

The Acquisition
Lindz McLeod

Zero Sum
J. Daniel Stone

Bad Night at the Office
Emma K. Leadley

X-Treme

By

Callum Pearce

Josh and Luke edged closer to the beautiful creature handing out flyers in Liverpool town centre. Neither could tell if this person was male or female. They seemed a beautiful mixture of both. They were tall and slim with dark, immaculate skin. Their lips were dark red, their features strong and sharp. Their face looked as though it had been carved from a beautiful gemstone. Their short cropped hair and perfectly fitted suit gave the lads no more clues about this stunning person's gender. They were intimidatingly beautiful so you wanted to pull away and hide yet something was pulling both of them closer.

"Oh my god," Josh gasped seeing the name on the front of the flyer. "It's X-Treme. That would be an amazing first proper date for us."

Josh and Luke had met nearly a month ago and fallen into a sort of relationship but had yet to go on a proper date. Luke was always mocked by Josh for, as he said, wanting to live the straight life. Luke wanted all of those customs and expectations that Josh had always been happy to be free from. Josh liked to have Luke on his arm. At nineteen, he was eight years younger than Josh but Josh had been out as a queen since he was in school and visiting gay bars since the day he left the miserable place. Luke had only just sneaked out on the gay scene just after his nineteenth birthday. Sometimes, there seemed to be decades between them. Josh was enjoying saunas and dark rooms with multiple men whilst Luke had been at home summoning up the courage to look at the men's underwear section in his mother's catalogue. What was shocking and dirty to Luke had been a regular night out for Josh. The night they'd met, they'd fucked in the back alley behind the club. Anyone would think Luke had just done his first skydive the way he talked about it. It was his first real taste of danger and excitement. This only drew Josh to him, it was as though he could claim back some of his lost innocence by being closer to the innocence of others. Being young and attractive, he had something Josh could use.

"They wouldn't just be handing out flyers in town, It's the most exclusive night of the year," Luke mumbled ignoring the evidence right in front of him.

"Well, they are and I say we grab one quick," Josh replied pulling him closer to the androgynous creature that now held the key to a perfect first date.

X- Treme happened once a year, every Halloween. The venue would change each time and only those that had managed to get a ticket would receive an email informing them where to go.

Everybody knew about it and everyone had seen the logo sprayed in places around the gay scene. Neither Josh nor Luke had ever met anyone that had been.

"You, boys. Come closer." The stunning thing in front of them shooed away the people hanging around and beckoned Josh and Luke. At first, they both froze but then Josh pulled himself together and dragged Luke towards them.

"You seem very interesting," they said to Josh holding their hand out.

Josh was grinning from ear to ear, beaming with pride at being singled out. As he reached out for the hand they grabbed his and pulled him close. Leaning into his face they ran their tongue up his cheek then leaned back savouring the taste. Josh managed not to pull away or look surprised he knew that he had to look cool for this one.

" Nice. You will be very welcome," they sighed. The words seemed breathed out rather than spoken but they carried well to their intended target.

"Can I get a flyer then?" Josh asked trying to sound cool and hide the excitement that was building inside him.

"I think we can do better than that," the promoter breathed. Reaching into their pocket, they pulled out a small envelope. "Someone as special as you deserves an invitation."

Josh almost gasped but managed to hold it in. "Can I get one for him as well?" he asked, suddenly remembering that Luke was still with him.

"You're entitled to bring a guest," they said but turned and grimaced at Luke. "I would suggest a more interesting guest than this boy but it is of course your choice."

Luke was devastated hearing those words it felt like all of those times he had been the last to be picked for sports teams in school or the few times he had tried to chat someone up in a bar and they had looked right through him. He was even more gutted that Josh had said nothing in his defence just snatched the invitation from their hand. He was about to say something himself but the promoter just waved their hand to shoo them both away and gazed into the distance as if they no longer existed.

***

"I've just got the map in my email," Josh was buzzing with excitement.

"Great, can't wait," Luke grumbled.

"You can't still be sulking. Just grow up, you child," Josh snapped. "I'm sorry I didn't defend your honour, you poor, fragile, little lady. People would kill for an invitation to this night and I managed to get one for both of us. You could try being grateful instead of a whiny little bitch."

Luke hated the way Josh would speak down to him and it seemed to happen more every day. He was nothing like the man he had met that first night. Every time he wanted to push Luke into doing something that he didn't want to do, Josh would change. He would turn cold and dismissive. Sometimes, he would completely blank him for days until he got what he wanted. Usually a trip to the sauna or walk around the cruising area. He felt that he was being used as bait in these places to get men for his partner that would usually ignore him. Josh would always insist that twenty-eight in gay years was at least forty in regular. Luke had always imagined he would find a man and they would be enough for each other but his boyfriend always had his eyes open for something more. He had given up objecting because when he did, Josh would treat him like some naive child that needed to learn the ways of the queers.

"I'm sick of arguing about it," Luke said quietly. "let's just try to enjoy tonight."

"Go and get ready then. The invite says no costumes so you can wear those jeans I've put on the bed, your package looks brilliant in them. We'll have people swarming around us." Josh was laughing but Luke felt like shit. He was just some young bit of flesh for Josh to parade around in front of others. Of course, he did as he was told.

When they were both ready, Josh grabbed the invitation and the map that he had printed earlier and they rushed to the bus stop. They sat in silence for the journey. Josh was too excited and Luke too nervous to say a word. Luke could already imagine Josh mincing about like Mr Popular while he trailed behind either getting leered at or looked at like a skid mark on a hotel towel. He fidgeted and adjusted his cock and balls in the far too-tight jeans Josh had chosen for him.

Arriving at Dale Street, Josh pulled the map from his pocket and they hopped off the bus.

"It's supposed to be this way," Josh said marching ahead. "I don't recognise any of these street names but it should be a couple of turns off this one."

Luke stumbled along behind Josh who was checking out every street name they passed.

"Here! It should be one of the streets off this one."

They turned off Dale Street into a road that Luke didn't recognise. The area looked run down with grey, dull warehouses all the way along. There only seemed to be one street leading from this one so they both aimed for that. Josh gasped as they reached the corner.

"Not even a queue outside. This is super exclusive and classy," Josh declared.

"Or just not very popular," Luke teased.

"You still fucking sulking? You're not making a show of me in there."

"It was a joke, I'm quite looking forward to it," Luke lied.

Approaching the main entrance they saw a doorbell next to the closed door. A scream came from inside as Josh pressed it which made them both smile. The door opened slowly and a tall drag queen dressed as some sort of demon or vampire loomed over them. She must have been about seven feet tall in her platform shoes. She held out her hand and Josh went to shake it.

"The invitation," the drag queen hissed. She looked at Josh's outstretched hand as if he was trying to hand her a dead puppy.

"Sorry, yeah, erm, I've got it here." Josh stammered as he rummaged in his pockets. "Here you go."

The envelope was snatched from his hand. She didn't open it to check the details she simply held it under her nose and breathed in. Grinning, she waved them in. Luke realised she must have been dressed as a demon rather than a vampire as he had at first thought. He noticed that every single tooth was sharp and pointed rather than just the two fangs you would expect.

"Love those," he said pointing to the teeth and smiling sweetly. The drag queen ignored him completely and locked the door behind them.

There was a short corridor before they hit the main bar but they could already hear the retro, eighties, electronic beats and feel the vibration of the music. Pushing open the double doors, they made their way to the bar the smell of smoke, beer and poppers wafted around them.

"Please sir, take a seat," the man behind the bar said before they had the chance to speak. He had the same teeth and a masculine version of the same make-up as the drag queen from earlier. "Somebody will come to take your order. The first show is about to start."

"Well, this is fancy," Josh laughed leading Luke to a table that he liked. "You don't get this kind of treatment in Paco's bar."

"No, you usually need treatment after going though," Luke laughed. He was determined to enjoy this night as much as possible. Drinking and shows shouldn't be too much hard work.

The atmosphere was strange, Luke put it down to being a more classy place than those he was used to. Most of the tables had people at them, drinks sat in front of them and bar snacks but nobody seemed to be talking much nor eating and drinking. Every so often, one would lean into another and whisper something but nobody was talking properly. With the loud, eighties music blasting around them he expected a bit more shouting. He reasoned it was because the show was about to start but it still felt strange. He was happy when the barman came over to take their drink order as Josh had already fallen into his people-watching mode. Josh would check out the whole room and likely pick one or two to give the hard stare to. Luke always hoped that nobody would return it but they often did. Then, Luke was stuck in a threesome he didn't want or three days of mental cruelty for refusing. As inexperienced as he was, part of him knew that not all Gay relationships would be like this but then he only hung around with Josh's friends and Josh surrounded himself mostly with people like him.

The lights lit up on the stage and the music stopped the moment the barman put their drinks on the table. Josh pulled out his wallet.

"We take our payment at the end, sir," the barman said spinning around to leave them.

The curtains opened on three of the demonic drag queens, Different wigs and skin colours but the same strange make-up and teeth. The one in the middle walked down a few steps into the audience and took one of the guests from their seat. They didn't protest or act shy, they walked with her as if in a trance.

"He looks familiar," Josh whispered. "Do we know him?"

Luke shrugged and carried on watching the show. The drag queen attached the man's arms to some chains hanging at the back of the stage then proceeded to cut his clothes off. The man didn't resist at all and the other queens slowly approached. Each pulled out a knife like the one the first had used on his clothes.

"He must be a plant in the audience, no queen would let you cut their outfit up like that," Josh laughed.

The drag queens started running the knives over the young man's skin then one of them sliced clean and deep down the middle of his chest.

"What the fuck!" Luke gasped.

"It's make-up dumb-arse. Look he's not even reacting."

It was true. The man just hung from his chains as the other two drag queens sliced deeper and then pulled the skin away with their claw-like nails. He turned his head and looked towards their table staring straight into Luke's eyes.

"That's amazing," Josh exclaimed. "I'm sure I know him from somewhere though."

Luke could guess where Josh knew the man on stage from but said nothing. He couldn't take his eyes off the disgusting spectacle in front of him. The queens were ripping chunks of flesh from the man's body and chewing on them with their sharp teeth. Blood ran down their chin and neck and chunks of flesh stuck to their costumes. Music started to play, it sounded like monks chanting in tune. The queen that had brought the man on stage dug into his chest and pulled out what looked like a beating heart. She danced around the stage with it before devouring it in front of a silent audience. The other queens danced around her holding other organs that they had stripped from the hanging body. The man just stared towards their table, this time he was staring at Josh . He was staring back, seemingly loving every minute of the show. As the first queen danced at the front of the stage, the other two went back to the hanging man and started cutting off small chunks of flesh and placing them on silver trays that sat on tables at either side of him. The main queen hit her grand finale and backflipped twice on the stage before disappearing. There was no puff of smoke or sparkles, she screamed as flames seemed to rip through her body in seconds. Then she was gone. The other queens took the trays out into the audience.

"I wonder if Penn and Teller have seen this act," Josh Laughed. "They would shit."

"Might be too much even for them," Luke had to look away from the sight on the stage. The still living man with his organs and flesh now being passed around the audience as hors-d'eouvres. Luke was glad that the trays had emptied before the drag queens had made it to their table. He knew it couldn't be what it seemed to be but he didn't want to have it thrust in his face either way.

When the drag queens had returned to the stage and the curtains had closed the happily familiar eighties tunes started up again. A few men got up from their tables and walked towards the back of the bar. One of them winked at Josh causing him to follow him back with his eyes.

"I think they've got a dark room," Josh seemed excited, Luke's heart sank. "Let's go and take a look."

"What you're feeling horny after watching that?"

"We don't have to do anything just take a look. This is a one-night-only thing it would be a shame not to see all of it."

Luke knew exactly what Josh wanted to see but he downed his drink and made his way to the back of the bar with him. The dark room seemed pretty typical of others Josh had dragged him through. Tub of free condoms and lube, corridors with private rooms and some less private rooms for the exhibitionists. Men hung around watching to see if anything nice came their way. The first room they passed was set up like a jail cell. Through the bars, they could see a man standing naked and a man kneeling in front of him. The man was moaning and rolling his head in ecstasy.

"No fucking way, I know him. He's an ex." Josh said gesturing to the naked man just as the kneeling man turned round with a face full of blood and those sharp, spiked teeth. Blood was gushing from the top of the legs of the naked man.

"Jesus!" Luke exclaimed. "what the..."

"Oh that's brilliant, even the darkroom is part of the show. Genius." Josh was pretty impressed. "I didn't even know he was an actor, can't remember what he did, shame they've covered his cock with all that make-up though. It would put even yours to shame."

Luke felt the words like a knife, the only thing Josh ever complimented him on was his dick and now even that was being overshadowed by someone that was currently pretending to have his chewed off. Josh moved quickly to the next room and turned pale.

"Something isn't right here," Josh seemed panicked all of a sudden. "This isn't a show."

Luke looked into the room and saw a man nailed to a cross grinning out at him. He followed Josh as he rushed to the next room. After looking in there, he turned and threw up on the floor.

"What's going on?" Luke was panicking now too.

"They're all exes."

"Well, that's hardly surprising. The gay scene isn't that big round here and you've kept yourself busy on it..." Luke stopped because he could see something was very wrong with Josh, he was shaking and his skin was like chalk.

He looked into the room and saw a man staring back at him. There was no gory scene just a man standing alone staring at people who passed.

"It's just a weird coincidence. Very weird but so a few of your exes are involved."

"That one killed himself five years ago," Josh was sobbing now. "I found his body in my fucking living room. He can't be here."

Luke grabbed Josh by the arm and dragged him back the way they had come. As they left the dark room area, they didn't come back out into the bar. Instead, they came out into a small room with a hospital bed at one side and the androgynous promoter that had given them their invitation sat behind a large desk. A door slammed shut behind them, Luke turned and tried desperately to open it but it wouldn't budge. By the time he turned back, he saw that Josh was lying on the hospital bed and the Promoter had moved over to stand beside it. Luke's feet and arms felt as heavy as lead, he couldn't move anything but his head and face. The promoter took a scalpel from her pocket and ran it around Josh's face as he screamed in agony. Luke felt sick but could do nothing to stop her.

"You know he thought himself to be quite the most beautiful thing to walk the earth." She peeled the skin from his face in one piece Josh had stopped screaming but his eyes still flicked from left to right. "I don't see it myself," she laughed holding the face skin out in front of her. "Boy, he hated you for your youth and beauty. He hated them all so much."

"Why are you doing this?" Luke managed to whisper.

"It's my job, I lead people from this realm to their next." they were slowly removing Josh's clothes. He put up no resistance. He just lay there as they adjusted him to make it easier but his bulging, lidless eyes flicked this way and that.

"Why us?" Luke began, "What did we ever do?"

"Oh not you dear, you're an innocent. I can't touch you. I was hoping he would bring a more interesting guest." They laughed a deep raspy laugh. "The nights are wild when we get two sinners and it tends to take longer before they figure it out."

"This whole event was just for him?" Luke asked. "What could he have done that was so wrong."

"Not just for him," The creature explained. "A hundred tickets are given out each year and a hundred people walk through that front door. But the door leads to many different places. Everyone gets their own waiting room until it is time for the main event."

She plunged her hand straight into Josh's chest and ripped something dark and hard out of it. "See, his heart really is cold and black as you have suspected at times," she rubbed the cold wet thing against Luke's cheek.

"But why?" was all Luke could think to say.

"He has been doing my work for most of his life. All of those men you have seen tonight and many more have been ushered to hell by your charming friend here." The demon explained. "He pollutes them and tortures them, drives them insane, makes them hate themselves and everyone else. Of course, he pretends to be helping them, these innocent boys that cross his path even to himself. Helping them to grow up faster than they should, showing them the world he would like them to see."

"He's not evil, he's a good man." Tears were running down Luke's face.

"He was a charming man, I will give you that. That doesn't mean good. This man has a body count worthy of the greatest serial killers, he just managed to do it without getting his own hands dirty."

Luke noticed that Josh's eyes were still moving around in the raw flesh. The demon was running its claws over his stomach, Scratching deeper with every stroke. The room shifted around them. Now all three were standing next to the cell in the darkroom that had caused Josh to react so badly.

"This one was abused all of his life by his family, Your friend here saw him as perfect fodder to practice his manipulation on." The young man in the cell was sobbing and slicing his arms with a Stanley knife. "The trouble with these fucked up kids though is that whilst they are easy to manipulate, they become tiresome pretty quickly to a man like our Josh here. Whining, crying, trips to casualty when they go too far with their self-harm. But they're oh so easy to push over the edge when you get bored.

The light flashed off and then back on. Luke could now see the living room of a home with the man's body lying in the middle of the floor, grey skin and wide-open, dead eyes. An empty bottle of tablets lay next to him. He saw Josh walk into the room and casually step over the body with a glass of wine in his hand. He sat down drinking it for a moment then started practising crying for when he called the police.

"He beat them all down and destroyed them. They came to us perfectly primed. Some went on to murder or abuse others. Many went into drugs and crime or just abused themselves until they destroyed the lives of all around them. All because of the pollution and cruelty your friend here dripped into their souls. The little shit could end up with my job when he has served his sentence." The demon laughed again. "Speaking of... you should run along now, we need to get on with everything we have in store for him. She nodded to the faceless, heartless shell of what used to be his partner."

"You're not just going to let me go," Luke began.

"Why on earth not, will you bring the police to this empty warehouse and tell them all of the horrors you've seen?"

Everything around them including Josh disappeared. Luke and the demon stood alone in an empty, derelict building.

"Now run along, I'm sure I will be seeing you again before long. Sin finds everyone in the end. Especially ones who choose the kind of men you are drawn to."

Luke suddenly thought of the ranting priests and words of his parents.

"Ah you're wondering about the gay sex, you've been told that was a sin." the demon laughed.

"It is though isn't it?"

"Nope, not on the list," The demon smiled. "Now run."

The demon's words dug deep into his mind and his body turned and ran from the building without him even intending to. The door slammed shut behind him and he stopped to catch his breath. He could see the building was empty through the broken windows, the street was empty too.

Husk

By

James Bennett

I'm a face in the rain. A sketch of shadows under streetlight. Mostly I'm a memory, a ghost of myself. Adam was my name. It's confusing, but every time I even the score for us, I grow stronger. Isn't that why I'm here, standing outside the restaurant, born of tears and blood? I'm the *shadow* Adam. Your husk.

The wind, a swirl of dead leaves gives me shape. The rain silhouettes my shoulders. Fumes from a passing car lend the hint of a jacket, a turned-up collar. My hair wet, the half-remembered colour of rust. A fluttering crisp packet picks out my face – a face you'd know if you looked out of the window. You'd see me, standing here on Blank Street, Nowhere. Know me like your know your own reflection.

I'm what you left behind.

When you look out, you see only rain. The city in your eyes, a washed-out limbo. Buildings that don't care about you, that don't know you like I do. You're laughing and drinking, amused by something the man sat opposite you has said. Miles? I caught his name as I followed you from the station, you a torch in the dusk. I can see what you see in him.

Those dark looks you were always a fool for. His rich brown skin. The voice you could bathe in. The hands that'll grip you as you fuck... It's your birthday. Why wouldn't you flirt? You don't know about Brick yet. Or the killings to come.

We're the same, two sides of a mirror. One silver. One black. But I can't say it's my birthday. I began in the garden shed, in the mosaic on the floor. In the rage and the fear you cast aside.

Ghosts don't have birthdays. But the living sometimes have ghosts.

Oh, Adam. What happened to us? We used to be so close.

Where did it start? This seed?

"I see how you look at me, fag."

Ah yes. You were on your way home from school. Aged sixteen, circa two years ago. Brick said that as he stepped out from behind the big tree. I remember the smell of grass on the playing field. The janitor mowing it, the slaughter of bugs in the air. Brick blocked your path. You saw his fist by his side, trembling. The fist of his *face,* screwed up in disgust. His smirk at the cruelty to come.

"Don't flatter yourself." You knew he meant the changing rooms after football practice, Adam. You knew what he was getting at, same as you knew he was wrong. When the boys in class were showering, you tended to look at your feet.

You tried to laugh it off. Brick wasn't laughing though. In fact, he looked hurt by your rejection. There was this… atmosphere, I remember it well. It made no fucking sense whatsoever. There wasn't time to examine it, because Brick was punching you. You fell to the ground. Blood in your mouth. Your ribs on fire as he kicked you. It went on and on. Was it a relief when he ripped your face from the earth, spat on you? Shock carried you like the wind, borne with laughter in your ears. Across town. To your house.

In the garden shed – there was no way Dad could see you like that – you sat and licked your wounds.

Tears and blood fell to the floorboards, bright in the dust.

A beginning.

Ghosts have memories. How weird is that? Mine, of course, are only recent. They began last Thursday at the 'party' in your apartment. You had to make a song and dance about it, didn't you? You stood there in your tee-shirt. *Nevermind.* Was Dad going to kick off again? Hit you like when you were ten? Hit *us,* I should say. Only you remember the *feel* of it, his knuckles... That day you spent in the shed thinking on your sins. Like you did after Brick beat you up. Like you did after Dad. The tears and the blood. The shame. It's an abstract. A recollection torn from me like tears and blood. Like skin and bones were torn from me when you decided to up and leave.

"I'm sorry," you told Mum and Dad. You'd promised yourself you weren't going to apologise. "This is who I am."

Shouting ensued.

"No son of mine is a poof", Dad said.

Mum cried. She held her pocket Bible in trembling hands. "How could you do this to us?"

I'm sorry, you wanted to say. *I'm sorry for not being who you think I am. But every day, every hour, I was fading, you see. Rubbed out by your expectations. What you think of me. What you want for me. What you want for yourselves. Soon I would've disappeared completely...*

They cried. They mourned you to your face. No one asked you if you were in love. If you were alone. If anyone had hurt you. So you showed them your scars. Another thing you'd sworn not to do. Oh, how you betrayed us, Adam. My little Judas. All eighteen years of us standing in the living room on Any Street, Anywhere, showing them the lines you'd made with the razorblade.

Don't you understand? you said. Shouted. *I hated myself. I wanted to die.*

They didn't understand. They left, the door slamming on a November night. Like the door of the garden shed. Or a coffin. The funeral was over before they'd put you in it.

But a part of you *did* die last Thursday. It honestly did.

And I came back.

I see how you look at me.

They don't call him Brick now. *He* doesn't call himself that now. The Arsehole Formerly Known as Brick got a job in the local shoe shop. No one likes grownups with nicknames, so he's plain old Bill now. Oldies don't take us seriously as it is and Brick was a bully's name. A hero on the football field. In the Court of the Changing Rooms. That kind of shit doesn't fly in the real world. Bill found that out last Friday night. He was polishing the shoes in the window display. Then he locked up shop for the manager and got on his bicycle.

In a swirl of dirt and leaves, I followed him. The first time he looked back, his pug of a face squinting in the gloom, I saw the unease in his eyes. The dark comes on quick in winter. So did I, hissing through the trees beside the cycle path. He sensed something then. He pedalled a little faster, through the cut towards the railway bridge. Keeping up wasn't a problem; I'm empty enough to ride on the wind. In some way I was attached to him. I could see his trophies gathering dust on a shelf, a reminder of past glories. It pulled me on like a rope, passing through whatever lies behind the air and pushes against the emptiness. The next time Brick – let's call him that for old time's sake – glanced over his shoulder, he saw me. Saw *something,* at any rate. Swooping under the streetlights, invisible, I saw him look up. His eyes were full of sodium, circles of fear. I gusted towards him, viciously. He had to cover his face. He let go of the handlebars to bat at the swirling grit.

You hit us, I said out of the darkness.

His bike pranged. It crashed into the wall of the bridge. Flesh met tarmac with a satisfying thump. There was nothing to him but meat. Brick groaned, but he didn't sprawl there long. He had bigger concerns. A troubling of the branches above. A flicker of the streetlights. A voice that belonged to no one. One he might've recognised, if he'd had time.

When we got home and took off our shirt, your shoe had left an imprint on our back.

"Please," Brick said. He thrust out a hand, flailing at the murk. No one can fend off a shadow. "It was years ago. We were in school..."

Sweet that he remembered.

It isn't over. It never is.

Brick was crying. He covered his face. There wasn't much for him to see. Only the bridge. The trees and the night. A spindle of dirt. He didn't want to look anyway. I pushed against the wind. Against his face. A damp patch spread across the front of his trousers. Thank God I couldn't smell it.

In the distance, the rattle of a train.

"He was looking at me in the changing room!"

That isn't true. It's what you tell yourself.

Adam was too scared to look. I know that. I was there. How the tiles, the noise pressed down on us. Every snap of a towel a bullet in our ears. Adam was too scared to look. He thought that if he did a siren would go off above his head, flashing and wailing.

And everyone would see.

"Get the fuck away from me!"

Brick was climbing to his feet. Fear will do that to a person. He was brawny once. Much like that day on the playing field, Adam still wouldn't have stood much of a chance. But Adam didn't have the wind on his side. It was a simple thing to blast the bastard over the wall. I'd timed it just right. The six o'clock train slammed into Brick's tumbling body at a hundred miles per hour. He burst apart like a melon. His spine went one way carrying his head. His legs another.

When I found him beside the track, he looked uglier than usual.

Still, he tried to crawl away in the undergrowth.

He didn't get very far.

Soon after that day on the playing field we started to use the razor. One night we got up and went to the garden shed. Dad was right. We were a waste of space. We'd come to suspect we were different, anyway. When the lads in class talked about girls, boasting about a hundred dirty things, Adam, well… we found we had nothing to offer. We knew we were supposed to be turned on by it. The other boys were. We could tell by the way they shifted themselves, plucked at their trousers. Chuckled and coughed. It became clear that *they* were turning us on. Making us hard. Burning in our cheeks.

Desire has a smell, I think. So does fear. We must've stunk of it. That's where the idea of the siren started, invisible and waiting. We started pushing it down. Burying it. Us. We started to change the subject. Then, when Brick laughed at us – *virgin!* – we avoided the guy talk completely. We went to the library. Hid in books. It's the story of a thousand boys like us, Adam. It's corny as fuck. But none of their stories are like ours.

We thought we could get it out of us. We thought if we associated the thought with pain, it would fix us. God was useless. There was nothing in His book but blame. We gritted our teeth. We sat in the dark. Drew steel over our skin. We wept, holding ourselves when no one else would.

Make it stop. Take it away.

It isn't always God who listens.

Blood and tears speckled the floorboards. Enough over time to make a mosaic.

All that hate. It had to go somewhere.

I'm stood here on this rainy street, remembering. Why not? I'm a memory, after all. Well, a little more perhaps, seeing as I get to even the score. It's something to do with the fear, I think. And the blood, which gave me substance. I'm half-shadow and half-air, but litter flutters to a stop when it hits me. Puddles ripple when I pass by. The more I remember, the more the world allows for my presence, it seems. It makes sense that blood would form a bridge from the emptiness. *The blood is the life.* I read that somewhere. Saw it in some dumb film. Blood is where I came from, that's for sure. Leaking in drops. Fed on tears. Blended with dust on the shed floor. With rags and dried paint. The husks of dead insects. A nightmare brewed behind doors.

I got bored of watching you in the restaurant. All your laughter, the way you stroke your throat as you talk to Miles or whoever. It's such a come on and he knows it. His eyes never leave your face. He thinks it's happening, first date or no. When he pays the bill and you exit, his arm is around your shoulder. I whirl through the rain and the headlights of cars to follow you. That's what shadows do.

At the door to your apartment – you're such a cliché – I watch you from the stairwell as Miles leans in to kiss you. He touches your hair. Looks into your eyes. If you weren't so distracted, you might notice me there, a not-quite-solid shape. A puckering of angles and space. Of course you're not paying attention. Jealousy, cold and bright, stabs through me. How fucked up is that? Part of me envies you. Part wants to rip the guy away from you, hear his bones crack against the hallway wall. What happened to *my* say in matters? Six months ago you'd have gone to the shed for even thinking like this. We were together. *Together.*

It was all that counsellor's fault. Rachel Marsh.

When did it begin, the pain? She asked us.

Adam, you're kissing him back. He's taller than you. His weight is pressing you against the door. The edge of the frame is between your buttocks like a promise of what's to come. And I'm thinking about the counsellor, Marsh. Whether I should pay her a visit as well. The throbbing in my head makes it hard to focus. When there's heightened emotion like this it's uncomfortable. It makes perfect sense, seeing as I am you. Or *was*. I can feel you growing hard. The same way you can feel Miles growing hard. You shiver at his size through his jeans, another unspoken promise.

"Miles..." you say. "I'm not -"

That's when the lightbulb shatters, dousing the hallway in darkness. I don't want to look. I don't want to see.

"What the hell?" Miles says. His jacket is up, shielding you from the flying glass. I guess you like that he did that.

Still...

"Miles, I'm not ready for this."

Miles takes a breath. You expect snark. Resentment. Maybe he'll call you a timewaster like that other guy did. Instead, he smiles and strokes your cheek.

"They hurt you too, huh?"

You're no longer thinking. You turn to unlock the door and you drag him inside.

I'm a whirlwind. I'm a fury. I'm out of here. The hallway window shatters, not that there's anyone around to hear it. And I take to the night.

I am *not* going to watch you fuck.

Anger is a magnet, drawing me to the source. You better believe I was pissed off. And the truth is the both of us know where the pain began. When you were six years old. When you saw him punch Mum for the first time. You thought about it yourself, the razorblade between our fingers in the shed, slick and red. We wondered, our sixteen-year-old self (*selves*), whether we shouldn't take it out on him in the room upstairs. We stood there, watching him sleep, his mouth a well. His throat bared. It was only our fist closing on the blade that forced us to step away. To forget the whole thing. It doesn't matter now. Whether we imagined it or not. It's *in* us. It's a thing. And it gives me a foothold in the emptiness.

I roll with the wind. That's how I find myself flying along the freeway of all places. Lights leave an orange smear above. The shutter speed of passing bridges. *Click. Click. Click.* Dad is driving home.

He's the boss at the factory now, grey haired and bellied. Respected. He gets the job done. He's changed his shirt for one identical to the one Mum laid out for him last night. When she was downstairs, he made sure to pack it in his briefcase. He took a shower in the hotel. It's the only way to be sure there's no lingering trace of perfume on him. Mum would notice a change of clothes, he thinks. She doesn't know about the girls downtown. At least she tells herself that. Dad genuinely believes he's doing what any man would. That it's part of who he is. It's funny when you think about it. He sees his needs as reasonable even when he's cheating on his wife.

You're the pervert, remember.

Dad is listening to Elton John ('Tiny Dancer', I think), crooning along without a shred of irony. *Elton!* It doesn't help my mood much. On the one hand, I lack the bond you two have. You took that shit with you, Adam. Your daddy *issues.* On the other, I'm grossed out by looking into his soul. Seeing all his dirty little secrets.

That's where Brick comes in handy. Or the mess I made of him. I have enough juice to fuck with the car radio. The music washes out in a blast of static. There's the whine between stations. Then he's listening to his own voice. His Bible bashing over the airwaves.

"It's against nature. Against God. You're contributing to the death of the human race."

He said this, glaring at you over the pages of the Book in his lap. You'd gone to see him with beers on Saturday, tried to talk to him about it. *I can't help who I am* et cetera. He didn't even ask you to sit down. Blamed you for all of the evils in the world. The destruction of everyone, everything. He called you a plague. His only son. These people… they never think about the pain they cause. That it never goes away.

I won't go away.

"Jesus!"

Dad – *your* Dad – might well invoke the name of his Lord and Saviour. I am filling up the car. I am shadows uncoiling, a black serpent in the cramped space. Just like I uncoiled in the shed. He thinks I'm smoke, I guess. First thing he does is slam on the brakes. Then, one hand on the wheel, he tries to roll down the driver's side window. But I'm holding it fast. He gives a little wail as darkness engulfs the car. The streetlights, the motorway eclipsed.

The radio squeals. Half music. Half bigotry.

Homophobia. The greatest hits.

There's a second, a moment of regret. He thinks about you, Adam. Honestly he does. *Sorry.*

The wheels screech on tarmac – he's struggling to recover control – and the car is slewing to one side. I don't think I can hold him like this for much longer. I'm writhing shadow and wind. So I let myself go. I'm a whirlwind of blood and glass (I kept the shards from the hallway window), exploding in the car.

Dad screams. I'm in his cheeks. His eyes.

We are a flower of flame as the car slams through the railings of the freeway.

Acceptance is a terrible thing.

"Learn to accept who you are," Rachel Marsh said, sat in her plush green armchair in her office.

Marsh was the kind of woman that people admire. She looked crisp in her nice grey suit. Marsh emanated patience. It was an aura around her. She wore just enough make up, but that's up to her. There was a photo of her with another woman on her desk. They looked happy, but we were never going to be friends. We went there full of shadows. It wasn't a good starting point for pleasantries.

We were on the couch.

"I hate myself and I want to die."

OK. We didn't actually say that. But that's what it amounts to. Kurt Cobain said it best. I'm sure he wouldn't mind us borrowing it, considering. Hey, maybe I could ask him. But then I'm in the emptiness and Kurt...well, Kurt is really *gone.*

"Hate is a poison, Adam," Marsh told us. "It seeps into every corner of your life, polluting everything. Most of all you."

Soon after that you locked up the shed. The shed in your mind as well. You threw away the razorblades. They had become blunt. It was hard to see which bits were blood and which rust. You hadn't used them in quite a while. Into the trash they went, wrapped in newspaper and a faint, frightening hope.

Soon enough, we found ourselves in bars. Under mirrorballs. In strange beds. We were *trying.* Under every sweep of laser, with every discarded condom, you were growing brighter.

And I was fading, Adam. You didn't care. You left me behind. Dust. A pile of rags. A mosaic of blood and tears. A husk.

But Marsh was right all the same.

Yeah, she was right about that.

Poison.

Somewhere. Some town. Miles is walking home from your apartment. It's dawn. We're in that dull grey light that seeps into everything at this hour. The suburbs smell of dog shit and dew. Miles left you sleeping. He has to go to work. The truth is he's pretty pleased with himself. You can see it in his step. Annoyingly, Miles really likes you. That just won't do.

The streetlights are blinking as he reaches the underpass. *Blink. Blink. Blink.* One by one they go out. Through each pool of shadow I drift. Low to the ground. Clothed in litter. If it wasn't for the roar of traffic, Miles would hear me, the tinkle of glass in the wind. Oh, I'm more than that now. More than blood, rags and glass. More than *hate.* The car crash was fuel too, you see. Your Dad's dying scream has sharpened me. I'm less empty than before. But I wait until Miles is halfway through the underpass, passing graffiti that wishes him dead, and then I make my move.

Shadows engulf the entrance to the underpass. *I* engulf the underpass. At first, Miles doesn't notice it. Concrete makes everything grey. The tunnel stinks of piss and death. If Miles runs now, he could probably break through the web of shadows. I'm not strong enough to hold him. I have to move fast. Still, there's a certain satisfaction in watching it dawn on him, the same way it dawned on Brick and Dad. His eyes grow wide. A curtain falls over the end of the tunnel. There is no light at the end.

Smoke? he wonders. *A collision?* He knows it isn't the case. Sweat glitters on his brow. He doesn't know what to do. When he turns back he sees me. Me and my cloak of shadow. Blood and dirt floods the underpass. Rags weave in the wind. An odd spot of paint. He makes out the chips of glass that pass for my eyes. The flames of my smile.

"Adam..?"

He knows I'm not Adam.

He isn't yours, I tell him. *He's mine.*

Miles is trying to speak. There's a sound in there somewhere. It's no surprise he can't get it out.

I burst into flames. I carry the car crash with me now. I'm feeling much stronger. *Brighter.* If I push, I can fill up the underpass in no time. The shadows have him cornered. If I push, the flames will rip through the tunnel from end to end. It's all over for Miles.

Grief will bring you back to me, Adam. All the fear. All the hate.

This time, you'll never leave.

If I *push* -

"Stop this."

I spin in shadow and flame. And I see you. Adam. The real you. You're standing in your jeans. An open shirt. You pulled your trainers on without socks. Fuck, you were in such a hurry, weren't you? The space in the bed next to you got you running for the door. You didn't know what you were going to say to him. You don't know now.

Oh, Adam.

Miles screams, a shatter of echoes. He tells you to run. To get away. But we're not listening to him.

You left me, I say. *You left me behind.*

Fuck, I am angry. I'm a fucking funnel of fire. I'm a shoeprint on your back. I'm a razorblade in the dark. I'm a pocket Bible in trembling hands. I'm rags and dust and blood and glass. I'm your shadow. Your husk. And you should be afraid of me.

You only smile.

"No," you say. "I didn't."

Before I can stop you, you step forward. You step forward with your arms spread wide.

You embrace me.

Us.

The sun has gone behind the clouds when we walk out of the underpass. Miles is shaking. He winces when I take his hand. We're a little hot from our tantrum, you see. All the same we know that Miles likes us. *Really* likes us. Enough to overlook the darkness inside of us. The blood we've spilled. The shit we never wanted. The poison.

We smile at him. He smiles back, uncertain.

He understands. We know he does.

It isn't over. It never is.

Toy Box

By

Mark Young

Danny.

Slipping his coins into the machine, Danny hankered for his daily shot of cheap coffee. Piping hot brown water dribbled into the beige plastic cup that fell into the slot. He often found himself counting the drops before they fully drained into the cup. It had become a habit all too quickly since he began work at Manpower Inc. But the routine offered stability. It was also one of the biggest buzzkills for the excitement and adventure Danny craved – that he once dreamt of as an optimistic teenager. Being a goody-two-shoes was a stress-free life. It was also a very boring one.

It was a lesson learned within the first few months of starting his first job out of university. Two years of lectures, a ton of debt and an unfinished BA Honours in Civil Engineering was enough to prompt him to take up this data inputting job full time. It was as unfulfilling as his studies had been, but at least it gave him a modicum of income to rent a room in a flat-share with a guy who was hardly ever there. He could go out when he pleased. Treat himself to some clothes. Afford a few niceties in life.

Upon returning to his desk, he logged into his computer and stared into the screen. Mesmerised by the flashing green cursor and the scroll of text that followed. The monitor went dark while booting up and Danny was faced with his reflection. The dark circles under his eyes glaring back were the result of long hours staring into this abyss. How he longed for a night out. If only the tiredness had come from partying then at least he would've had something to show for it.

Then it was decided! Tonight would be the night he'd venture into town. It was Friday after all. Adrenaline must've kicked in at the excitement of it as he sat up and spun in his chair – the moment soured by the rows of empty cubicles waiting to be filled and no-one to share his decision. Getting in so early, he really didn't do himself any favours. It benefitted no one but the company. He had no-one else but himself to complain about when he got tired and felt overworked.

He took a sip of coffee. It'd be a while before the caffeine kicked in but at least the scorching water burning his tongue jolted him out of his funk.

Hmm. Now. Danny drummed his fingers on the desk. *Where to go? And what to wear tonight?*

***

The thump of the bass rattled the fire doors and echoed down the side street. The hum and chatter. He loved the buzz. The anticipation. The brewing excitement of what the night might unfold. Even if the night air was nippy and he shivered a little as he waited alone in the queue. Suffering the cold for a few minutes was always worth it. Because, once inside, Danny would skip standing in line for the coat check and head straight for the bar.

***

"Rum and coke, please, darling." Danny leaned across the bar and air kissed the barman Keith. Fully aware his arse looked good in his new tight jeans.

"Haven't seen you in a long while," Keith called out, pouring the drink. "How you been?"

"Oh, not bad. Working lots, you know. Debts to pay. Holiday to save for."

"Oh, nice. Where you thinking of going?"

"Dunno. Somewhere where there's a bit of nightlife, I guess."

"Gran Canaria. Sieges. Mykonos. That's where all the boys go."

"I'll have to look into it."

Keith handed over his drink and winked. "This one's on the house. Have a good night."

Danny raised his glass and bowed his head, turned and headed off into the crowd.

Eyes like invisible laser beams, darting across the dance floor. Mist pumping out of the smoke machine, bending the rays from the disco lights into weird and wonderful shapes.

The smell of sweat and aftershave and spilt alcohol.

The heat – caused by the gyrating mass of clubbers from all walks of life.

Then there was the music. Ah the sweet, sweet sound of music. Booming from the speakers and around the walls of the club. Shaking the body, head to toe. Voices from the crowd, rising into a rousing chorus. If this club was a church, then this huddled mass of clubbers were the congregation.

Danny was more than happy to follow this fold and dance the night away.

***

Several rum and cokes later, Danny's cheeks flushed along with the perspiring glow that came from a good night out. After ordering another drink, he meandered upstairs to the chill out room. The grinding beat of the mellow music gave this part of the club a more relaxed vibe.

The alcohol coursing nicely through his veins, he'd left his inhibitions on the main dance-floor hours ago. He propped himself at a spot where a couple of cute guys were hanging out. Who knew? Maybe one of them was single.

But it was the guy in the cowboy hat and black leather jeans and vest who caught his eye.

Hmm, Danny thought. *Now there's a tall drink of water I could sip all night long.*

He tried playing it as cool as a cucumber, but awkwardness reared its ugly head and his elbow slipped from the bar he leant on. He jumped out of the way of the split drink to avoid getting it down his jeans.

"Shit!" He felt the fool.

The cowboy chuckled.

Is he laughing at me? Or with me? Danny smiled, rolled his eyes and shrugged his shoulders and turned to the bar.

"Here, let me get you another." The cowboy sidled up next to him and signalled the bartender for another two drinks. "Same again, please."

The bartender nodded.

"Thanks." Danny was clearly embarrassed. And annoyed at himself for ruining his buzz. "Nothing like making a good first impression."

The two young men chorused in unison. "And that was nothing like a good first impression."

That old joke broke the ice. They both chuckled which put Danny at ease.

The bartender served them their drinks and the cowboy paid with a note, leaving the change in the small tray. The man tipped. Danny liked that.

A whole string of cheesy one-liners ran through his mind. He took a large gulp of Dutch courage. He was about to blurt out something – because something was better than nothing – when the cowboy leaned in and kissed him.

His soft lips pressed hard against his own and he allowed the man's tongue inside. A wash of rum and coke followed, mixing with the taste of his cherry chapstick. The contact sent a rush of electricity throughout Danny's nerve endings. This cowboy's kiss was heavenly.

The cowboy pulled away. Took a sip from his plastic cup and leaned to whisper in Danny's ear.

"You don't know how fucking sexy you are." His voice was deep and smooth. He flicked his tongue on Danny's ear before gently blowing on his lobe.

Goosebumps washed over his flesh. The shiver of arousal ran up and down his spine. This man knew exactly what he was doing and Danny found himself submitting to the stranger's will. He gazed into the cowboy's piercing green eyes, losing himself inside his magnetic charm and beauty.

"Where the hell did you come from?" Danny asked, almost stupefied from that single kiss. "How on Earth can two people who've barely spoken make a connection like this."

The cowboy grinned. His teeth iridescent like pearls. Could he have any more redeeming features? Nobody was this perfect. Surely?

"Cute. Very cute indeed." The cowboy signalled to Danny's empty cup. "Let me get you another."

Danny hadn't realised how much he'd drank in the few moments they'd been in each other's company. He was about to say 'no' when he found himself taking another.

"Thanks. For the drink. That's very kind of you."

"There ain't nothing kind about my intentions, sexy man. I want to take you on an adventure."

Those feel good chemicals buzzing in his brain were firing on all cylinders. He almost pinched himself. Was this dream too good to be true?

"C'mon, let's get out of here." The cowboy kissed him full on the lips, taking Danny by the hand and leading him away.

"Wait." Danny stopped. "I don't even know your name. Am I supposed to call you cowboy all night."

"Well, if the hat fits…" The cowboy doffed his Stetson and winked, taking Danny by the hand again and leading him out of the club.

***

The two young men didn't talk much in the back of the cab. Spending the duration of the journey with their tongues down each other's throat. Oblivious to the presence of the driver – who seemed to pay them no mind.

"So where are we heading to?" Danny held the cowboy's hand. "For this *adventure.*"

"All will be revealed." The cowboy smirked and looked out the window. "In fact, we're almost there."

The cab pulled over and the cowboy paid.

Danny stepped out of the car. There was a slight chill to the air, causing his nipples to harden. Standing on the pavement he stood, waiting, with his arms folded to keep himself warm. He clocked the cowboy overpaying the driver and thanking him for the ride. He was impressed with the man's generosity.

"Aren't you cold?" Danny asked.

"Nah!" The cowboy put his arm around Danny and kissed his forehead, leading him towards a large house on a very well-to-do street. "I'm a red blooded man, me. You'll see."

The cowboy jumped over a low-bearing wall.

Danny hesitated. "This isn't your place?"

"You wanted an adventure, right?"

"Well, yeah. But…"

The cowboy held out his hand. "Come on. Let's go have some fun."

A small voice in his head said *turn away. Go home.* But as the cold breeze caressed his skin, he shivered. Desperate to get inside and into the warm, he threw caution to the wind. *Fuck it! You only live once. This is what you wanted, after all.*

He sat on the wall and swung his legs over, cantered over to the cowboy and took his hand. His heart raced as his curiosity got the better of him and his concerns melted away.

Still a little drunk, he was amazed by the gothic grandeur and the architecture of the mansion before him. Made of dark bricks. Tall windows. High turrets with small windows. There really was a gargoyle mounted above a grand door.

This really is turning out to be a damsel in distress story, Danny thought as he pictured a demur drag queen with extremely long hair cascaded out of highest window.

Under the cover of the trees, he followed the cowboy across the grass and down the side of the house.

"This isn't your house, obviously."

"Are you ready?"

"Not until you tell me what's going on. No way."

The cowboy sighed. The charm. The façade. For the first time that evening the pretence fell away. A more serious expression drew across his face. One of concern. Fear. Almost.

"The man who owns this house," he said. "Is not a very nice man."

"Then let's get out of here. Go some place else."

"I can't."

"Why not?"

"Because he has my boyfriend in that house. Locked up."

"What?" The news was sobering. Hearing the news the cowboy was spoken for Danny couldn't help feeling selfish. He took a moment to process the situation. "Are you kidding me?"

"This is no joke, my friend." The cowboy looked pitiful. "I'm sorry. I shouldn't have lied to you. But if I'd have told you the truth, you wouldn't have come."

Danny softened – he couldn't help feel sorry for the man.

"We have to call the police." He reached inside his jeans for his mobile phone to find it wasn't there. "Shit! My phone. It must've fell out in the cab."

"Please. I'm desperate. I can't do this on my own."

Be careful what you wish for. Danny stood, hands on hips. Trying to decide what to do. *You wanted adventure – and now you've got it. What if it was me in there? I'd want somebody – anybody – to come rescue me. But no. Fuck it. I don't know this guy. The bastard has already lied to me. What else is he lying about? I can't trust him and I don't owe him anything."*

Danny turned and marched back toward the main road.

"No, wait!" The cowboy ran after him. Grabbed his shoulder and jumped in front of him. "What are you doing? Where are you going? You can't leave."

"Err, I think you'll find I can. And I am." Danny pushed passed him, but the cowboy followed and stopped him again. This time placing his strong hands on Danny's shoulders. His grip sent a tingle rushing through Danny's body. He tried to ignore it but found himself drawn nearer to the cowboy.

"Please." The cowboy looked him in the eye. "I meant what I said earlier. If things were different..."

Despite his body yearning for the cowboy, Danny shoved him. "No! This is a bad idea. I want no part of this."

"How would you feel if it were you in there?

Danny stopped in his tracks, closed his eyes and took a deep breath. His mind said *no,* but his body said *yes.*

The cowboy's arms folded around him. Bringing him close to his chest. His lips gently kissing Danny's neck.

Danny weakened. A cool breeze caressed his skin and the cowboy's kisses – all rational thought gone in a second. He turned, pulled the cowboy close and kissed him. His hands exploring his body. His muscular chest. His tight arse. And the hardening between his legs. The connection they had was electrifying. Danny would've given himself to the stud right there and then had things been less tempestuous between them.

He pulled away and gazed into the cowboy's eyes.

"Okay, I'll help you. But we get in – we get your boyfriend out. And after that I don't ever want to see you again. Ever!" It pained him to say but that small voice of self-preservation in his mind made itself heard.

"Oh my God!" The cowboy pressed his palms together. "Thank you. Thank you. Thank you."

Danny took a deep breath and exhaled. "Why do I feel like I might live to regret this?"

***

The cowboy picked the back door lock with ease.

Danny was surprised alarms didn't go off. His voice dropped to a whisper. "The man who owns this place. Is he home?"

"I don't think so."

"You don't *think* so?"

"I *know* so. Okay. But you can never be too sure."

"How do you know where to find him?"

"I have a rough idea."

Danny grabbed the cowboy by the arm. "What do you mean you have a rough idea?"

"Well, it's not like I've been here before."

"I mean, how do you know he's even here?"

"Because he's done this before. It happened to a friend of a friend of mine. Except he got away."

"A friend of a friend? Are you kidding me with this?"

The cowboy glowered.

Danny felt bad. Who was he to imply that the lad was lying. "Well… Didn't he go to the police?"

The cowboy gestured to the opulence around him. "Look around you. People who live like this have friends in high places. People who live like this can afford to build rooms beneath rooms. Walls behind furniture. Locks. Soundproofing. Cameras and alarms. Money talks. And when you've got lots of it, you can buy anything. Have anything you want. Even if it ain't right. Even if it's immoral and unethical."

"What happened to your friend's friend?"

"He disappeared. Everyone knows he's dead. This bastard killed him."

"I'm sorry."

"Why? It's not your fault."

Danny didn't know what else to say. Struggled to find the right words. Over his support – because that's the kinda guy Danny was. But the more flustered he became, the more determined he was to help the cowboy. He followed him into the hall. "Do you know where he is?"

"Down here." The cowboy opened a door under the stairs. It was nothing more than a coat cupboard. Until he reached beneath one of the coats and pulled on a hook, releasing a lock. He pushed the secret door forward.

Danny stepped in behind him and looked into a dark abyss.

The cowboy pulled out his phone, switched on his torch and took his first step down the stairs before him.

Danny followed. He didn't like this one little bit. As he descended, he kept glancing over his shoulder to make sure they weren't being followed. The anticipation of someone reaching out of the gloom set his nerves on edge. But it was the hanging cobweb that made him jump as he turned back to follow the cowboy.

Moments later they reached the bottom of the staircase to find an iron door. A relic from a time gone by – something that had been there for many, many years.

A creaking floorboard made Danny spin round. "Can we hurry up and get this over and done with."

"Will you just relax! It's just the house resettling." The cowboy reached to the ledge above the door, feeling for a key.

"Yes!" As luck would have it he found two – one large, one small.

"Relax? We've broken into the house of a highly dangerous man and you're telling me to relax?"

The cowboy put the chunky key in the lock and the bolt clunked as he turned it. "Thank you. For doing this. You don't know what your help means to me. You know, had things been different you and I could've really hit it off."

Danny's heart fluttered. Despite the deceit he was still attracted to the cowboy. Maybe his boyfriend wasn't down here at all. Maybe he didn't exist and this was all part of a silly game to tease and excite him. If that was true, maybe they could spend more time getting to know one another after all this. Spend more time fucking each other's brains out.

The cowboy pushed the door. It opened with a grinding shriek.

Danny followed him in. The temperature dropped. He wrapped his arms around himself. The air was dank and musty. Concrete walls surrounded them as the cowboy scanned the room with what little light his phone emitted. The ceiling was low but the space opened out with an offshoot of rooms either side. Whether it was the cold, his nerves – probably a combination of both – Danny shivered.

Together they searched each room.

Slings. Toys. Cameras and large video screens. At first, Danny felt a tingling of excitement. Was this what the cowboy had in mind when he invited him on an adventure?

But that notion soon disappeared. Whoever owned this house had a sadistic mind. The further they moved into the space – inspecting each playroom – the more ill at ease he became.

A dentist's chair with straps and harnesses. A trolley with a selection of tools. A rack and selection of tools intended for whipping and flogging displayed in another.

But it was the next room that filled him with horror.

His stomach churned and gurgled so loud, he half-expected the cowboy to turn around and be the funny, charming and wildly aloof man he'd encountered back at the club. But the stranger had more pressing matters on his mind to notice. The man he'd met at the club no longer existed. That magical moment of hope was gone.

And all that mattered now was *the box.*

They entered the room but kept their distance from it.

It was about a metre and half squared. Solid. Encased in black leather with a couple of air holes at the top.

Danny knew who was inside and he almost turned and ran out of this pit of pain and degradation, up the stairs and out of the house. But he didn't.

Instead he stood there frozen like the cowboy. Staring in anticipation at what they might find when they opened the box.

Danny took the cowboy's hand. "Come with me."

The cowboy frowned. "What?"

"Let's leave now. You and me."

"Are you serious?"

"You open that box now and you might not like what you find?"

"What do you mean?"

Danny knew exactly what he meant but just couldn't bring himself to say it. He stared at the box. There were no smells coming from it. But no sound either.

"You think he's dead?" Shear horror seemed to course throughout his body. From the expression on the cowboy's face it was clear he hadn't considered that his boyfriend was gone. His body became rigid. He was not the confident young man Danny had first met. He shook his head, stuttering to speak. "I can't look."

Grabbing the cowboy's phone, Danny took the bull by the horns, strode over to the box. Shining the phone's torch into one of the holes, he peered inside.

He gasped.

There was someone inside. But it was hard to see who he was looking at. Still there was no response.

"Is he alive?" The cowboy folded his arms, pacing back and forth. "Is he? Tell me. I can take it. Just be honest with me."

"Sssh!" Danny rested on the box, leaning down and placing an ear against one of the air holes. It took a few seconds to measure and then he heard it. "He's breathing."

"He's okay. My baby's okay. He's gonna be alright."

Danny tried to ignore his thoughts, he couldn't help but feel left out. Jealous even. Why hadn't he found someone yet? Someone to care for him the way the cowboy did for his boyfriend?

"Keys?"

The cowboy was confused at first. "Huh?"

"Keys! There's a padlock on this side of the box.

The cowboy tossed them to Danny who then placed the smaller one in the padlock. It clicked. "Bingo!"

Danny released it and dropped it on the floor.

He and the cowboy unthreaded the chain through the hoops that kept it bound tight. Together, they lifted the heavy lid and tipped back where it rested on solid hinges.

"Oh my God." Tears welled in the cowboy's eyes as he pressed his fingers over his lips, stifling a whimper. "He's alive."

The poor kid looked bruised and beaten. Gaunt and discoloured. His breathing shallow – just as Danny had suspected. His eyes opened. The only thing about him that had any colour left. Deep green. Like his own. It wasn't often he came across someone with green eyes. His dirty blonde cropped hair was dull and greasy – with traces of flaking hair product. He wore a white t-shirt spattered with dried blood. Jeans but no shoes on his feet. And the stud in his left ear. Much like his own. In fact, his clothes were the same too. His hair the same colour and style.

Danny chuckled. Not because of what and who he was looking at. But in disbelief. He looked at the cowboy, quizzically. About to say something but he couldn't quite find the words.

He leant over the top of the box and studied the lad again.

It was like looking at version of himself. Even though he wasn't. But the similarities were astonishing.

"Uncanny. isn't it." The cowboy didn't seem so upset this time around.

"I don't understand." Danny kept glancing back and forth between the two young men. "Is this a joke? Is this all part of the game? This so called adventure you said you'd take me on?"

The cowboy said nothing, just stood there and scratched his chin.

"Because it isn't very funny."

He glanced at the young lad in the box, unsure what to think. What to do next. Should he help him? Or was the kid faking it? Should he just sod these two pranksters, leave them to their sick game and make a run for it.

Danny looked up.

The cowboy was gone.

He felt a fool. He still didn't know the guy's name. He patted his pockets for his phone, cursing when he remembered he longer had it. "Shit! Fuck! Shit!"

Panic set in. He rested his hands on the edge of the box, dropping his head to try and catch his breath. He was about to turn and make a run for the door when...

Two cold and clammy hands gripped his wrists. Danny yelped. He tried to pull away but in spite of his weakened state the young lad in the box was surprisingly strong. He was, after all, fighting for his life.

The lad in the box pulled himself up. His breath reeking of sickness and internal rotting.

Danny gagged. But it was the boy who vomited all over him.

Pulling himself free, Danny stood in shock. He wiped the putrid bile away from his eyes and the rest of his face.

The boy was slumped over the edge of the box. He reached out a hand. His voice a raspy, gurgling noise. "Help... me."

Stepping towards the boy, Danny was about to reach for his hand when he stopped.

The boy wasn't looking at him.

But behind him.

A shiver ran down his spine as he turned.

The last thing he saw was the cowboy's fist heading straight for the middle of his face. His nose cracked as he stumbled backwards. The pain spread like a burst of dark light into his eyes. Blinding him. He tried to find his feet, almost falling. The sense of nausea and vertigo didn't help but he managed to stay on his feet. He found the box behind him, leaning on it. Blood gushed down his face. He coughed and spluttered as its tangy metallic flavour trickled from his nasal passage, into his throat and mouth. He tried to pry his eyes open.

"Why are you doing this?" Danny cried out, trying to stop the bleeding. "What did I do to you?"

"Nothing." The cowboy had moved. His voice coming from the left and passing to the right as he spoke. "You are just unfortunate. It's nothing personal."

"Nothing personal!" He tried to open his eyes again but all he saw was feint blotches of colour in the darkness. His head spun whenever he tried to stand. And his nose wouldn't stop bleeding. "How can I not take this personal?"

"You are nothing more than a replacement. Everything I said to you was true."

"What do you mean?"

"The only way I can save my boyfriend is to trick the monster who did this to him. Make the bastard believe that you are him. Giving us time to escape the country before he realises the switch."

"You bastard!" Danny ran forward, blindly. Arms swinging aimlessly.

It took no more than a shove from the cowboy and Danny found himself back against the box.

Arms wrapped around Danny from behind.

It was the boy in the box.

Danny struggled to break free, but fear had weakened his resolve. "I'll tell him I'm not your boyfriend. I'll tell him what you've done and where to find you. You won't get away with this."

"There is one way around that," said the cowboy.

Danny felt a slug to the gut, winding him. Fingers intruded his mouth, holding his mouth open as he gasped for breath. Another set of fingers pulled at his tongue.

It all happened so quickly.

The edge of a sharp cold blade scraped against his front teeth before slicing deep into his tongue, filling his mouth with blood again. Copious amounts of blood. He tried to scream, but could only produce a nonsensical gurgling noise. He choked, projecting blood spatter. This was it. The moment his light would no longer shine. The place he was going to die. The pain. The terror. Intensified by the lack of sight. Lost in the dark. Alone without his own cowboy to save him.

A vice like grip — arms around his body — pulled and dragged him kicking and flailing into the box.

Two pairs of hands forced him in and when he clambered to escape, the two strangers reached inside the box and punched him down.

Danny had no fight left. He slumped to the floor.

"Remember," the cowboy said, "it's nothing personal."

The lid came down. The padlock clicked into place.

And all traces of light and colour disappeared from behind his eyelids. There was a brief scuffling and muttering. The cowboy and his boyfriend were moving towards the door.

It slammed shut.

The lock turned and clunked.

Silence.

Darkness.

Danny was truly alone.

***

The sound of a door unlocking. Opening. Danny roused. Opened his eyes. Blinked away the drowsiness. His sight was returning. He saw light through the holes in the roof of the box. He tried to move but his body cried out in agony. He feared he'd cracked a rib. Or something equally damaging. Whatever it was his movement was limited. If he had any chance of getting out, he'd have to push through the pain.

That's when he heard...

Footsteps.

Approaching the box.

Walking around the box.

They stopped.

He held his breath. Froze. Remembering where he was. And whose lair he'd been trapped in. From what little information the cowboy had given him, this bastard was a sadistic murderer.

The sudden rush of images flooded his mind. The next few minutes. Hours. Days. Weeks. Who knew how long? Being this man's plaything.

Danny barely had any strength to move let alone fight the monster and escape. The thought of dying like this shredded what was left of his nerves.

He wept.

Sobbed.

Whimpered like a helpless dog. Left high and dry. With no one to come to his rescue. He had no contact with his family. No boyfriend or friends to miss him. Only work might wonder why he hadn't turned up. But would they contact the police? He abandoned all hope.

Danny was broken.

The padlock clinked and the key turned.

The lid opened.

Through blurred vision, Danny glanced up at his captor. The silhouette of a man looked down. He was a beast – a hulking beast of a man. Six or seven foot tall. Muscular. Broad shoulders. Thick arms. Huge hands with chunky fingers.

The dark shape was still and silent. All but for the rise and fall of his accelerating breath and the motion of his chest.

Intense fear reignited in Danny's mind, shooting through his body. He tried to move. Tried to talk. But couldn't. Remembering his tongue had been removed. He sounded like a Neanderthal. But he'd been mutilated. A piece of his body taken away. Discarded like unwanted meat. He felt humiliated. Degraded. Something less than the young man he'd been before.

The man growled – clearly angry. Had he realised his prize had escaped? Been replaced with some second-rate look-a-like?

The lid came down. His roar shook the room. Danny almost felt the vibrations of his fury. The murderous monster was enraged. He threw things around the room. Pounded his fists on the lid. Kicked the sides.

Danny braced himself for his final moments. It would soon be over.

He mustered one final burst of energy. One last cry for help. One last plea for mercy.

Danny screamed.

The beast stopped.

All was silent but for the sound of his own breath and the pounding in his chest. He closed his eyes. Body tensed. The boring life he once knew had come to an end.

The man approached.

The lid opened.

Danny looked up.

The man roared again. Grabbed Danny by the scruff of his shirt. Dragged him out of the box with ease. Flung him to the floor.

Danny yowled as he landed. Another explosion of pain shot up his back as if barbed wire tightened around his vertebrae. A large, booted foot came towards his face. Survival instinct kicked in. With a burst of energy, Danny ignored his screaming injuries and rolled to avoid the murderous blow. He scrambled backwards on his hands and knees to the nearest wall. Held up his arms to shield himself from the knife that came towards him, that sliced into his forearms.

Bloodied saliva dribbled from Danny's mouth as he cried out for the man to stop. He spat into his captor's eyes.

The man stumbled back, wiping his face, mewling like a wounded lion.

Danny pushed up, using the wall to stand. He made for the open door. Stabbing pain in his side. His back throbbing. Dragging a leg as he reached for the handle.

But a hairy hand crushed and twisted his wrist, crippling him. His body contorted under the strength of the gorilla-sized hand, bringing him to his knees.

The door slammed.

There was no escape.

He had no choice but to give in. Submit to this man's will.

For the first time, Danny was able look into his eyes. And he into his.

Despite his deformity and out of sheer desperation, Danny uttered the words as the thought appeared in his mind. "Let me help you."

The man picked him up and slammed him against the wall. Another shot of pain coursed through his body. Danny clenched his teeth, now determined, one last ditch attempt to fight for his life.

"Let me help you find the boy who escaped. Let me help you get the man who freed him."

The man drew back. Snorted as a change formed in his expression. Had he understood what Danny was trying to say? Was he considering his proposal? The man slammed him against the wall again. Danny was either becoming numb to the pain or the man wasn't shoving him so hard. Was Danny getting through to him?

His captor's face *was* softening. Less angry. More contemplative.

Out of pure desperation Danny leaned in and kissed him. He didn't know why. But what else was there left to do? He allowed his lips to linger for a moment. Hoping for a connection to be made. It was all he had left. A kiss.

And it was that simple kiss that saved his life.

The man loosened his grasp, catching Danny as he crumpled to the ground. Lifting him in both arms, he carried him out of the room. And into another. The light brightened.

Danny succumbed to an overpowering wave of lethargy. Found himself drifting towards the white light.

***

The room was clinical. Clean. Disinfected. The air fresh. Daylight subdued by half drawn blinds.

Disorientated, Danny felt muzzy. Confused. Where the hell was he?

Then he remembered.

A score of images flashed in his mind.

Adrenaline kicked in. Panic ensued. Danny tried to sit up in bed, only to find himself strapped down. He struggled against his constraints, but the fight was brief when his poor aching body cried out in pain. He groaned in agony. Then spotted the intravenous drip next to his bed. Tubing connected the device to his wrist. A bandaged wrist dotted with blood.

The cuts.

The slicing.

The vicious attack. How he fought helplessly. He wept at his own anxiety. Sobbed at his own weakness.

He traced the tube protruding from his arm, finding a valve. He reached for it and pressed the button. Whatever painkiller flowed into his veins he was thankful for the rush of chemical relief.

***

When Danny woke again, he had no idea what day it was. No clue how much time had passed. He was still lethargic but the drip was no longer attached and the straps had been removed. No longer was he a prisoner.

Too spaced out to panic, he shimmied to sit up in bed. His body still ached but nowhere near as much as it had before. Time would tell how much he'd healed — he'd have to wait for the medication to wear off. The bandages had been removed. The cuts on his wrists had turned to brown-green crusty scabs. His mouth was dry. There was a jug of water and a plastic cup on the bedside table. He stretched and winced as the pain in his side throbbed. But his thirst took priority. His mouth was sticky and dry. He was gasping.

Managing to pour some of the water into the cup, he attempted to place the jug on the table, but missed. Water spilled over the floor. The plastic jug made a racket as it bounced to a standstill. Danny paid it no mind as he chugged down what little water there was. He dribbled down his chin. Bloodied water stained the bedsheets. And then he remembered. He opened his mouth and reached inside. He touched the stump where his tongue once was, pulling his fingers out quickly. A lump in his throat formed. He sobbed into the palms of his hands until he could cry no more.

Why me? he asked. *What did I do to deserve this?*

The effort tired him. Shuffling back down the bed, he pulled the covers over as he rolled onto his side and closed his eyes.

A door opened. Footsteps drew near.

Danny prised his eyes open for a second but was too tired and too bleary eyed to care.

As sleep began to take him the fingertip of the gentle giant standing by his bedside brushed aside his hair, stroking his brow. But it was a tender kiss upon his forehead that bid him goodnight – sending him to the land of dreams.

***

Violent nightmares woke Danny from his slumber. The same nightmares he'd had the last few nights. The events once real were now an intense memory imprinted deep within his psyche. Forcing him to relive his trauma – over and over again. There was no escaping them.

He hadn't seen or heard his captor/saviour in the moments he was awake but it was clear that the man was taking care of him.

But why? Why had he beaten him to near death and then changed his mind?

Then he remembered. The cowboy and his boyfriend.

Waves of anger. Hurt. Shame. A whirlwind of emotions. He'd never felt so stupid in his entire life. To allow himself to be duped like that. He only had himself to blame, surely? He screamed. Shouted. Cried until he exhausted himself.

All he wanted to do was sleep, hoping the darkness would take him so he wouldn't have to dream, think or relive that night ever again. But as the nights passed, it seemed the universe had other plans for Danny.

***

It was the smell of a cooked breakfast that roused him. A tray on the bedside table with a plate full of bacon, sausages, eggs – the whole works – waiting for him. Along with a glass of orange juice. And a note. It simply read:

'Eat. Get your strength up. We have work to do.'

***

The Cowboy.

Gran Canaria's Pride parade was already in full swing when Brad and Ricky joined the march. They'd missed the starting ceremony due to dropping a pill and shagging each other's brains out in the kitchen at home.

Decorated floats, each with its own theme, blaring its own brand of thumping party music, clashed discordantly through the crowded streets of Maspalomas. Drag queens and scantily clad Adonis' danced and pointed at the adoring crowds while DJs spun their records. Most were there to celebrate their identity, their sexuality. Others there in support. There were a few disgruntled old codgers put out by the affair, but nobody paid them any mind. The atmosphere was electric and everyone else was having a great time.

"You are a disco bunny through and through." Brad fingered his boyfriend's fake furry ears, straightened his bow tie, slipping his hands inside Ricky's glittering shorts to pinch his cute little arse before planting a kiss on his lips. He stood back and admired his diminutive beau. "Those shorts leave nothing to the imagination."

"Hmm, that's coming from the cowboy donning a pair of white arseless chaps covered in faux diamantés, along with a matching sleeveless jacket opened to expose his smooth chiselled torso." Ricky rubbed his hands over Brad's chest, gently flicking his newly pierced nipple as he leaned in and returned the kiss. "A torso to die for mind you."

"Well, today is the day we celebrate coming out of hiding." Brad smiled as he put on his sunglasses. "Let the world know we're here and we are here to have fun!"

"With our online presence, I think people already know who we are… hello there!" Ricky got distracted by a fellow partygoer asking for a selfie with them. "Of course, you can."

Photo moment over, Brad draped his arm over Ricky's shoulder. The couple were lapping up the attention. And the two of them bathed in the adoration. After two years spent keeping a low profile, they were both determined to make the most of it.

But it wasn't just Brad and Ricky getting noticed. A bulked up young man wearing a string vest caught their eyes the moment he stepped into view.

"Well, well, well." Brad eyed the stud over the top of his shades. "Looks like we've found our plaything for tonight. What do you say, babes?"

But Ricky was already sauntering off in the man's direction. The crowd folded around him and Brad lost sight of him and their potential playmate.

"Hey? Ricky!" He pushed through the throng of people singing, whooping and blowing their whistles. The mob closing in the further he went in. "Wait for me."

The music seemed to get louder. Faces laughing in his direction. Brad became overwhelmed, a little dizzy. He panicked. Much to the dismay of his fellow partygoers, he forced his way passed them to the sidewalk where he caught sight of Ricky disappearing into an alleyway.

"Fucking hell." Brad ran after him. "This is the last time we pop pills and go out in public."

Upon reaching the dark and narrow passage, Brad stopped. He noticed the string-vested stud walking off down the street, away with the parade.

Ricky's laugh bounced off the walls. But he was nowhere to be seen.

Brad entered with caution.

Ricky giggled.

Was his boyfriend playing one of his games? This twink liked his kinky adventures, but it was normally something they'd plan together. While Ricky was off on a happy high, tormenting him, Brad wondered if he was on a come down already as paranoia set in.

"Snap out of it, Brad," he said, talking to himself. "Don't be a party pooper."

Maybe it was time to take another? So he retrieved a pill from a packet in his pocket, broke it in half and swallowed it down with a swig of water from the bottle he'd been carrying.

Upon reaching a dead end, Brad found an open door. He peered inside.

"Ricky?" He stepped in. "Oh, Ricky! I'm going to find you. And when I do, you're gonna get it, you sexy little fucker."

Brad loved Ricky's little games. They'd never played them in public before. Except out in the dunes when they went cruising for guys. This was something entirely new for them. It was a huge turn on. Brad adjusted his cock as it stiffened inside his chaps.

A noise to his left caught his attention just as the ecstasy kicked in. He followed the sounds through the darkened hall, pushing through sheets of plastic that had been left hanging mid-job by a workman. And there was Ricky. Naked. Tied to a rack with his arms out and wrists above him. And his legs spread wide.

"You horny little fucker." He couldn't take the strain no more. He had to have him now. Dropping the bottle of water, he unzipped his chaps, took his dick in his hand and stroked it as he approached his boyfriend. He reached inside his jacket pocket for a bottle of poppers. He twisted off the cap. Placing a finger over one nostril while he sniffed deep with the other. He reached over Ricky's shoulder, shoving the bottle under his nose and then put the bottle down. He spat in his hand and massaged the saliva on his cock and slipped inside his boyfriend with ease. Hard. Rough. The way they both liked it. It didn't take long for Brad to come. That's when he collapsed forward onto Ricky and wrapped his arms around him. Kissing the back of his neck. Gently nibbling his ear.

"You're as sweaty as I am," Brad said, whispering. "That was so fucking horny. *You* are so fucking horny."

Beads of sweat trickled down Brad's forehead into his eye. He wiped with the back of his hand to realise just how wet it was. How dark it was.

Something wasn't right.

He did up his trousers and pulled out his phone. The device illuminated. He swiped the screen with blood. His hands shook. They had blood all over them.

"Baby?" He reached for Ricky's shoulder and shook him. More blood. "Baby, say something."

He stepped round in front of him.

Brad dropped his phone. Fell to his knees. And screamed.

Ricky's torso had been sliced. Deep. From the neck down to the pelvis, across his belly from which its entire contents dangled, dripping onto the bloody mess below.

A lurch in his stomach broke Brad's state of shock. He turned away from the corpse he'd just made love to, fucked, whatever. The point was he'd just had sex with a dead man.

Once the entire contents of his own stomach had been emptied onto the ground Brad tried to stand, resting his hands on his knees while he caught his breath. The pill he'd popped just minutes ago was really working its magic. He turned back to Ricky, his beautiful face still so angelic. He never knew if what they had was love but there had been something special between them these last few years. Ever since he had rescued him from…

Dread overwhelmed his drug-induced state. Cascading throughout his body – an attack on his nervous system. The realisation was all too much. How could he have been so careless, so stupid? He'd left an online trail. Allowing anyone to track him down. And boy, had he made plenty of enemies over the years. But none so ruthless and brutal as the killer who'd previously captured and tortured Ricky two years ago.

And now, Brad had blood on his hands. Was this the monster's plan all along – to kill Ricky and frame Brad for his lover's murder?

"I can't go to jail." Brad shuddered, running his red hands on his trousers in a panic. "I'm not cut out for it. Too pretty. They'd eat me up in there."

He turned to run. The head of a shovel hit him right in the centre of his face.

And all he knew was darkness.

***

Brad came to in the strangest position. Knees up to his chest. Arms wrapped around his calves. Mouth gagged. And naked. He struggled to break free of the heavy-duty tape and cable ties keeping him bound.

The dank room reeked of sex and death. Enough for him to taste the stench, causing him to wretch. His nose was blocked – encrusted with dried blood. He tried looking around but there was very little room for movement, so his view was limited. The gag in his mouth wouldn't budge. It was buckled tight around his head. There was no escape.

For Ricky. For his own stupidity. For his imminent death. He wept. But his time and his sorrow were cut short when the sound of a door opened behind him. Footsteps followed. Slow.

The wait was agonising.

"Let me out of here," he pled. "I won't tell anyone. I promise. Just let me go. Please."

The monstrous man who once held Ricky captive rounded and stood before him. He wore a leather mask – shaped like a bear – to match his leather harness, trousers and boots. Hulking in stature. Looking larger than any man was supposed to.

"I'll do anything you want. Please, just don't hurt me."

A fist struck his left cheek. It came not from the monster of a man before him but from the left. The blow stung. Something on those hands tore into his flesh. Blood trickled down his face and over his lips.

A muscular young man – a lot shorter than his companion – circled round. Blood dripped from the short claws on his right leather glove. He too wore similar S and M clothing. But unlike his friend, this one donned a wolf-shaped mask. In his left hand he carried a mobile. The wolf tapped the device and a distorted voice spoke.

Brad listened.

"You must be wondering who I am, Bradley. I know you are familiar with my friend here. It seems you stole something precious from him a few years back. Thought you could fool him, deceive him by replacing your little *disco bunny* with another. Hoping he wouldn't notice."

"I'm sorry." Brad fired out excuses like a machine gun. "I just wanted my boyfriend back. Please, please let me go. I won't say nothing. I pro-"

The recording continued, cutting him off.

"But he noticed. And he was very, *very* angry about it."

The wolf removed his mask.

Brad squinted. His jaw dropped. "You. You're alive. But how? I don't under-"

"And so was I. I convinced him to save me. Even after you cut out my tongue." The wolf knelt down and opened his mouth to show him the twisted nub of flesh where his tongue had once been.

"And after several years of love and care, pain and torment, gruelling hard work and hell of a lot of planning and surveillance, I wish to return the favour."

"No, no, no!" Brad tightened his lips, turned his head away as far as he could.

The bear stepped forward. Crouched beside Brad. Forced his fingers past his lips and his teeth. Prising his mouth open.

Brad glared through the gaps between the bear's fingers.

The wolf had placed the phone on the floor and from one of the hoops on his harness, unhooked a blade and a pair of pliers.

Brad screamed. But resistance was futile.

The wolf unbuckled the gag, letting it drop to the ground.

The pliers gripped Brad's tongue. The wolf pulled, and gently teased the blade across the lump of flesh. The tongue wept a crimson tear. He raised the blade, about to make the blow when he stopped. He tapped his phone screen again and another voice file played.

"I won't cut out your tongue. The suffering would be over too quickly." The wolf grabbed his crotch. "Besides I may have use for it later."

He returned the blade to his harness but kept hold of the pliers.

"Let's take the teeth instead. We have no use for those."

The cold steel scraped against his teeth as the pliers grabbed one of his wisdom teeth. Yanked. And twisted it free from the gum.

Brad shrieked. Nearly choked on the gushing blood. The pain so excruciating he nearly passed out. But he fought to stay conscious. It was his only chance of escape should the opportunity present itself.

The wolf played another audio file.

"You will suffer like I did. I want you to feel what I felt. The pain you subjected me to, the pain I endured… I let it go. It is my gift to you."

The bear lifted Brad from the ground. Carried him into another dark and gloomy room. Inside it – a solitary box. The wall around it full of sex toys and instruments used for torture.

He tried to fight with every last bit of energy. But in the end all he could do was cry like a baby cradled in the arms of the bear.

His arm cracked as he met with the floor when the bear dropped him inside the box. He cried out as the shock surged through his body.

The wolf and the bear peered over the edge and into the box. The wolf played one last file.

"Welcome to your new home, cowboy." He tossed in Brad's Stetson. "I hope you hate every moment of it. You belong to us now. You are our plaything. And this is our toybox."

The bear lifted the lid. The wolf played one last message.

"You must understand one thing, cowboy." The voice mocking in tone. A sinister smile drawing across Danny's face. "It's nothing personal."

The lid came down.

My Cin

By

Maxwell I. Gold

A thousand statues, conceived through foggy perceptions,

wretched and bleak and lost to my own pathetic desires.

My halls were filled with the bodies of the brazen, bold, and broken dreams,

but never good enough for me.

No one was good enough for me.

Not even him, the last statue I'd ever conceive in a crumbling palace

towards the edge of a wild, deranged infinity.

Sculpted from clay and blood I objectified that thing which needed, no, desired a dark, starry curiosity. Gods, I didn't mean to do it. I loved him, and more than any of the others. Cin was my favorite, the most beautiful creature I'd ever laid my eyes on. The most beautiful creature I'd ever created. Pulled from an iron forge his bones coalesced into something I'd only ever imagined in my wild, bizarre fantasies. Cin's first breath was like a thousand-million decades suddenly craving a single touch from my grace, yearning for my kiss.

"Not like this," a voice whispered into my ear.

It wasn't supposed to happen this way though. Really, it wasn't. Trickster, some called me, protector, healer, even messenger.

Murderer though?

I'd never kill anyone, at least not on purpose. It's difficult being in my position. I got so lonely through the ages, pulling the sun across the horizon in endless repetition, forged new stars in the unendurable solitude of merciless infinity. I've tried others, too. True, his antecedents were legion before him and the creative process was arduous and cruel. New bones crackled and seethed like newly forged iron; eager flesh sheathed muscle as if, scalding molten glass spread across the surface of a metal plate. I enforced my own indifference to the awful screams, though I could've made them without the ability to feel pain. The pain was truth, and it was something I never felt. Still, the dreadful cacophony tore its way from ragged throats and died in the echoes of the countless millennia as I looked upon their horrified countenances which infested my halls.

Sculpting them, I even gave some of them their own names; Crocus, Smilax to recall a few, but never before did I feel the seething conflagration strangeness of emotion kindle inside me like that for the love of Cin. The forge itself was a massive piece of craftsmanship, older than the most wondrous palaces where the gods had dwelled for untold millennia. A great brass-colored kiln looming high above even the most Herculean builds, the forge was an imposing structure. Belching with flame and gas, it sat at the heart of my palace, deep in the confines underneath the beauty and splendor of everything else. I was entrusted, no, *expected,* to stand watch as the steward of the forge for as long as my eternal soul might dare to burn.

These were expectations, easily constructed into coherent shapes and memories; and how simple it was for me, every piece of flesh writhing its way into place, muscle and tissue enshrouding blood, and luminous synapses coruscating incandescent spheres of light so terrifying in their intensity that they became something almost dreadful. Still, I pressed further, the heat of the flesh-forge too great and I knew Cin was going to be different.

Who am I kidding? He was mine. I made him. He was mine.

Cin wasn't like me, though his precious, unmatched beauty would never fade even when his body had passed from the plane of the living to dwell in the land of Someday. I couldn't prevent the tears escaping from my eyes as I stared at that broken, imperfect soul, blood and beauty emptied onto the cracked marble. They say gods *can* die, which felt preferable in the dreadful, appalling moment when I saw the lifeless body of the clay man whom I loved beyond reason or sanity.

In the agony of that moment, I remembered the day I pulled his body from the forge, bulked, bronzed, and burning, birthed from the molten fury of my loneliness, I knew everything was going to be different, and yet at the same time, I wished it never happened.

We were playing a game, my choice of course, and Cin always obliged so willingly with a serene attentiveness to my needs, no matter the request. There was only so much to do when time was nothing more than a useless afterthought. Games and statues were all I had to amuse myself. My opinionated siblings, who hadn't the moral authority to judge me, called me manipulative or even overbearing. I simply didn't see what they were complaining about.

Still bathed in ash and dust, he twirled in the flesh forge, gaping upwards.

"Where am I? Who am I?"

"You're here in my home," I lied, "and you are my devoted, sweet love, Cin."

"Cin? That's a funny name," he always had a strange curiosity about him and `way of things, "Who are you?"

Of course, I didn't want to tell him anything of the world I lived in, or the gods and stars who composed the nature of existence. I also didn't want to tell him of the loneliness of living in a city of beautiful gods and ugly clay men. I tired of their gray countenances, insipid laws, and ever-changing litany of lopsided justices and relative moralities. There were reasons, *expectations,* in keeping certain parts of our world shut away from those like *Cin.* Intention was a naïve, monstrous thing and despite its purpose there always existed the possibility of some undue calamity that not even the gods could foresee.

I took his hands. "I am *everything* to you, my sweet Cin and you to me. Nothing else," I smiled while his head was caught in a silly angle that made him look like a child.

"You seem confused," I said.

"I'm not sure what to think," Cin said, though his eyes told me another story as his nimble mind devoured every possible visual clue to his new life and surroundings.

I knew then, Cin was a scintillating light that changed everything for me. The fickle concepts of death and entropy had their own agendas and endless mechanicians, and I, for once, didn't care. I had *him*. I had an object that would cause the stars themselves to implode with impotent, jealous rage. Others might try to have their way with him, take what could never be theirs, and I found a happy satisfaction in knowing they'd never take him from me.

"This is a strange place. It's so bright as if I've been here before."

"You could say that. This is my home, a small sanctuary I've taken for myself built of gold, marble, and tricks in a city where gods dwell and pray on idle dreams. Sounds fun, right?"

"I suppose, but what is this room? These chains, those fires, and metal baths?"

He was so new. Innocent, fragile, constructed with all the compelling aesthetic desired by any being designed from flesh and clay. Terrible thoughts ravaged my mind as to what I could do to him. I could envision the necessity of presenting to myself dark, demented reasons to justify Cin's existence in *my* world, reasons that he could never understand and that I could never explain. Such ruminations assaulted the ramparts of my mind, only to be destroyed under the inescapable truth that he was here to love and be loved and perhaps placate my erroneous fantasies.

The expectation was everything in my world, but I had decided the illusion of control was just that. So, in a sudden moment unencumbered by rationality or reason, I made a choice. "This is where you were born, Cin. Where I *made* you, to bring me the pleasure of your company and the light of your insight and wit. You're a being reanimated from flesh and clay, but I want so much more for you than a pile of water and mud." He *almost* smiled, but there was a sadness in his gaze.

"What troubles you?"

"Does this mean I am but an object? A mere toy for your amusement?" He asked.

The illusion was usually much more powerful, for Cin to be considered, and remain, an object and I had hoped it might stay like this forever. The overwhelming intensity of my own damned loneliness shattered something inside me, and I suddenly felt like I was like staring into a broken mirror. "Normally, yes, but I want more for you, Cin. I want you to be more than an object or plaything."

The sadness melted away, "Must I live here? In these metal confines?"

"No, not at all. You will live upstairs with me if that's what you would like."

Cin smiled, "I would like that very much."

Upon emerging from the deep forges, he saw the light for the first time. Alabaster walls festooned with gold and silver crown moldings, a bit over the top perhaps, but I enjoyed myself. There were hundreds of statues composed from bronze, copper, and certain other calcified materials, their faces dripped with misery and wretchedness; decaying before our eyes, their crumbling mouths seeming to accuse me of countless cruelties, their leprous presence a mute reminder of my myriad pathetic attempts to find some semblance of companionship. I hoped it wasn't too startling for him.

"You really live here?"

"I do," I gleamed.

"I've never seen such a house before," he said.

"Well, these are your first moments of existence, so I wouldn't expect you to have seen any house at all." Though I tried, I couldn't help my own laughter.

Cin, confounded with a naïve gawk, turned towards the center atrium where jade pillars held aloft a great rotunda with various mosaics of men and gods, dancing together in scenes of wild, reckless abandon.

"Are you all right?" I asked.

He examined the mosaics above, carefully. "Who are those men? Are they gods like you?"

"Sort of," I smiled. "You're quite the curious one, aren't you?"

"Why do they look so sad? They look as if they're all...

He lowered his eyes until they met my own. I saw a shadow fall upon his countenance which seemed to drain the light from his eyes.

"All what?"

"Dying," Cin whispered. His brow furrowed. "Why do you have such awful images? Is this the fate of all men? Of me?"

I took his face in my hands and held his gaze, "All *other* men yes. You? Not you! Your existence defies the material from which it is made! You carry within you the very flame of the Flesh Forge! Your heart beats with the fire of eternity itself. Your fibers weaved with the very clay and salt of the stars. Like other men? Foolishness! So do not fear, my beloved Cin. Neither Fate nor Death have a claim upon you."

He took a step away from me, and my hands hung in the air for a moment, suddenly emptier than they had ever been before. "There's nothing of what you have said depicted in the pictures above me. Those men died, I can see that clearly. Were they mere playthings to be cast aside? Shall my face be painted upon your ceiling one day?

Or a plaything that was not cast aside? A toy that was kept. I mean, unless that's all I am to you. A model for pleasure." The first conviction in his life of flesh and air, and it was a moment of pride for me, despite the fear in my belly.

"No. You are *mine.* I created you, Cin with the expectation you'll love me and in return I'll give you everything. An undying fealty to protect you from whatever shadows that creep outside these palace halls." I took a step toward him, but he placed a hand upon my chest to stop me.

"And if I do not? I will be like *other men*? My continued existence is contingent upon my obedience?"

"There *are no other men,* Cin," I grabbed the much larger hand over my chest.

"So, you say," his eyes locked with mine.

"My Cin. Those men, the ones up there had an expectation, an illusion which could never be reached, and the gods who hungered for more, willingly, blindly tossed them into the mouths of oblivion. Those men, Cin, never understood what was on the other side, never saw that hot, burning light. You're nothing like *other men.* You're nothing *like those men!* You're the light.*"*

Something changed. Silence inserted itself between us, awkward but thick with worms of worry that made me feel for the briefest of moments, small and vulnerable. And weak like gods were never supposed to be.

"Cin?" He stared up towards the mural once more, then back to me again.

All at once, and for the first time, Cin's face lit up with a smile that'd I'd never forget, "No," pulling me against his broad chest, "No – I certainly am not."

A thousand statues, conceived through foggy perceptions,

wretched and bleak and lost to my own pathetic desires.

My halls were filled with the bodies of the brazen, bold, and broken dreams,

but never good enough for me.

No one was good enough for me.

Not even him,

I wasn't good enough for him,

the last statue I'd ever conceive in a crumbling palace

towards the edge of a wild, deranged infinity.

Too late I'd come to understand

His smile the last I'd ever know.

Despite the expectations of my world, or my own lack thereof, everything within my power – I gave him - Cin grew to be the most beautiful and handsome man in the world, as immortal as any god, even holding the power to sway hearts and minds. Some called him Adonis others Hyacinth, but to me, he was *my* Cin. The envy and lust of the gods was great, yes, but nonetheless a bothersome and, at times humorous consequence of his perfection. Even Drag, the Queen of the Underworld attempted several times to seduce, capture, and abscond with him to her shadowy realm. If the fat adoration of gods wasn't enough, their thirst could only be quenched by their fervent desire that Cin replace me. .

That heretical thought never crossed my mind until I found Cin once again pondering the mural in the atrium one evening. His ivory skin and sculpted frame iridescent in the cold moonlight; his eyes held captive by the fresco and a contemplative expression on his immaculate face.

"I thought I'd find you here," I mused walking towards him.

No answer as Cin continued gazing upward.

"Is everything all right, my Cin? You created quite a stir the other day when you refused Drag. It's not often the Queen of the Underworld is turned down even if she chooses an unwilling suitor," I laughed. "The fire that burns within her is cold compared to your own."

"I'm aware of these things. You didn't seem much help when she was trying to kidnap me," Cin quipped.

"I think you've grown to be able to handle yourself, Cin," I gestured towards his powerful frame.

"Have I? Or was this always a part of your plan for me?" He stood firm in his accusation, obviously feeling betrayed and angry. It was a side I'd never seen of him, before.

"Why haven't you ever spoken of the ones you created before me? Those twisted statues arrayed like an army of broken toys imprisoned in their own carcasses above the flesh forge. I've dealt with you in this place for as long as I can remember, but those *men*, the closest souls I have to kin, stare lifeless into the cold, empty night, as if they once had a story to tell or an urgent warning about the unfeeling gods they wanted to give – but somehow – too late they were unable to utter their last refrain.

Tell me truthfully, am I wrong? Please, tell me I was more than just another enervated statue in your troubled, ceaseless search for the diversions of pleasure. Is that why others were trying to take me away from this place? From you? Out of jealously or was it something else? Was it really just because you had succeeded in forging a better statue than they had? Or some way to protect me and to stop you from destroying more souls? Is this the secret you've hoped to keep from the innumerable statues that continually stare at you?"

His anger was clear and cold as every muscle fiber and follicle tensed and twitched with every wrathful phrase, "Tell me!"

"Clearly I have upset you, my Cin? Not only have I given you your very existence, but I've also given you everything any mortal could dream of. And yet, with the lips that only move because I willed it to be so, you heap upon my brow the unwarranted scorn of these… silly, inventive thoughts, bereft of any argument that can boast a reasonable foundation. Do you really think I'd toss you away like some piece of broken marble?"

Cin looked unfazed. Unmoved, really. He stood with his back toward me, his face lifted to regard the fresco above him. His muscles were taut with a tension that I had never seen in him before. I suddenly felt uneasy and took an involuntary step away from him.

"Do you tire of me, and this place?" I asked. "Do you tire of the tiered walls of Someday? Do you grow weary of the admiration of the gods? *My* admiration for you? Do you grow bored of their passionate worship of your perfection? stone faces and old stars which hunger for your perfect face and ennobled body; Would you cast aside all of this in favor of the empty and cold tombs on that dirt clod that churns in a swirling froth below us? You've heard the stories. The plastic cities and broken spirits, bereft of hope who'd forsaken us for artificial gods of their own creation. If you, in all sincerity, tire of me, of this place, then Cin, I remind you that there are other places for you, places that are populated with a great number of things worse than those statues that you abhor, that you proclaim I've erected in the pursuit of my own desire."

Finally, he turned to face me, his eyes filled with a seething passion that almost looked as if he wished to transmute me into stone. He spoke in a voice like I'd never heard come from him before. "I only wish you didn't hide the truth from me and hadn't kept me hidden away in here as if I were some nymph brought to sate your desires. If I were anything more than that to you, you should have been open and honest with me. This, you have not done, and as a result, your initial intentions have been laid bare by your own deceitful actions. You wear a cloak of lies, and have swaddled my eyes in untruth."

"If I have failed you thus, I can do no more than promise that I will always be truthful with you in the future, Cin," I said.

"Then swear to me, " hands gipped my shoulders, "Never lie to me. Again."

"I swear."

His expression hardened, and his hands tightened around me.. There were no more tender or kind words between us from that moment onward. Our only reality, all that we had left was that all expectations both his and mine, were dead.

"Good."

My own fall, my descent into lunacy nearly too complete to endure, began with his silence. He spoke to nobody, neither god nor man. He wore his contempt of me, of the gods, of all things, like a suit of armor. His touch became reluctant and it his own desire as if I were the very statue made for his enjoyment, now, and held within it no hint of the tenderness that we once shared. My very essence suffered, a wound inflicted by a sword of my own forging. My heart bled until I had no strength left. That was when he struck his blow. Despite it all, the rest of my days were filled with the darkest, twisted sanguinities and spent languishing in what little cruel copulation Cin might objectify me in; my self-imposed nightmare.

Dark clouds filled my mind, impeding any clarity of thought. *"What did it matter? I created him. Right? I was created to brighten his night. No, wait. He was just another statue from the flesh forge!"* Everything was turning upside-down and my days and nights blurred together in an excruciating panoply of undifferentiated, feverish vignettes.

The world grew heavier as the days dragged onward. It all happened so quickly – I cannot fathom the depth nor the celerity of the collapse, nor the swiftness of my descent into the lunacy that followed, but perception is easily subverted, warped, and manipulated by those who want only one thing: control. This was Cin's desire, perhaps his *only* desire. He nurtured and succored my pain, sowed and harvested my agony, and took everything from me. My home, my position, my godhood. I ceded to him everything that I could, allowed him to take what was never his to possess, and it left me broken and bereft, a wispy remnant of a shadow of who I once was.

I should've been flattered, though forgot I was no longer living in my own *house.* Banishment, for the cruel flesh experiments and thoughtless actions was the punishment I was to endure according to Cin. The other gods granted him permission over my domain, and my fall was complete. He consigned me to a corner of the flesh forge, ostensibly to remind me of my transgressions, but also to illustrate just how far he had risen, and how far I had fallen. Always he was filled with jubilance, like some mad lunatic, grateful to remind me of my fall from grace. At least he would speak to me now.

He was a conniving bastard.

Nights grew cold, passionless, and riddled with animalistic fervor underneath a wide metallic sky, coarse with distempered wrath; unchecked and bloody. My fingers broken, bled over his chest, childish cackles erupted at my pain like some juvenile game. A game where he was quickly losing interest.

"I'm growing bored," he mused, wiping the dried blood off his chest. "You don't put up much a fight anymore like you did in the beginning," he cooed, manipulative and sinister, my mind lost in the pool of his mercurial eyes.

"It's your favorite though, I thought?"

"It was...but I'm not the man I used to be when you sculpted me so long ago. I grow bored of this place," he said.

"Could I at least come down off these chains?" My bones were brittle and shaky.

"It's funny to me."

"What is?" I said.

"How even gods which seem as if they would outlast us, are as delicate and shallow as the water crashing over the salt rocks. You probably thought me the same, didn't you?" Cin's long fingers squeezed my wrists

"I mean, I don't know...I suppose I thought you naïve, yes," I saw the anger boil in his eyes.

"And?"

"I don't know," he squeezed, an intensely brilliant pain flashed and snapped as my hand fell limp.

He was a monster, a picturesque creature imbued with my own baneful reflections of existence and still, I couldn't help my sick attraction.

Cin constricted his body around me as the chain pulled taught against my arms. "You meant to say that if all failed in your design for companionship, I'd end up another statue in your grand halls? Another regretful piece of botched flesh; metallic and broken unable to breathe, dream, fuck, or leave your demented house?"

"That's not what I had in store – not for you. Not like this," I pleaded.

"And what about the others? You never gave them this choice. What makes me so different? Is it that I'm more beautiful? Taller? More well sculpted compared to the others, or perhaps better suited for perverse lovemaking in your eyes? *Your eyes?* What about their eyes? The ones that are filled with metal and oxidized tears."

He had finally met my fears as my head hung deep in shame and regret. Cin stepped back, the light muddled with particulates and dead skin.

"I have an idea, how about one more game? For old times' sake, hm?" A black smirk curled across his face, "indulge me this last time?"

"Do I really have a choice?" I sighed.

"You're so sweet when you flirt. It's like I made you this way," Cin laughed.

His games always began like this, filled with a murky eroticism and dank sense of misplaced self-worth. His eyes, which sparkled with all the hopes of my future, now grizzled with a bleakness I'd only known but once. My body was thrown into the air, held loosely by thin chains, it was a matter of time before my arms completely ruptured under the immense force.

Rage combined with blood fashioned from an indiscriminate worthless yearning where meaningless cracks, bruises, and scars dotted a model that was my now body. I had become his sculpture, soon to be one of many for *his* eternal pleasure. The world began to move faster and faster without consequence or remorse for any actions taken or pain he caused me. A numbing paresthesia crawled up my arms where I met his cruel face. At least, whatever was left of them.

Cin's blood-sport was interminable and his laughter strangely edifying while the stars melted away into fragmented light and all my expectations for what was and whatever might be, were blasted into the far reaches of oblivion.

"Not like this," I said.

"Say it again," he smiled my frail body bestrode by his frame. "You remember, don't you? The first words I said when you brought me into this world, don't you?"

"Not like this, please," I watched the world bleed into nothingness as my body felt like some malleable tool within his grip.

Never had I conceived a creature so deadly, or derisive whose destructive passions resulted in my undoing. Disbelief was the ultimate nemesis, the wraith who flies in the face of all probable outcomes or possible circumstances, perceptions altered when the light was dampened by that which is unseen in the dark. Disbelief, guided by the hand of mistrust and fear who ultimately sealed my fate. Not the bloodthirsty monster sculpted from clay and flesh, though my subjective reasoning was muddled under a murky daze after the second time thrown across the hall.

He stood up again, walking away from my chained body, dreadful footfalls echoing through the flesh forge.

There above me, I remembered the first time I saw him beneath the rotunda where he spied that despicable painting, gods cavorting and men dying; a youthful and simple exuberance ignited in his gaze. And while the last pieces of my soul fell to a tenebrific end; I stared into the eyes of my horrible desire, "please, not like this..."

The Ride

By

Brandon Ford

Vince glimpsed the dashboard clock. It was closing in on 10:30 by the time he'd had the chance to thoroughly cleanse the back of the Toyota Corolla. Nearly an hour in the CVS parking lot, hunched over the backseats while the blistering December winds numbed his lower half. As minutes ticked on, fewer and fewer patrons passed the automatic doors to enter or exit the store, but each time they did, he heard the echo of one of many holiday standards playing at top volume.

Reminders of the Christmas holiday were everywhere he looked. In shop windows he passed, in the multicolored lights adorning residential streets, spread along the front lawns of the many drop-off points. The rosy cheeks of an illuminated Santa Claus and the painstakingly elaborate mangers had become reminders of his many responsibilities.

Vince pulled in to pick up April and her co-workers just after 8:00 PM. As the majority of those leaving holiday parties so often had, they tried to squeeze more than the allotted number of passengers into the vehicle. When Vince shot down the leggy redhead who insisted she could easily squeeze in the back with the rest, and the swaying executive who couldn't grasp why he wasn't permitted to sit in the front passenger seat, Vince was certain there'd be trouble on the horizon. After signing up with the ride share program, he'd never been called a piece of shit, or told to suck a dick with such regularity.

All because he deemed it mandatory to follow the rules clearly printed in the app, not to mention the law.

Vince assumed the amount of alcohol the group gleefully consumed impaired their natural-born ability to argue, for their speech was so slurred he could hardly decipher a word, and when he did, they'd just made the same points repeatedly. He'd been on the road only a few hours by then, but already, Vince felt his patience and tolerance wane. In a stern voice, he told the party he'd be taking three passengers and three passengers only. If they had an issue with that, they could find another ride, or use the app to file a complaint. Most passengers despised hearing their paid monkey wouldn't bend to their will, thus began the profanity and petty name-calling by adults who more often than not worked in a variety of prestigious fields, this he knew because they insisted on telling him. However, their intelligence and achievements never stopped them from behaving as though they'd recently been freed from a wildlife sanctuary. Vince felt the jolt of shoving hands on the back of his seat as less than cordial clients exited the vehicle. Had to cleanse his windshield of spattered phlegm by stopping at a gas station before returning to the road. Had to file an insurance claim to cover the cost of a large dent in the driver's side door, as well as a busted taillight, both of these the effects of a large booted foot as he pulled away from what was meant to be a pick-up site.

The women that night frayed his nerves thirty seconds from the high-rise building. Each had something imperative to convey to the group the very instant the other two started in on some office politics, or professed disapproval over who'd be climbing the corporate ladder after the New Year. And then there were the suspicions regarding how he or she had gotten there. Vince immediately realized his mistake when he politely asked they decrease the volume to a dull roar, for that was when they started in on him, throwing a host of personal and impersonal questions in the direction of the driver's seat.

"Hey, what's your name?" was one he received more than any other, especially when the passenger clearly had a few too many. Politely, he'd oblige, despite the presentation of his name, photograph, license plate, and car type visible on their version of the app. "How long have you been a ride share driver?" almost immediately followed. And then came demands regarding what kind of music they could listen to during the course of the ride. Vince liked it quiet, namely because his passengers left him with a migraine. But if they asked nicely, he'd switch on the radio and tune it to the channel of their choice. He'd raise the decibels just below midlevel so he could still be well aware of his surroundings. This often posed a problem, for the intoxicated riders were still looking for a good time and wanted their music loud.

Tonight, however, April committed what Vince considered to be a cardinal sin: reaching forth to fumble with the radio's controls, thereby invading his personal space and raising the potentiality of an accident. Like all others who committed this offense, April wanted to switch on the Wi-Fi so she could pair her phone with the car's speakers and crank her favorite songs to an insufferable level. When Vince immediately shot her down and insisted she take her seat, she begrudgingly obliged. The women began chatting quietly with one another, but their version of quiet was far from traditional. Within minutes, they were back to drunken cackling and slurred sentences—until April claimed she suddenly didn't feel so well. Vince felt a hand lay upon his shoulder. He assumed she'd ask that he pull over, but there was nowhere to pull over *to*. They were on the expressway and still several miles from their destination. In the rearview mirror, he watched in muted horror as April turned from her friends and lunged for the door, as if it were open. She proceeded to vomit along its side, armrest, and the edge of the cushion. Simultaneously struck ill, by the scene or the alcohol creating a very hazy scene, another of the three dropped her head between spread thighs and purged onto the floormat. The stench filled the car with unmerciful strength, temporarily bringing tears to Vince's eyes. He gripped the wheel to keep from swerving and cracked the window.

"I'm sorry," one of them called. "We're so sorry..." But her words bled together, making them almost incoherent. Even if they were, it wouldn't have mattered. All the apologies in the world wouldn't remove the odor or clean the upholstery.

"Are you mad?" another asked moments later. "Are you mad at us?"

Vince gave an exhausted sigh. "Right now, I'm just...just trying to get you guys home." The remainder of the ride concluded in silence, until one of the girls passed out and began snoring. She woke when the car pulled alongside an apartment complex and Vince slammed the door as he exited the vehicle. One by one, he guided them to the main entrance, a courtesy that wasn't even part of his job. But he wanted to ensure they got where they were going safely and most importantly, that he got them out of his car. Weaving them around snowbanks and ice patches, he took them by the shoulders and did his best not to touch them. More apologies as they fell upon a bench outside the building.

"Hey," he said, clapping both hands as they teetered before falling shoulder to shoulder, heads lolling. "Don't pass out. You *have* to get inside." He looked up at the building and silently considered. Would they have neighbors who'd be so kind as to help them negotiate the lobby?

His concerns abated when April rose and tugged on their jackets. Holding on to one another, they hobbled past him, one slurring something that could've been "Merry Christmas" before a keycard was produced and they entered the building.

Vince turned to face the Toyota. The back doors open wide, he could see and smell the mess they'd left behind. The incessant chime of the bell acted as a warning, but not for on-road safety. His time was rapidly running out. Looking down to ensure he hadn't inadvertently gotten anything unsavory on himself, he stepped over a snowbank and pulled for the passenger side door. He snapped dozens of pictures with his phone, capturing the multitude of stains in the highest quality available. He'd send the images to the company and tell them what happened. They'd compensate him based on the severity of the mess. Knowing the amount of money he'd have to put on his credit card to purchase the necessary supplies, not to mention the amount of time he'd have to dedicate to returning the car to its previous condition, Vince was certain he'd receive the maximum.

Watching the vaporous exhalation of his rapid breaths, Vince traversed the CVS parking lot, where he deposited spent towels and brushes he'd never use again into a Dumpster. With what remained of the various cleaning products stored in the trunk, he planted himself in the driver's seat and closed his eyes. Hand on the keys, he breathed in. Searched for remnants of the odor. He'd used a spray disinfectant, as well as a fresh-smelling deodorizer once he'd successfully removed the stains. He only hoped these would eliminate the stench entirely, as opposed to simply masking it. He smelled nothing objectionable. Even still, he lowered the back windows for a few minutes while regaining his bearings.

The phone lying in his lap came to life. He glimpsed the screen and sighed. Another pick-up. He should've logged out of the app, but pressing matters eclipsed other obligations. He squinted at the screen. Aldamoore. At least a 45-minute trip. But he'd rake in some decent cash, which was what being a driver for a ride share was all about. He accepted the ride and rolled up the windows. Breathing in deep, he searched for an odor, turning his head this way and that. Satisfied, he raised the phone to dial Angela.

"*Please* tell me you're on your way home," she panted.

"I just accepted another ride," he said and winced.

"What does that mean?"

"It means I probably won't be home for another hour or so." It would probably be closer to two, but he sure as hell wasn't going to tell her that, especially when he noticed the dashboard clock.

"Vince," Angela said with restrained fury, "we have a mountain of toys to assemble. The kids will likely be up before sunrise. I doubt we'll get more than a few hour's sleep before we head out to your mother's tomorrow."

"I know…" he muttered.

"I've—" she started to rage before checking herself, beginning again in a softer tone. "I've started on some of the smaller stuff, but you know I'm not good with my hands."

"Just read the directions."

"Vince…"

"When I get home, I'll grab a screwdriver before I even take my coat off," he said, trying to calm her.

"I hope you don't mean a cocktail."

"I could sure as hell use one, especially after the night I've had."

"What happened?"

"I'll tell you all about it when I get home," he said, turning the key in the ignition. "Let me do this last pick-up."

They exchanged I-love-yous before Vince disconnected the call and placed the phone on its mount. The screen switched to the ride-share app, where a GPS showed where he was and where he'd be going with a glowing map of multicolored lines. He sighed when he saw how long the trip would take, according to the calculations before him.

Snow flurries fell upon the windshield. The wipers washed them away as he eased into traffic, unable to stop from sniffing the air. The last thing he needed was a bad rating due to a lingering odor. As he drove, Vince thought of Angela and their little boys. At 6 and 9, they became more demanding when birthdays and especially Christmastime approached. Even with combined incomes, the young parents struggled to make ends meet. Angela had been working for a call center for four years, making good use of that Musical Theater degree she'd spend the rest of her life paying off. Vince spent the past year as assistant manager of a department store specializing in various electronics. After clocking in the mandatory hours and kissing enough corporate ass to leave his lips raw, he moved up to general manager, sights set on regional management. Even with their combined income, they were barely scraping by. With a monthly mortgage, two car payments, insurance, private schooling for their children, they could quite easily slip beneath the undertow if every penny wasn't calculated and designated. Taking on the ride share job was meant to keep them afloat for the holidays, but with the way things looked, Vince would be behind that wheel for several months to come.

If not years.

He switched on the radio to occupy his mind, eyes fixed on an endless stretch of moistened blacktop lit by twin headlights. He found nothing but holiday standards as he scanned the stations. What else did he expect to find on Christmas Eve? He considered switching to a music app on his phone, but feared what catastrophes the minor distraction could potentially cause. Even with rides available at the push of a button, irresponsible drivers continued to hit the roads, regardless of the amount of alcohol they consumed. Vince need only avert his eyes for fractions of a second to collide head-on with another motorist.

With the holidays, one could never be too careful.

A lengthy ride led to an upper middleclass area festooned with twinkling lights, mechanical Santas, reindeer, and a variety of other accoutrements. He lowered his gaze to glimpse the map. Saw he was only a few houses from his destination. He rolled alongside the curb and pulled to a park, granted only a moment to marvel at the storybook Tudor before the front door swung and two female figures emerged . Faces lit by flickering lights, he observed a woman in her late forties sporting a heavy red sweater and dark-rinse jeans.

On her arm, an older woman with white hair and heavy coat, orthopedic shoes on her feet. They advanced slowly along the walk, side-stepping ice patches and windblown vegetation. Vince strongly considered getting out to lend a hand, but the ride share's strict policy regarding making physical contact with the passengers kept him rooted to his seat. As they stood before the door, he slid the window down a few inches. The younger of the two smiled, vaporous breath fogging the glass,

"Ride for Victoria?" she said in a pleasant voice.

"Yes, ma'am," Vince said, glimpsing the picturesque suburban home one last time, hoping he could one day provide something equally as beautiful for his own family.

"I reserved the ride for my mother," Victoria said. "Can we get her inside?"

"Yes, of course." Vince fumbled with the control panel to unlock the doors. Behind him, Victoria helped the older woman into her seat, speaking to her in a soft tone while buckling her safety belt. She closed the door and stood before the driver's side window once more.

"We should've known to expect this," Victoria said. "She does it every year."

"Pardon?" Vince said.

"She joins us for Christmas Eve dinner and then we sit around the fire opening presents. She has every intention of sleeping in the guestroom so we can all spend the morning together, but by about nine o'clock, she starts complaining that she'd rather sleep in her own bed. Usually my husband drives her, but it's so late and we still have lots to do in preparation for the morning."

Vince nodded, holding his tongue while recalling his own obligations. Things Angela was now doing on her own.

"It took a while to find a car," Victoria went on. "There aren't very many of you on the road tonight, huh?"

"Not tonight," Vince said. "Not at this time."

"Well, I'm glad to have found you." Victoria took a step to the left and called out to her mother. Vince lowered the automatic window so they could exchange final words before venturing off. "Stan will be by early to pick you up tomorrow, okay?"

In the rearview mirror, Vince watched as the elderly woman gave a half-nod. He raised her window when Victoria reappeared at his side.

"Thank you so much for taking her," she said.

"No problem," he said. "Will she need any assistance getting inside?"

"I'm sure she'll be fine, but if you could wait just a minute or so to make sure she gets in safely, I'd certainly appreciate it."

"Of course."

"Merry Christmas," Victoria called, waving a hand as she stepped backward toward the house.

To the frosted back window, she hollered an I-love-you.

With a half-smile, Vince raised the window and pulled away. Adjusting the rearview mirror, he spied the older woman, who appeared pleasant enough in the passing lights and shadows. "Is there anything I can do to make you more comfortable?" he said. "Turn up the heat, or…?"

"No, no," she said, her voice strained. "I'm fine, thank you."

"You're warm enough?"

"Yes, thank you."

"Would you like me to turn on the radio?"

"No, that's quite all right."

Driving without music made Vince feel obligated to entertain his passengers by engaging them in polite conversation. Something, however, told him she wasn't interested in chatting. As he glimpsed the GPS, he spied the dash cam and considered switching it on. He made it a point to record every ride, then wiped out the cloud when he returned home if the evening transpired without incident. Returning his focus to the road, he left the dash cam off and readjusted in his seat. Glimpsing the older woman through the rearview mirror, he saw her seated motionless, head facing the window.

"Did you have a nice evening with your family?" he asked.

"Mmm-hmm," she replied in a pleasant tone.

"Good," he said. "You're my last ride, then I'll be heading home to my wife."

She said nothing.

"We have a lot to do. Very demanding kids." He gave a low chuckle.

More silence from the backseat.

As he turned onto the highway, he heard her fidget. Preparing to help in whatever way she needed, Vince glimpsed the rearview mirror, only to find her slipping out of her coat. Beneath it, she wore a floral-patterned dress better suited for a spring afternoon, as opposed to a chilly Christmas Eve dinner. She raised a sleeve to regard an expensive-looking watch with a gold band. He wondered if it'd been a gift from her family.

"Is the heat up too high?" he said. "I can turn it down, if you'd prefer."

"I'm fine," she said. "Just a little stuffy in that coat. Thank you, though."

As he carried on, he watched the cars around him. Several families traveling for the holiday. If he managed to make it through the night, he'd be back on this very road tomorrow afternoon. Things generally went harmoniously. The boys would entertain themselves by playing video games with their cousins. Angela would help in the kitchen in between sharing nuggets of gossip. Before dinner, the men would kick back in the living room, drinking beers from longneck bottles and discussing the potential future of whichever football team they favored. There'd always be an uncle who'd ask Vince more questions than he cared to answer. Wanted to know his exact job title, though he already knew full well. By way of forced politeness, Vince would make it a point to answer every question, but couldn't help wondering why *he* was always stuck entertaining the relative who shared the least in common with the group.

By the time they sat down to a delectable baked ham dinner, the women would have had more than their share of white wine and gossip would be out in the open, as opposed to kitchen whispers.

In his twenties, Vince never would've pegged this as the sort of life he'd have in his early-forties. Marriage and children never appealed to him. He enjoyed bachelorhood. Dating casually and bedding down with various women. But when he met Angela, he realized what he truly wanted.

In the back, the elderly woman let out a strange noise. Sounded like a grunt. When Vince again glimpsed her reflection, he found her sleeping, head slumped to the side. His attention returned to the GPS. He frowned as he remembered a line from a Robert Frost poem.

Still miles to go before I—

An inhuman cry filled the car, causing Vince to jerk the wheel. He motioned to turn, but two hands grabbed him from behind and tightened around his throat. He tried to call out, but could barely gasp the oxygen he so needed.

What the hell was happening?

When he saw the floral pattern, he knew the old woman was choking him.

She was trying to kill him.

"STOP!" he managed when a few breaths entered his lungs. *"STOP! WHAT THE HELL ARE YOU DOING?"*

Vince looked around him. At the steady flow of traffic. At the highway that left him with nowhere to yield. He leaned on the horn, praying it would draw the attention of another motorist, or startle the woman into submission. Behind him, cars honked. High beams flashed.

In the rearview, two glowing eyes looked back at him.

The woman had changed into something monstrous, two rows of impossibly sharp teeth revealed as she pulled her lips back to snarl. Vince looked around him. Scanned the passenger seat, as well as the dashboard, for something to protect himself with. But had anything strong enough been there, could he hurt an elderly woman, even if it meant saving his own life?

But this *wasn't* an elderly woman… This was something else. Something evil. Something inhuman.

Something that wrapped it's jagged claws around his throat, once more squeezing the life out of him.

Vince moaned as she dug into his flesh. He took one hand off the wheel in a pathetic attempt to pry hers away. The car veered off course, swerving from lane to lane, invoking the rage of other drivers, who cursed him from behind closed windows. As he reached to reclaim the wheel, her hand encircled his forearm, leaving scratches deep enough to draw blood. He screamed as her teeth sank into his neck.

She didn't stop there, however. As blood gushed from the open wound, spilling into the neck of his sweater, she leaned inward, forcing herself forward, as if trying to feast upon his flesh. When he heard the sound of his own skin tearing, the world around him spun and darkened, sending him far off into some alternative reality. A place without miles of highway, blaring car horns, and a demented creature ripping the meat from his bones.

Inadvertently, Vince leaned on the gas. The car accelerated. He knew he had to let go of the wheel in order to somehow fend her off. Where this would take them, he couldn't be certain, but he knew there would be nothing left of him if he let this carry on. The car drifted to the left as he grasped her forearms and pulled them from his oozing flesh. He begged her to *stop, stop, stop*, but hearing anything over her monstrous snarls and growls grew impossible. He reached for the wheel with one hand, using the other to thrust blindly behind him. As he stopped them from swerving into oncoming traffic, he felt the pressure of her body against the back of his seat. Again, she sunk her claws in, this time tearing back from the start of his hairline. A shrill, feminine cry escaped him as the warmth of fresh blood streaked his cheeks and neck. If he hadn't seen his stained reflection in the rearview mirror, he would've sworn she'd ripped his scalp clean off.

For Vince, any reservations about hurting the old woman—if she were indeed an old woman—abated the instant he saw the scratches and deep lacerations. When he saw the crimson mar the otherwise smooth skin of his left cheek. If he didn't fight back, his boys would wake without a father. Angela would wake without a husband. What remained of both he and the ravenous creature would be found in a fiery blaze in a ditch somewhere.

When he saw the exit, he launched himself forward and grasped the wheel with both hands. His chest against the horn, his body folded like an accordion, he floored the gas and led them down a dark road leading God only knew where. A few moments of respite and she was on him again, the claws of her gnarled fingers reaching for his collar and pulling him back toward her. As the wounds bled onto the wheel and onto his fingers, he shouldered her off and swore to himself that he wouldn't allow anything to pull his focus from the road until he saw bright lights and some indication of people. Again, she tried to feed upon him, to maneuver between the seats and crawl into the front with him. Using his right elbow, he sent her sailing back. He was certain that if the harshness of the last-minute motion had caused any injury—had broken bones or harmed her in any way—he would've heard. But there was nothing. She carried on the attack as though he'd done nothing at all.

Thank you, God, Vince thought when he lifted his eyes to a lit billboard advertising a well-known chain of restaurants, the parking lot leading to one of which just a way's off. If he could only make it a little further, everything would be okay. He was *sure* everything would be okay.

Still leaning on the horn, Vince jerked the wheel, doing well over ninety. He felt the force, suddenly terrified they'd be up on two wheels, but by the grace of some miracle, the car squealed into the parking lot right side up.

He knew he'd just rolled a pair of dice with limited sides, for the chances of the restaurant being open at this hour on Christmas Eve certainly weren't in his favor. He pulled the key from the ignition and screamed the moment he saw the emergence of figures. Three men and four women, all dressed in regulated attire, entered the lot, phones held ahead of them.

"CALL THE POLICE!" he yelled toward the largest of the men.

A man he was certain would've been the chef.

It appeared the man ceased recording and used the touchscreen to punch a few keys. He then had the phone pressed to his ear as others approached. Some asked if he was okay, which would've made Vince laugh under different circumstances, for he clearly wasn't. The rest screamed for the woman to stop, for she'd bitten into his hand and removed a clean chunk the moment he reached to unfasten the safety belt. More blood oozed from the wound branded by her teeth marks. Vince had fractions of a second to glimpse materializing pus before she wove through the seats, now successfully reaching the front of the car.

Pounding on the door commenced as she took his face in both her hands and used her fanged teeth to remove his bottom lip. He felt the pain. *God knew he felt the pain.* But there was little fight left within him. Little fight and little air to scream as she continued to bite and used her claws to slash through his coat. He felt the tips of those claws graze his chest, immediately drawing blood. If he didn't get her off of him, or somehow find a way out of the car, she would've long since made hamburger out of him before the police or anyone else came to his aid.

Fists pounded the door's glass.

"Unlock the door," commanded a male voice Vince saw as belonging to one of the servers. "Can you hear me? Open the door and let us get you out."

I can't, Vince wanted to cry, but he was too weak to respond, let alone reach for the key fob, which had fallen somewhere out of reach.

He burned with a sudden fever as his body retaliated against innumerable infections, further blinding him and weakening his resolve.

And she was biting, clawing, *ripping him to shreds.*

Hysterical voices all called out at once, some aimed at co-workers, some aimed at Vince, and some aimed at the woman who appeared less human with every ounce of flesh she swallowed.

"Stop! Let go of him!"

"The police are on their way!"

"What the hell is wrong with her? She looks like a rabid animal. Is that even a person?"

More banging on the glass.

More urgent cries for Vince to open the door.

Lazily lifting his left arm, he curled his thumb and forefinger into a C.

If you're ever beneath the force of an animal you're clearly no match for, Vince remembered his father telling him during an adolescent hunting trip, *remember to always go for the eyes.*

And so he did, thrusting his hand forth, thumb and forefinger penetrating the sockets of the creature incapable of reason. Though all fight within him had long gone, he somehow found the strength to finally cause harm, for the woman roared again, this time in physical agony. As he thrust harder, dug deeper, her weight lifted from his torso and her back met the wheel. The horn blared as she lifted her hands to shield her bleeding eyes, while in the parking lot of the family oriented restaurant, hysteria reached new heights. The staff screamed louder now, possibly to be heard over the deafening car horn, or the wail of police sirens as flashing red and blue lights rapidly approached.

Vince seized the opportunity to unsnap the safety belt and thumb the driver's side door lock. Thankfully, a member of staff had been watching closely and pulled the door open the moment Vince found a way to allow access. A multitude of hands grabbed him by the arm and clenched the torn fabric of his coat, pulling him from his seat as several patrol car doors opened and slammed shut. Vince fell upon the icy blacktop as one of his many saviors used a blunt instrument to send the woman sailing into the passenger seat. The door snapped shut and she threw her weight against the glass, scratching at the pane and releasing guttural cries from within the vehicle.

"Get him away from the car," someone panted, hysterics clearly audible.

"Don't move him," replied a female voice. *"Wait until the ambulance gets here."*

"Where is the fucking ambulance?"

Sirens sliced through the cold as a vision in red sped into the parking lot. Bleary-eyed, Vince watched with gratitude, with relief, as paramedics exited the large vehicle, toting a gurney. They lifted him onto the thin mattress and immediately began checking vitals. A sphygmomanometer strap encircled his arm as a pen light burned into his left eye, then his right.

"Can you hear me? Can you see me?" one of the paramedics asked, speaking in a loud, deep voice so as to be heard over the fervor.

"We've gotta bandage these wounds and get him to the ER now," a female voice pled.

The already shredded coat was pulled from his back. Temporarily lifting him from the mattress and inflicting additional pain. He moaned.

As two paramedics worked on cleaning and covering incalculable lacerations, another jammed an IV needle into his hand. To keep him awake, endless questions were thrown his way. What was his name? How old was he? Does he have any family? Where had he just come from? Who was the woman raving maniacally inside the car?

The smashing of metal and breaking of glass startled him for the second time. Ignoring the constant inquiries, he turned to glimpse the Toyota. To watch the large fireman lift and throw an axe, breaking through the driver's side door. As it fell away, the creature burst from the open cavity, howling and squealing with rage. Onlookers gasped and cried out in terror. Much like them, Vince was sure the creature would continue her wrath.

Two gunshots.

A body fell upon the glass-littered blacktop.

"That should be good enough until we get to the hospital," one paramedic said to another, ignoring or disinterested in the insane activity only six feet away.

They started rolling him toward the ambulance. Strained grunts filled the air as he was hoisted off the ground. The gurney slid effortlessly into place before one of many faceless paramedics hurried to lock it. One door slammed, but fractions of a moment before the other followed, Vince saw the creature now lying flat and motionless upon the asphalt, her floral patterned dress spattered with blood. He would've inhaled a long gasp, had an oxygen mask not covered his nose and mouth.

It could've been the effects of blood loss. Could've been the drugs flooding the IV tubes and flowing through his veins. But Vince was certain that in the instant before the ambulance door slammed upon that night, ending what felt like countless hours of torment, he saw her face.

And she'd changed back.

Gone were the jagged fangs and monstrous features. She'd returned to the sweet old woman he saw standing outside the home of her daughter, Christmas lights and mechanical Santas behind her.

"Vincent? Vincent, can you hear me?"

Vince looked into the eyes of the pretty blue-eyed paramedic hovering over him, hair pulled back in a neat braid.

"Don't try to speak. Using your fingers, rate your pain on a scale from one to ten."

Vince had no trouble holding up ten fingers.

The paramedic nodded her understanding. Turning toward the front, she called for the driver to hit the gas. Vince heard the wailing sirens, felt his body jostle, as the ambulance took off. He then slipped into immediate unconsciousness.

Drop. Rock. Death.

By

James Lefebure

He hadn't slept properly all week. His eyes bore the brunt of this. Usually a soft brown, now they were red and bloodshot. The bags living under his eyes were not designer.

Every night for the last week he had found himself jolting upright in bed. Covered in a cold sweat, a scream teasing his lips. The first night had been the easiest for him. He shook off the feeling of unease the next day and looked forward to getting into bed that night to catch up on his sleep. The day had been spent ignoring a voice at the back of his mind whispering a secret warning that something was watching him. That something was hunting him.

'Sleep came harder each night, leaving him increasingly drained. Last night was the worst yet. Last night he had dreamed something that refused to leave him. There was no sleeping after that. He remembered nothing much of the nightmare; *"They are coming for you. Your lies have fed them."* He had cried then. The truth weighed on his heart. He allowed himself to wallow for an hour. Then, as he had his whole life, he shut it up. "Let them come to this stupid island." He muttered to the darkened room.

He'd been born in Kirkwall and never left. It was a big city in his eyes although to the rest of the world, it would pall in comparison. Aberdeen wasn't far, just a ferry ride away, but he knew he would get lost in the labyrinth of granite and steel. *Listen to yourself you big pansy,* his mind chastised, *you're going to give yourself the blues if you're not careful.* The time for his moping was done. Tightening his laces he stood and stretched, taking a deep breath of the heady mix of sweat and testosterone which would only be found in the gym.

He walked over to the water fountain and drank deeply. The metallic taste refreshed his tongue and soothed his throat, he could faintly hear a laugh that could only belong to Tank; deep, menacing, and full of presence.

Mick "Tank" Phillips had gotten the rather solid nickname due to his physical resemblance to said machine. At six-feet-two he was a thick wall of muscle and anger. Steve had been friends with him for the last ten years, ever since Tank had invaded his twentieth birthday party and knocked out two of the guests.

Steve hadn't minded; the party had been crap and the guests boring. He was after a bit of danger. That danger had presented itself in the form of two things. The first was the Tank's dependence on their friendship. He saw a kindred spirit in Steve. An endless well of anger lived inside both men. They were both aware that anger was always the answer. Regardless the question. The second was Steve's desire to grab his friend of ten years and kiss him. He knew that if he did his life was over. Tank hated gays. He'd been reminded of this numerous times when he had dropped his guard too much and got a touch too close to Tank. "Move, ya queer" was usually spat in his direction. Pushing through the door he left the sanctity of the changing room behind and entered the warzone. His game face was on.

He was greeted with a wall of testosterone; this one was charged. He could feel the rage and aggression in it, the power of the men who had contributed to it. This was their battlefield. This was where men came to war with themselves and their bodies. This was where he was the happiest with himself, happiest with his life. Where his own desires could be ignored in favour of sweating and pushing his body to the limit. He had been coming here since he was sixteen years old. He had even introduced Tank to this gym, effectively letting him into his inner sanctum. It was the closest he had ever felt to trusting someone.

It had been his headmaster Mr Towers who had suggested he find an outlet for his rage. Mr Towers was the only person at that point in his life who took an interest. Who saw past the orphan who lived with his Nanna. The other children hadn't. Merciless name calling and lonely lunch times had been his only companion as long as he could remember; that and his never-ending rage.

The day had started easily enough. He'd gone to biology and sat with dead eyes while the teacher waffled on about cells and blood and other things that he knew he would never need in his life. His eyes lingered over the round behind of the boy in front of him, an inner battle commenced between eyes and brain as to the dangers of looking at his classmates behind. A male classmate behind. That was when Stephen Bryman caught his attention. Namely by pointing and whispering something to the block of lard that was Daniel Leckie next to him. Both boys turned and stared at him with a mixture of hatred and disgust. They saw! His mind screamed as panic did a nervous lap inside his brain.

Steve knew what he was going to have to do. He was going to have to fight. That break saw him stood behind the bike shed smoking to calm his nerves for what was about to occur. He sensed the two boys and the crowd before he saw them. The air around the tree changed as he heard the trample of footsteps and slowly, he walked out onto the field to be greeted by a battalion of students, led by Bryman. Exhaling the last of his smoke Steve eyed the crowd, his face set in stone. "I seen you!" Bryman spat at his feet. "Seen you looking!" the sneer on his face was enough for Steve to get his rage started.

"I saw you, fucking moron" he said with no emotion in his voice. A few chuckles from the spectators but the air was tense, they had come for blood.

"And what did you see?"

"I seen, I mean, saw you looking at Robbie's arse, you poofter." There was spittle on his lip as the last of his words came out.

Steve nodded slightly; he could feel the stares of the people around him. Tension filled the air as they tried to decide who they wanted to be victorious.

He'd always been a loner, never been invited to a birthday party, never stayed over at someone's house. He didn't know these people; he didn't want to know these people. He just wanted to be left alone. "You're not even going to deny it?" The horror in the voice was obvious, this wasn't how it was supposed to go. "I wasn't looking at his arse.

You might have been, but I don't tend to notice what other boys are looking at." It was a weak argument, but it provided another weak ripple of chuckles which gave him the distraction he needed. Within seconds his fist had connected with Bryman's right cheek. He felt the soft skin, then felt the pop as his fist knocked out a tooth and sent Bryman flying to the ground. A chorus of noise erupted around him as he kept the momentum and started kicking. He was still kicking as the silence fell around him and two sets of arms roughly grabbed him and pulled him to the ground. He could remember thrashing around, screaming, and spitting as his anger at the world roared. A French teacher, who had never taught him, frog-marched him to the headmaster's office and there he sat, awaiting the verdict.

The man in front of him was thin and old. They were the best words that any student at the school would use to describe him. At six foot his rake-like physique made him look as though he were likely to snap in half at any second. Most rumours put him at seventy-five years; adding twenty years to his true age, However this gave him an air of learning and respect where the students were concerned. Steve sat sullenly in the office his eyes full of anger. His fist red and sore. This was not his first trip to this office.

"So, what started it this time?" It was a weary yet familiar tone.

"He called me a poof" he answered.

The man in front of him looked at him sadly. "Ah I see. And you were merely defending your honour?"

There was no emotion in this, and Steve struggled to understand where the conversation was headed.

"Well? Am I right?" the headmaster probed.

Steve merely nodded his answer.

"I see, well we can't just have you going around punching everyone who you think has insulted your honour. You do understand that don't you?"

He nodded his answer. This was greeted by a weary sigh from the other side of the desk. "Listen, Steve you know that I don't like to punish you; but there are some things that you just cannot get away with."

Guilt started to gnaw at Steve; the man before him had never shown anything but kindness; despite his frequent visits. He lowered his eyes and felt the feelings showing on his face. "I'm sorry Sir." It was a feeble word, barely covering the emotions that he was feeling, but it was the best he had.

His mentor's eyes softened as he gave Steve a welcoming nod' "I can't just let you off though Steve, that wouldn't be fair on the other student."

"But he said – "

"I'm not interested in what he said." The teacher said, cutting him off "I need to suspend you for two days." He could feel the horror showing on his face as Mr Towers delivered his sentence. "But you will use it effectively. My brother-in-law runs a gym, it's very good for getting your anger out of you. And when you're ready to commit, it can help you unlock the real person you are under that facade". The rest of the meeting was spent sorting the logistics. Steve never forgot the risk this teacher took for him and every time he stepped into the gym, he pushed himself to the limit.

Snapping out of the painful memories, Steve scanned the room; there were the usual sorts in tonight ranging from skinny guys trying to bulk up to sculpted gods who were trying to maintain. He fell in the middle of both. From his frame it was apparent to anyone who looked at him that he went to the gym frequently. Hours of bicep curls and triceps dips had given him the arms of a wrestler. Thick, muscular, and tight they lead to a chiselled chest, thick with blonde hair. He knew there were men in here with much better bodies than his. Hell, Tank was built more solidly than him, but he was happy with the body he had. He knew that a change in diet would allow him to slim down and an increase in weights would help him bulk up. But Tank always complimented his body. He couldn't change it now.

Popping in his headphones he turned his music up and felt the beat, matched it with his breathing and walked towards the treadmill. He had a lot he wanted to think over tonight, the dreams, his life, his future, and he knew that the treadmill would be the perfect place for him to do that. He didn't need to see Tank yet, he knew that he would be here for hours, probably long after all the other patrons had gone; it would just be the two of them in the gym. Three if you included Pete, Tank's weird little brother - Steve never did.

With a press of the button the ground under him juddered and slowly started to move. Picking the pace up a little he felt his body getting into a natural rhythm. He could run all night if he needed too. With a conscious effort he got his breathing in check and let himself enter the zone to let his mind work through the issues that were plaguing his sleep.

By the 5k mark the world had completely faded away from his view. He was in the zone now. He didn't notice the crowd thinning, the people showering and leaving. He was too busy thinking about what had been plaguing his nights. His dreams usually started the same, there was darkness. He was always aware of the darkness, of things moving around in the darkness. Fear was never present here, more a sense of confusion. He didn't mind the sensation, but the whispering did bring back memories of being excluded and hard words. The whispering would normally start to get louder. Words would start to form from the gloom, its speaker never clear. He would never understand the words at the start but slowly they would come through, bit by bit he would understand more.

"Lies". The word echoed around him. Always the same. Night after night. The last few nights the dreams had been the same. Blackness pulsated around him. With each whispered sound of the word, hungry darkness would tighten its grip on him. He was being crushed by an invisible idea. Then he would hear screaming, he knew that his screams were mingled in with them, after the first night he had woken up at this point. Sweat dripping off him as the bed sheet clung tightly to his body as he shook in the secret hours of the world. The second night had seen him get beyond the point of screaming. he had heard the other screams and had managed to identify two others mingled, and the loudest seemed to be coming from a person he couldn't see.

It sounded like he was hearing the beginning of a conversation. He did his best to walk towards the source. The ground below him had started to crunch, he looked down but couldn't see anything below his knees. The crunching was a familiar sound for him living in Scotland. He was starting to walk through snow. He felt that he was walking in the right direction but when there is nothing around you, it was easy to assume right meant current.

He had carried on walking. Whispers about lies surrounding him. The darkness had faded to a thick foggy grey. He was more aware of the potential of surroundings as he walked. He had begun to feel as though he were trespassing. Suddenly from in front of him he heard an unfamiliar voice; whereas the other had been steel and iron, this voice was secrets and whispers. It had no real strength, as it whispered.

"The rift is opening."

'What did it mean? What rift?' His stomach churned, his mouth filled with the sour taste of bile trying to think of the meaning. His footsteps were getting slower as the snow below his feet started to get deeper. Slowing a bit to try and make it easier to wade through he heard another voice.

"I seen you. Seen you looking!"

He knew it instantly. Tears sprung to his eyes; sorrow heavy in his chest. The wounds of the boy he once was had never healed. The foggy darkness had thinned to the point of enabling him better a vision of his surroundings. He could see shapes in the distance, grey and unidentifiable. The ground below was now clearly snow; it wasn't a great shock, but it did make him curious as to where he was headed. He was still fighting his way through the murk when a male voice spoke again;

"Help you unlock the real person you are under that façade"

The anger from before awoke in him as though his voice were the match it desired. It sped through him, filling his veins with the same white-hot rage he had encountered before. He really despised the truth that had been uttered. If only it were that easy. There hadn't been a chance. The façade had kept him safe.

"Your lies feed them"

He felt all the air rush out of him. The light grey mist that was surrounding him thickened and grabbed at him, slowing him at first before constricting him and grinding him to a halt. Before he could think any more the darkness tightened around him, its thin grabbing fingers working over his body, around his face, down his throat, exploring, choking, killing. He always woke up gasping.

Back in the gym he had hoped that the physical exertion would have helped to improve his mood, to help sort out the jumble of thoughts that had gotten tangled inside his brain. Looking at the screen on the treadmill he saw he had run 15k, his t-shirt was stuck to him with sweat, his breathing hard and his chest tight. Keeping momentum, he pressed a button which bleeped its understanding as the machine started to slow. When it had ground to a halt, he allowed himself to stop. His legs were shaking as he drank deeply from his water bottle his heart beating loudly in his chest.

He noticed that it was a lot quieter in the gym now than it had been when he arrived. Scanning the room, he spotted his friend's bulk and made his way over to him. He was greeted by a red strained face as Tank worked his arms with weights that would not have looked out of place in the home of a professional wrestler; huge metallic discs that any normal mortal man would have laughed at the idea of lifting were being moved slowly up and down as Pete spotted. Steve hung back a minute, he really didn't have the energy to play nice with Pete; he just wanted to speak to his best friend.

When Tank had finished, he let out a bellow fuelled by testosterone and rage. He looked at Pete and growled. "Drop Rock. DEATH!" smashing his fist into his palm as Pete patted him on the back. "Stevie" he smiled as he pushed Pete out of the way.

"Alright mate." Steve smiled back, he could already feel his spirits lifting, although the smell and appearance of his friends' bulked physique was threatening to lift something else.

"Hiya Stevie" Pete interjected.

"Been here long?" Steve enquired, completely ignoring the attempt at interaction, with Tank it was hard to tell how long he would have been here, he had been known to spend up to nine hours in here working each muscle group with precision and effort. The following conversation was merely a façade, both men knowing that they were merely getting the niceties out of the way before entering battle together.

They were preparing to train together, enter a battle of endurance and pain together - each pushing the other further than they would have gone on their own. Today Steve needed that, he needed to scream in pain and rage, feel his body be punished and more importantly he needed to be close to someone while he did it. He was feeling a deep sense of loss and isolation he hadn't felt since early childhood. He knew that Tank was the answer. The two-hour session of weights and screams, pushing himself further than his body was prepared to, was just the catharsis that he needed. All the while trying to ignore the words that were floating in his head. The words that his dreams had spoken; *"unlock the real person you are under that facade"* and for a short while it had worked.

Back in the deserted changing room his body was screaming as waves of pain rippled through him. Both Tank and Pete had gone for showers as soon as they had entered the changing rooms leaving Steve alone; he was in too much pain to move from the cold wooden bench he was currently glued to. Closing his eyes, he did his best to focus his mind. He could hear the soft soothing patter of the water as it fell from the showers in a constant downpour. He knew that Tank would be a long time in there; he always was. He could feel his body relaxing as his mind wandered to the showers.

He could just imagine Tank in there, the water massaging his grizzly chest, coating the course black hair, straightening it closer to his pale skin. The soap frothing and foaming, a stray cluster getting caught in a trickle of water, travelling down over his chiselled stomach, coating the luxurious hair there, sliding down, mounting his thick, rough pubes. The silence of the showers turning off brought him back to his senses. Sitting up quickly he felt fresh embarrassment shoot through him as he tried to hide the remnants of his daydream by sitting forward. He waited for his friend to leave the shower room. What came out of the showers was not his friend.

The thing in front of him was not human; he knew that much straight away as terror tried its best to paralyse him. A battle had started in his head; fight or run. Looking at the thing in front of him he tried to work out where his best friend had gone. It was a bulk of stale grey muscle, thick ropes of black veins protruded from his limbs. Its legs were squat muscular things, its face was a mask of scars; black deep-set eyes glared back at him. Its wide, wet mouth unable to shut as two thick black tusks jutted outwards. With its mouth partly visible Steve could see a row of short pointed yellowed teeth.

His mind was reeling at the horror before him. A menacing smile slowly spread across the creature's face as a thick gruff voice spoke; "Bet you don't like my body now eh Stevie?"

For a second the terror in his mind eclipsed and fear got a tight grip. "T-t-ank?" His voice was shrill; the fear dripping from the short word.

"Drop Rock. Death" he growled and with speed unbecoming its size the Tank-creature lowered its head and ran for him.

Instinct kicked in and Steve's body screamed as it hit the floor and rolled. He was bouncing to his feet as the creature smashed into the bench with a roar. "Tank - what the FUCK!" he shouted. His mind was reeling as he tried to make sense of what was happening in front of him. It couldn't be his friend before him.

"Thanks for the feed, mate" Tank taunted. Its hand moved to its groin and gripped something thick and bulbous. "Bet you don't want me to feed you this now, eh?" It laughed cruelly. Steve's head was reeling. This couldn't be his friend. The only person he'd ever really loved. It couldn't be the person that not half an hour before had pushed him to the limit of his physical capabilities.

"Years you've kept us going." It laughed as it's blood thirsty eyes glanced behind Steve.

"You always forget about me you fucker." The Pete creature as was in life didn't have the same bulk as his brother. His body was thinner, quicker and the tusks longer. He roared as he ran at Steve who lunged to the left, his arm barely missing the razor-sharp tusk. The two brothers circled him together; their eyes locked onto him. "You know you can't beat me, Stevie," the larger creature goaded as he faked forwards.

Steve ignored the bait; his eyes locked onto the wall behind the brothers. Faking a run to the left where the exit was situated Steve threw himself to ground and slid. He heard the creatures thudding into the wall as he raced across the room. The fire extinguisher locked into his sights. Lifting it, he spun as the Pete-creature came rushing towards him. With a shout of exertion Steve swung and he felt the satisfying thud as it connected with the side of the creature's head.

Taking advantage of the confusion the blow had caused he raised his arms and brought them down with a loud crunch.

The Pete's creature sagged to the ground, dazed. "

"STEVIE!" a voice roared behind him. He had forgotten about Tank for the first time in his life. Not daring to look at the source he risked the impending danger and delivered a fatal downward smash upon Pete's skull. With a wet crunch the weapon sunk in as rotten black blood burst forth. He could hear the heavy footfall of the advancing threat. With a grunt of effort, he pulled the extinguisher free with a wet squelch. He spun to face his enemy, weapon dripping the remains of Pete. The pain of loss was evident on the creature's face as it ground to a halt. Its black eyes fixed on the bleeding corpse of its brother. Blood dried on Steve's face

"What the hell, Tank!" he groaned; "What the hell?!" He was begging for something. An answer. An explanation or simply proof that his friend was still there.

Slowly the creature tore its gaze away from the remnants of its brother. "You were supposed to die today. my friend." Its voice was deep and thick with anger.

"Why? If I'm going to die you might as well let me in on the secret,." he implored. "I don't think I'm going to tell you," it snarled as it rushed towards him.

Stepping forward Steve turned his body and brought the extinguisher forward to meet the approaching opponent. His plan only partially worked as Tank snapped into another direction. His speed did not befit his size. Steve's blow missed the desired spot. Cursing he spun on his heels, but his foe was already advancing on him again. He didn't have time to formulate a counter move. All he could do was try and reduce the damage he was going to receive. The blow that he received was what he had imagined running into a brick wall would feel like. He felt the tusk piercing through his right shoulder, the pain was hot and intense.

Instincts kicked in and he automatically pushed his arms forward, screaming in pain as the tusk pulled out. Blood pulsed from the wound He didn't know where his attacker was, but he knew it would be close. He knew that if he lost, he would be losing his life. It was a good motivator as he pushed himself to his feet. The importance of his next move weighed heavy on his mind. He knew that his fire extinguisher would not be of much use to him now. His foe was circling round the room, eyes burning with hate. His eyes were drawn to the mirror on the far side of the room; his own face stared back at him. It took him a second to realise that it was just his head and shoulders in the mirror. He felt like he was seeing himself for the first time. A plan formulated in his head.

The Tank-creature seemed to sense his newfound resolve and growled at him. Pulling the pin out of the extinguisher he pressed down on the handle, filling the room with breath stealing smoke. He could hear the roar of frustration from Tank.

"You're not even strong enough to come out Stevie!" Tank taunted. "You think you can take me on?" It laughed deeply. "Fucking closet case." It sneered. The words hurt almost as much as the bleeding wound on his shoulder. Quietly he felt along the lockers until he got to the mirror.

"Your misery and secrets have been keeping us going you know. From that first night, I've been living off your pain."

Steve knew he didn't have long to act; he was being played with and they both knew it. "You're a coward Stevie. I'd probably have fucked you if you had the balls to actually make a pass. The misery you'd have felt afterwards would have been a banquet for me and Pete." Tank's voice wavered on his brother's name.

"Wasn't too scared to stove Pete's head in, was I?" Steve quipped back. He got the exact reaction he needed. Tank's bestial roar filled the changing room. Using the noise to get a rough location for Tank, Steve swung the empty extinguisher and smashed the mirror. Grabbing a large piece of the broken glass he walked forward.

"Still got his brains on my top you know Tank." He heard movement to his right, "well, what little there was in there." Stevie pushed his heels into the ground and braced himself. He could feel Tank bearing down on him through the thinning smoke. He felt the tusk ripping through his shoulder. The pain white hot, exquisite, a reminder that he was *still* here. He felt the blood flowing down his hand as he thrust upward. Tank's body went limp, momentum carried them both to the floor. The glass had gone through Tank's throat and upward. There was no life left in the black eyes.

"Drop. Rock. Death." Steve muttered with a sob. Pushing with what little strength he had left he got out from underneath his friend. He caught sight of his bloodied reflection in the remaining shards of the mirror on the wall.

He saw himself.

There would be no more façade.

Effigy

By

Mark Allan Gunnells

"Nice Halloween decoration, Mr. Rogers."

Hank was at his mailbox at the curb, pulling out various EXCLUSIVE OFFERS addressed to "Current Resident," when the Sampson kid from down the street coasted by on his bike. At first, Hank assumed the boy was being sarcastic since Hank never put up Halloween decorations. He'd been in this house for five years now and never put out so much as a single pumpkin in all that time, even though many of his neighbors went all out with lights and ghosts and witches. At the end of the block, the Needleman family put skeletons all over their roof, some even hanging down from the gutters. By comparison, Hank's lawn always stood out for its lack of seasonal displays.

He glanced up at the Sampson kid and noticed he wasn't even looking at him but was instead staring off into Hank's side yard. Hank followed the gaze and actually gasped softly to himself when he saw someone standing in his yard right near the fence that separated his property from the vacant house next door.

But no, he realized no one stood in his yard. That was only the old moss-covered statue that had been on the property when Hank moved in, a remnant of the previous owners. The house had come full of furniture and yard decorations because the family had defaulted on their mortgage and moved abruptly, which was one of the reasons Hank got the house for such a deal. He had gone through the items left behind, keeping what he liked and throwing out the rest, including photo albums full of snapshots of the unfortunate family who lost their home and this evidence of their past.

The statue, a replica of Michelangelo's David, wasn't particularly to Hank's taste, but the damn thing was made of stone and heavy as a motherfucker. He kept telling himself that eventually he'd hire someone to haul it away, but he never wanted to part with the cash it would cost and over the years he had grown to ... not so much like it but he became accustomed to the sight of it.

But not the way it was now, covered in more than its usual outfit of moss and lichen. Over the face was a red Halloween mask, triangular in shape with a pointed chin and two horns sticking up. The devil's face. It was one of those suffocating plastic masks he remembered from his childhood, with a rubber band securing it in place. The body was obscured by a blood-red sheet or cape that went all the way around.

What really pulled the gasp from Hank wasn't merely the fact that someone had dressed up the statue in his side yard, but the fact that he recognized the costume.

"Did you do that?" Hank asked, his tone sharper than he'd intended.

The kid circled around on his bike and rode back to the mailbox. "Why would I dress up your stupid gay statue?"

Hank thought about saying something nasty back to the kid, but he'd just go tell his father who would make a big fuss about it because all parents these days thought their little snot-nosed, smart-ass kids were angels. Instead, he just turned and walked away.

Not back into the house but into the side yard. When he reached the statue, he tore off the mask and cape and marched over to the wheeled garbage container at the back edge of the house, the large leaves from his maple tree crackling under his feet. After tossing the costume, he glanced back at the street but the Sampson kid was gone.

Halloween was still two days away, but it looked as if someone were getting an early start on trick-or-treating.

Or at least the first part.

*

That afternoon, Hank sat down in the living room with a plate of chicken salad on his lap for his lunch. He turned on the TV and found the ball game.

When he glanced out the window, he wasn't looking for anything in particular, just a casual glance, but what he saw sent him flying up so fast that he nearly spilled the salad all over the floor.

Someone had put the damn devil costume back on the statue.

Tossing his plate onto the coffee table, some of the salad slopping out onto the surface, he hurried outside, looking around for signs of the damn Sampson kid or any other pranksters who might be lurking. As far as he could see, the street was deserted. He stalked across the side yard and jerked off the mask and cape for the second time then took them back to the trash. When he lifted the lid, he froze with his other hand poised to deposit the costume. Inside the container was the other devil mask and cape from earlier, meaning the ones in his hand were new.

So someone had not only dressed up his statue in this Halloween costume, but after he'd thrown the first one away this unknown trickster had replaced the discarded costume with a fresh one. But why? Seemed like a lot of trouble for a simple prank.

But what disturbed Hank the most was the costume itself. He stared down at the red mask with the painted on mustache and goatee. When he was a kid, this costume had been a dime a dozen, available at almost any store, and Halloween night would see an army of little devils marching through the neighborhoods demanding candy.

Yet he didn't know how common this costume was these days. Halloween costumes had become more elaborate affairs it seemed. Of course, cheap things like this surely still existed for the poor kids.

Like Frankie.

Hank tossed the new costume in with the first one and slammed the lid, hurrying back inside.

*

The next morning Hank was barely even surprised when he looked out the window and found the statue costumed again. What did surprise him was that the statue had been moved.

He walked across his side yard in his bare feet, kicking through the drifts of dried leaves, to make sure his eyes weren't playing tricks on him. But no, the statue was definitely closer to the house, almost a foot from its original location. Hank could pinpoint the original location because of the square of raw dirt where the base had sat. Oddly he could detect no grooves from where the thing had been dragged to its current spot.

Almost as if it had teleported from one place to the other. Or been picked up entirely.

This could be no kid pranking him. The statue was too heavy for even one adult to lift. So what did that mean? A group of people playing this stupid joke?

He wandered over to the road and took a stroll down to the end of the block and back. While most houses on the street were decorated, Hank's wasn't the only house that had decided not to celebrate Halloween. The widow several houses down was super religious and there was nothing in her yard but a slightly leaning cross; the old couple at the end of the block never decorated for any holiday, probably too much trouble for them at their ages; the newlywed couple renting one side of a duplex hadn't put anything out. Yet it didn't appear the prankster had visited these properties.

Which meant Hank was being singled out, and he couldn't help but think the choice of costume wasn't random. This had to be from someone who understood his connection to it.

Back in the house, he grabbed his tablet and pulled up Instagram. He found Doug's page, an old friend from his school days, and sent a quick private message.

"Hey Doug, you remember Frankie from school?"

After sending, he glanced out the window. He was sure it was just an optical illusion because of his vantage point, but it almost looked as if the costumed statue was a little bit closer to the house than it had been earlier.

*

It was nearly lunch time before Doug responded.

"Hey man, I don't hear from you for ages then you message me out of the blue asking about Feg. What's up with that?"

Feg. Yes, everyone's nickname back in school for Frankie. Frank Edward Gainey. Hank, Doug, and their crowd started calling the unpopular boy by his initials because they thought it sounded like "fag." The running joke was that his middle name should have been Andrew but it was close enough. The kind of shit kids find hilarious. Before long, the whole school was calling him Feg, including a few teachers.

"I know it's random," Hank typed. "But I saw one of those devil costumes like he was wearing that Halloween night we did that shit to him as kids. Got me to thinking about him. Man, I can't believe we were ever that mean."

"Don't sweat it, we were kids. That's what kids do, they pull pranks and tease each other. It's all part of growing up."

Hank mused about how innocent and almost wholesome Doug made it sound. A harmless rite of passage that ignored the screams and tears and blood. Somehow he doubted Frankie viewed that time through such rose-colored glasses. Especially when those glasses were broken.

Hank decided to change tactics with his next message. "You had any kids pulling Halloween pranks in your neighborhood?"

"Nah I live in an apartment complex. I'll be taking my kids out to one of the new housing developments in town myself."

It was still so odd to imagine Doug as a father, the guy who used to sneak into the girl's bathroom and piss on the toilet seats just because he thought it was funny. But Hank supposed people changed over time. Or in some cases became more themselves, which looked to the world like change.

Before Hank could respond, Doug sent another message. "What about you? When you gonna settle down and have some brats of your own? The bachelor life is fine when you're young but at our age it starts to seem sad."

Hank knew Doug was just joking, the kind of teasing they did back in school, but school was a long time ago now and Hank wasn't in the mood.

"I gotta jet right now but let's catch up for real soon."

After closing the app, Hank glanced out the window again, staring at the figure. For a moment it seemed to move but then he realized it was just the wind making the cape undulate.

As far as Hank knew, only three people were aware of what happened that Halloween night when Hank was twelve. Him, Doug, and Frankie himself. Doug would have no reason to be doing this, which left only one possibility.

Hank did a quick Google search for Frank Edward Gainey.

*

Todd came over at five. Hank had fallen down an internet rabbit hole and completely forgot about their plans. Well, not so much forgot but lost track of time and didn't realize how late it was until he heard the key in the lock.

Hank and Todd had been seeing each other for four months, the exchange of keys was a new and monumental step. Neither would dream of showing up at the other's place unannounced though, only when they had made definite plans.

Like tonight. Todd had worked a Sunday shift and Hank had agreed to make dinner for him.

Hank stood up from the sofa abruptly and stuffed his phone in his pocket. He realized this might look suspicious, like he was cheating or something. Part of him wished it was something that mundane.

When Todd saw him standing rigidly across the living room, he laughed and held his right hand to his forehead in a salute. "Standing at attention, are we?"

"I didn't make dinner," Hank blurted. "Sorry, time slipped away from me."

Todd shrugged and said, "That's okay. We can order Thai delivery."

That was one of the things Hank liked most about Todd, his ability to just go with the flow.

"I saw you decorated David out there," Todd said, pointing out the window. "How in the hell did you move it across the yard? That thing must weigh a ton."

Everything started to pile on top of Hank all of a sudden and he broke down in tears. Todd came to him quickly, put an arm around him and both of them sank down onto the sofa.

"If you're upset about dinner, it's really not that big of a deal. Delivery is fine with me. Let's face it, you probably would have burned whatever you tried to make anyway."

This got a laugh out of Hank, even through his tears. Ever since the morning after the first time Todd slept over and Hank had put the toaster setting too high and turned the Eggos into charcoal circles, the running joke had been that Hank shouldn't be allowed in the kitchen without a fire extinguisher on standby.

As Hank's tears tapered, he took a few deep breaths and wiped his eyes. "I'm sorry, that came out of nowhere."

Todd nodded but said nothing. He wasn't a pusher, he never tried to force Hank to talk about things before he was ready. Another thing Hank liked about him.

"I think we need to talk about something."

"You want your key back?" Todd asked, and Hank could see the genuine concern in his expression. He thought he was about to get a breakup speech.

"No, nothing like that. We're good, I promise."

The relief relaxed Todd's face and his lips curled into a smile.

"You know you're the first man I've ever dated, right?"

"Yeah, I know."

"I mean, I think I knew I was bisexual since I was young, and I had a few hook-ups in college, but this is the first real relationship I've ever had with a man."

Todd nodded again, urging Hank to go on but not pushing.

"In my youth, I wanted to hide it, wanted to deny my attraction to guys. It led to some pretty toxic masculine bullshit. I wasn't always a very nice person."

"That's not uncommon. Society puts all this pressure on guys to be a certain way, and when you know you're not, it can lead to some acting out."

"Yeah, but I did some stuff I'm really not proud of. One thing in particular. I never told you about Frankie."

"I don't believe so."

"It's not something I talk about. Hell, I don't even like to think about it."

"Hank, you're scaring me. What's going on?"

Hank took another deep breath and tried for a smile though he suspected it looked more like a pained grimace. "Sit back, it's quite the tale."

Todd did lean back into the cushions, but he kept a hold of Hank's hand. Hank appreciated the comforting contact, it grounded him, but he couldn't help but wonder if Todd would still want to hold his hand when the story was done.

"Frankie was this kid I went to school with. Since kindergarten actually, though I knew him even before that. He lived on my block and his mother and my mother were good friends, and so when we were really little we used to play together. That changed once we started school. You see, Frankie was one of those boys that really stuck out as different. He walked funny, he talked funny, he hated P.E. and all sports, he got along with the girls, and overall he just had this really prissy way about him. At five, most of us guys didn't really understand the concept of gay or bi or any of it, but that didn't stop the others from singling him out, making fun of him, calling him names and shooting spitballs at his head at lunch. It didn't take me very long to realize that if I continued to associate with him then I'd be subjecting myself to the same treatment. So I stopped hanging out with him, even outside of school. I even started to join in when other guys would call him sissy."

When Hank paused for a moment, Todd squeezed his hand and said, "Like I said before, that's not all that uncommon."

Hank held up his free hand. "Just wait. As we got older, things got worse. Everything about

Frankie seemed off, at least according to what we grew up being told boys were supposed to be like. The way Frankie held his books against his chest instead of down at his side, the way he crossed his legs one over the other when he sat down, the high-pitched breathy voice of his ... it all damned him in our eyes. People stopped calling him sissy and started calling him fag. Actually Feg because those were his initials, but you get the point. By the time we were twelve years old, Frankie's life must have been pure hell and I was one of the devils that made it that way for him. Kind of ironic, considering what happened that Halloween."

Another pause, but this time Todd kept his silence. Waiting for Hank to find the strength to continue, to lay his soul bare.

"A guy named Doug was my best friend back then, and we both considered twelve too old to dress up and go trick-or-treating. Although Doug didn't think it was too old to go tricking. He had this idea of going around the neighborhood, throwing eggs at houses and kicking in jack-o-lanterns and knocking over decorations. It's not really fair to lay it all at his feet. Yeah, he brought up the idea but I didn't take much convincing. I thought it sounded like fun and would be lying if I didn't admit I was all in.

"However, I was less enthused when he started stealing candy from the kids who were trick-or-treating by themselves. He only picked the ones that looked small and weak, and he'd threatened to beat them up if they didn't hand over their bags or buckets or pillow-cases full of treats. I thought that was going too far, but I didn't say anything. I didn't do anything to stop it.

"And then he saw the devil. A really cheap costume, just that plastic mask with the elastic band and the cape. Kind of pathetic looking, but the pillow-case was stuffed. When Doug stalked up to him and demanded the candy, the kid clutched it to his chest and said to leave him alone. The mask may have hid the face, but the voice was a dead giveaway. Frankie, just out trying to have a little fun, pretending to be someone else for the night and Doug and I came along and ruined the charade.

"Doug thought this would be the easiest score of the night, and honestly so did I. Neither of us were expecting it when Frankie swung his sack of candy around and belted Doug in the side of the face. I doubt it hurt all that much, even full of candy bars, but the bruise to Doug's pride must have been huge. And that's probably what led to everything that followed."

Hank fell silent for a moment. He didn't want to continue, he didn't want to dreg up his deepest shame, and he knew that if he chose not to finish the story, Todd would not force the issue. But he needed to finish the story. Hank wasn't a particularly religious man, but he did find some truth in the old adage that confession is good for the soul.

"You know where the strip mall is out on Ballenger Road?" he finally said, his eyes cast down and to the side. There was a reason confessionals didn't have you face to face with the priest. Sometimes confession was easier without direct eye contact. "Well, when I was a kid that side of Ballenger Road was undeveloped. It was a wooded area with a little creek that ran through it. So Doug grabbed Frankie in a bear hug, squeezing him around the middle and pinning his arms, and actually lifted him off his feet and carried him across the street and into the woods. I stayed behind for a few seconds, looking around to check if anyone saw, but it was getting late and the street was pretty much deserted. So I did what I always did, I followed along. I always followed along.

"When I caught up to them, Doug had Frankie on the ground and was kicking him. Not in the head or back, but in his arms and thighs. Doug wasn't trying to kill him or anything, but he definitely wanted to hurt him. Frankie was balled up in a fetal position, crying and moaning but not really doing anything to defend himself. I think that was what really got to me. He wasn't doing anything to defend himself. He never did. I mean, in school he could have at least tried to butch it up, try to fit in, but he just insisted on being his own weird self, drawing all kinds of unwanted attention his way. At the time, I didn't know why that made me so angry, but in retrospect I felt like it was some kind of indictment of my own fear and lack of courage. Whatever the case, I got in a few kicks too and I helped Doug when he stripped Frankie down to his underwear. I tore the cape into strips and Doug used them to tie Frankie to a sapling. I didn't help him with what he did next, but I did watch and I even laughed."

Hank kept expecting Todd to let go of his hand, but so far he didn't. When the silence stretched out for a while, Todd did say gently, "What did Doug do next?"

"Frankie was carrying a flashlight around with him like a dork, a devil afraid of the dark. Doug pulled down Frankie's underwear and he … well, first he took the remains of the ripped up cape in Frankie's mouth then … he sodomized Frankie with the flashlight. It wasn't a big flashlight and he didn't go in deep, but that sounds like I'm trying to make it sound less horrible than it was. And it was horrible, and I laughed. When Doug was done, I even took some mud from the creek bed and smeared the words 'Feg is a fag' on his scrawny chest. Then we tossed his clothes into the creek, put the devil mask back on him, and left him there.

"I have no idea if he stayed there all night, if someone eventually found him or he managed to get himself loose. All I know is we never got into trouble which means he never told anybody. But I noticed a change in him at school. He was even more withdrawn, even more twitchy. If I would pass him in the hall, he would move so far over he was practically melting into the wall. Halfway through middle school, his family moved away and I lost track of him, but I never forgot what we did to him. And I know he never forgot it either."

Hank waited for Todd to say something, but when several minutes passed with no response, Hank looked up to find Todd had averted his gaze. He still held Hank's hand but the grip was loose. Even though they still sat side by side, the distance between them suddenly felt huge.

Finally Todd cleared his throat and lifted his chin toward the window, toward the costumed statue outside. "Let me guess, that's the same devil outfit that Frankie was wearing."

"Yes, someone keeps putting it out there. I tear it off and throw it away but then a new one is up almost before I can turn around. And they keep pulling it closer to the house as well."

Now Todd turned to face Hank, but his expression was blank, unreadable. "So you think, what? That Frankie decided to track you down after all these years to mess with you?"

"That's what I thought at first, yeah."

"And what do you think now?"

Hank had expected this would be the part that was hard to tell, but after admitting to his greatest shame, he found that everything else was easy.

"I looked him up online, but at first I didn't find much. No social media accounts, which as you know in this day and age is bizarre. I kept digging, and I remembered hearing that when he left, his family moved to California. I remember that because some of the guys joked that he might end up in San Francisco with all the other fags. So I started searching his name plus California, and I got a hit almost immediately. His obituary."

This finally made Todd turn and meet his gaze. Todd looked pale and perspiration stood out on his face; he looked sick. "When did he die?"

"Two days ago. Of course, the obit didn't give a cause of death, only that it was sudden. But I found the notice on the website for the funeral home that did his services, and they had a place where people could enter testimonials. There weren't many but a few family members posted some things. One post from a cousin said he wished Frankie had called him so he could tell him it would get better, another post said something about how they knew Frankie had troubles but never thought he'd go so far, and a heartbreaking message from his mother where she talked about how Frankie had been unhappy since childhood and hoped he could finally find some peace. Those messages make it clear to me that he killed himself."

Todd didn't say anything for a moment. He took his hand from Hank's, ostensibly to scratch his nose but he put his hand back in his own lap after.

"And you think he killed himself because of what you ... because of what happened to him when you all were kids?"

"I'm sure that's not the only reason, but I can't imagine something like that wouldn't have continued to haunt him for the rest of his life."

"And now you think *he's* haunting *you*? Is that what you're telling me?"

"I don't know what to think. I mean, this seems too specific to be a coincidence."

"Do you think this Doug guy is experiencing the same thing?"

Hank shook his head. "I messaged him and he doesn't seem to be."

"So why do you think you would be targeted and not him?"

"Maybe because I was the one that used to be Frankie's friend. Maybe because Frankie recognized something in me, knew that we had more in common than I wanted to let on."

Todd's expression started to soften. "This could be related to Frankie and still not be a ghost, you know."

"What do you mean?"

"Maybe he told someone close to him about what had happened to him, and now that he's gone they've decided to mess with you."

"I deserve it. After what I did to him, I deserve it."

"You can't change the past," Todd said, which wasn't the same as saying Hank didn't deserve it.

"Maybe we can stay up tonight. You know, sort of stand watch. If someone comes into the yard, I can go talk to them."

"Tomorrow's Monday," Todd reminded. "You have to work in the morning. Not sure you should be staying up all night."

"It'll be fun. We can binge-watch something on Netflix and have a slumber party."

"I can't stay tonight," Todd said, and Hank noticed he averted his eyes again. "I have to go in earlier than expected tomorrow, so I should head home after dinner."

"You sure? I could – "

"Why don't I call in the pizza," Todd said, standing and walking toward the kitchen.

*

Dinner was awkward. Hank could see Todd trying to be normal and casual, but Hank's story had obviously left him feeling discombobulated. What Hank had done, he'd done as a kid, he'd done out of fear and self-loathing as much as any animosity toward Frankie, it was something he deeply regretted ... but he could see why Todd would have a hard time seeing Hank the same after knowing about it. Hank had a hard time seeing himself the same now that all those painful memories had been dredged up.

After Todd left, his goodbye kiss a mere peck on the lips, Hank settled onto the sofa, back against the arm, legs stretched out, staring right out the window into the side yard. He'd turned on the floodlight at the corner of the house so he could see the statue in silhouette. He thought again about the painful memories and how much of an asshole move it was to think about how painful it was for *him*. Hank hadn't been the victim; he'd been the villain. One of them anyway. It seemed almost disrespectful to be thinking about how the events of that Halloween had affected him when he had helped to crush someone's self-esteem.

He always kept a blanket folded over the back of the sofa, and he pulled it over himself and started his vigil. He would be no good for work in the morning, but he had to see for himself who was doing this.

He had to know, and if it meant a sleepless night, that seemed a small price to pay.

*

Hank woke up when the first weak rays of sunlight filtered through the window and kissed his eyelids. He turned his head and winced at the painful cramp in his neck. He groped at the floor next to the sofa, finding his phone and checking the time. 6:52 a.m. If he didn't get his ass in gear he was going to be late for work.

He sat up, for a moment wondering why he'd slept on the sofa and why Todd hadn't stayed over, but then the events of last night came flooding back to him. His confession, the awkwardness it caused between Hank and Todd, Todd's quick departure, and Hank's determination to stay up all night.

A determination he had not been able to follow through. He wasn't sure when exactly he'd drifted off, but the last time he remembered glancing at the clock it had been 12:48. Officially Halloween, the anniversary of the worst thing Hank had ever done.

As he pushed himself to his feet, he glanced at the window and couldn't even muster the tiniest bit of surprise when he saw the devil was now even closer to the house. Practically on the edge of the driveway. He went through the kitchen and out the side door and walked up to the costumed statue. How had the prankster known when Hank had fallen asleep inside?

Todd isn't around anymore, Hank thought. *You can stop pretending you think this is a flesh-and-bone prankster.*

Hank looked out across his side yard. He could clearly see the square indentions in the grass in spaced-out intervals, everywhere the statue had been placed as it drew closer to the house. Yet the grass between these squares was undisturbed, no evidence the thing had been dragged. It looked more as if the devil had hopped closer and closer.

Walking up to the statue, moving slowly as if afraid it would spring to life and lunge for him, Hank wrapped his arms around the thing's middle and tried to lift. He couldn't even get it an eighth of an inch off the ground. With a growl of frustration he pushed at the devil. He barely rocked. Planting his feet wide, he leaned forward and pushed with all his might. After a few minutes, the thing finally toppled over, dislodging the devil mask.

Fighting back tears, Hank turned and went back inside to get ready for work.

*

Hank's shift at the store ended at 5:30, and though it was still light out on his drive home, he saw many kids already out trick-or-treating. Mostly confined to the upscale housing developments that had cropped up all over town like clumps of mushrooms. It wasn't like when Hank was a child and kids roamed all over town, often on their own as they got older. Things were different now, parents almost never left kids unattended and stuck to specific parts of town. In many ways, that was probably a good thing. Less likely what had happened to Frankie could happen now.

All day Hank had tried to get Frankie off his mind, and succeeded only in thinking of nothing else. He'd been distracted at work all day long, gave customers the wrong change several times, dropped and shattered two coffee mugs while trying to set up a display, and he broke down crying in the bathroom around lunchtime. He was so off his game, his supervisor had asked if he wanted to go home early but he'd declined. The idea of being at home with the devil was not a prospect he relished.

By the time he turned onto his street, the sun was starting to make its nightly departure, the sky turning a pinkish purple with stars appearing like tiny pinpricks of light. As he pulled into his drive, the first thing he noticed was that the statue was no longer by the driveway. In fact, it wasn't in the side yard at all. Hank got out of the car and did a quick circuit of the house. No sign of the statue. Which meant it could only be one place.

He unlocked the front door and stepped inside, finding the devil right where he expected. In the center of the living room. In the dying light, the devil mask seemed more animated than normal, more sinister, and the cape flapped in a breeze that Hank could not feel.

He considered going back outside, getting in his car, and driving away. To where? Maybe Todd's apartment, but he wasn't sure the man would welcome him inside. He could get a motel room for the night, but he'd have to come back here eventually.

No, he thought as he closed the door behind him. *No more running from the past. Time to face up to it instead.*

He turned on a lamp and tossed his keys on the entry table before crossing the room and taking a seat on the sofa, on the end closest to the statue.

He looked straight ahead, the devil only vaguely visible in his periphery.

"I'm sorry, Frankie," he said in a cracking voice. "I know how inadequate that sounds, how inadequate those words *are*, but it's all I've got."

He knew this should feel strange, offering an apology to a statue, an inanimate object, but the strangest part was that it didn't feel strange at all. It felt like something he had to do, something long overdue.

"I hated myself. I made it about you, but I never hated you. In fact, if anything part of me was jealous of you. It's not like you were out at that age, but you were totally *yourself*. I mean, you weren't constantly chasing after the popular kids, trying to emulate them, trying to contort everything in your body and soul to fit in with them. At the time, I told myself I hated you for that, but really what I hated was my own lack of courage to be like that. I was so scared all the time of people finding out I was different, that I wasn't like them, it made me lose all sense of who I was and do things that I knew were wrong. Like what I did to you. I didn't hate you, I hated myself. I hated myself so much that it turned me into a monster which made me hate myself even more. Quite the cycle I trapped myself in."

In his periphery, Hank thought he had a sense of the devil head turning slightly toward him, but that could have been a trick of the scant light and the blurriness of his vision as tears welled up in his eyes. He chose to ignore it and keep his gaze focused ahead.

"I realize I'm probably romanticizing you. I'm sure like all kids you wanted to fit in, you wanted to be accepted, but you didn't seem willing to completely compromise yourself to achieve those goals. And I punished you for that. Punished you the way I wanted to punish myself. I thought something was broken in me and I directed that toward you instead of doing anything like self-reflection or soul-searching.

"I also realize that apologizing now doesn't change anything, but I don't know what more I can do at this point. I can't go back in time to change anything. I wish I could, I wish more than anything I could take away the pain I caused you. You didn't deserve it, and maybe if you'd had even one friend you could have turned to, talked to, who treated you with kindness … well, maybe things would have turned out differently for you.

"Hell, maybe things would have turned out differently for me. Here I am, with forty only a stone's throw away, and I still struggle with the fear of people finding out about me. My forays out of the closet have been tentative to say the least, and mostly consist of dating and hook-up apps. In many ways, I'm still the same coward I was at twelve. At least I'm not the same bully. I know that's little comfort now, but it's something I suppose."

He paused, letting the silence unfold like a quilt until it took up the entire room. He felt emotionally raw and hollowed out inside, but after being filled with such overwhelming regret and guilt, the emptiness felt almost like a blessing.

When nothing happened after a few minutes, he said, "So I'm sorry. I really am. There isn't much that can be done with sorry after it's too late to turn it into action, but I want you to know that I truly and genuinely am sorry."

He sensed movement off to his left again, and then there was a soft fluttering sound, and when he turned his head he found the devil mask and the cape lying on the rug, looking like the witch's dress and hat in *The Wizard of Oz* after she melted.

He stood up and walked to the window. From the streetlight at the corner, he could see that the statue was back in its original location out near the fence.

Hank wondered if he should be feeling something akin to awe or fear at what had just transpired here, something not easily explained by science or reason, but he continued to fill that hollowness. He also wondered if he should be feeling some semblance of relief since it seemed Frankie had gotten what he wanted, that maybe the young man's spirit had achieved some kind of peace.

But Hank didn't feel relieved, and he didn't feel at peace. And perhaps that was just as it should be. Maybe that could be the wind at his back that would drive him toward the courage he had always lacked.

Like Peonies

By

Caitlin Marceau

Emmie leans against the window of the bus, trying to make out the intersection she knows is too far ahead to see through the pouring rain. She pushes up the sleeve of her hoodie, checking the time on her watch despite having only looked a few moments ago. She frowns at the time on its small round face: 7:58 p.m.

I'm not going to make it.

She looks up at the sky, the thick grey clouds blacking out the stars she always admires on her commute home from work, and silently shouts for the bus driver to go faster.

The gas is on the right, pal.

She knows he's only trying to be safe. The main road is known for three things: potholes, the speed trap at the intersection of Hersh, and hydroplaning accidents. Thanks to the street's poor design and worse drainage system, water accumulates to a dangerous degree even after a light rainfall. Whenever there's a storm, the cars are forced to move at a snail's pace for days following the rainfall, and it's often faster to take the winding back roads until the road dries up.

Emmie looks out the window, finally seeing her stop, and her stomach plummets when the red tail lights of another bus, the 121 South, come into focus. She watches from her seat as the bus waits for any stragglers to climb aboard before pulling away from the shelter and driving off through the darkness, as her bus finally comes to a stop.

Slinging her backpack over one shoulder, Emmie descends the steps of the bus, nodding her disingenuous thanks to the driver as she exits the vehicle. The wind whips at her hair and rain soaks through her clothes as she runs for the warmth of the small bus shelter. The air is cold and cuts through her skin, biting deep into her bones. The bus pulls away, wheels kicking up ice cold water off the asphalt as it creeps down the road to the next stop. She watches it drive off from the doorway of the shelter and hopes the rain will ease up.

It doesn't.

Emmie pulls out her cell phone from the safety of her backpack and checks when the next 121 bus is arriving. The webpage takes a while to load, her reception spotty this far out in the middle of nowhere, and she wants to scream when the transit company confirms what she already knows: the next (and last) bus is at 10:30 p.m.

Soon, the rain is coming down in sheets, and Emmie dreads the idea of having to wait alone in the shelter late at night.

She eyes the forest across the road from her, taking note of the dark oaks and enormous maple trees standing guard. The massive greenspace is all that stands between her and her home directly on the other side of the trees. Thanks to local conservation efforts dedicated to protecting indigenous at-risk fauna and flora, people are barred from entering the woods. There are no man-made paths through the trees and signs posted around the perimeter promise that trespassers will be faced with heavy fines and possible jail time.

For a moment, she debates taking the ninety-minute trek around the protected property, but the heavy rain and harsh winds shut that idea down before she can even leave the shelter. She grumbles to herself and stares at the imposing woods. She can't help but notice how the trees, with their thick branches and dense foliage, would be enough to shield her from the violent onslaught of the rain.

As long as I walk in a straight line, it should only take me fifteen minutes—twenty minutes?—to get to the other side. Probably? I know there's a bit of thunder but I'm sure that if I walk quickly then I'll get home before any—

No.

She shakes her head. The last thing she wants is to get lost in the woods, especially when she's not supposed to be in them.

Emmie looks up at the sky, frowning as thunder rolls overhead. The rain is heavy, rattling the glass roof of the small shelter. Droplets splash against the ground and water trails across the sidewalk and into the small space, soaking through the fabric of her sneakers. She shivers, pulling the drawstrings tight on her damp hoodie and wishing she were home. She'd bought her house for pennies on the dollar; thankfully, rural Quebec hadn't experienced the same property boom as other parts of the province. Unfortunately, transit hasn't been quite as reliable as the real estate agent had promised, nor does it come as often as she was used to when she lived in the city.

Emmie looks back at the forest as thunder shakes the shelter around her, the air heavy with electricity. She fears the idea of going into the woods at night. As irrational as it is, she can't unmarry the idea of a darkened forest with monsters and sinister beasts hiding at the edges of her vision. She wraps her arms around herself, rubbing her hands against her body to try and heat herself up as she looks at the giant trees across the road. A gust of wind howls and shakes the walls of the shelter, blowing rain into the small space and wetting her clothes.

She stares at the forest, imagining the warmth of her house on the other side. She pictures herself on the sofa, wrapped in a thick fleece blanket as she drinks a glass of wine and watches bad TV with worse characters.

Another blast of icy wind hits her, storm water dampening the ends of her hair as they whip around her face.

Fuck this.

She tucks her hair into her hood, tightens the straps on her backpack, and makes a beeline for the woods, a knot forming in the pit of her stomach as the trees get closer. She exhales shakily through her mouth as she steps into the darkness, trying to focus on how glad she'll be to get home. She pulls out her cellphone, the canopy of leaves overhead helping to shield the device from some of the rain, and turns on the flashlight. She moves slowly through the foliage, careful not to catch herself on low hanging branches or unearthed roots as she makes a path for herself through the thick trees. As she heads into the woods, the streetlights quickly fade from view, and the blackness envelops her.

Emmie walks in silence, her eyes glued to the trees ahead of her. She does her best to walk in a straight line, but soon finds herself being forced off course as she avoids crushing wild mushrooms, getting tangled in thickets, or twisting her ankles on rocks and fallen branches. She checks the time on her phone, trying not to panic as what she thought would be a ten-minute walk slowly turns into a fifteen-minute and then twenty-minute one. She desperately searches for the edge of the woods as she walks, hoping to catch a glimpse of a streetlight, a headlight, or even the soft glow of a television through a living room window.

She doesn't.

As Emmie continues through the woods, the air grows thick and sweet. At first, she thinks she's imagining it, that she's breathing in her own perfume in the cramped space. But as she continues through the sharp branches that reach and grab for her, the smell gets stronger. It's rich like honey and clings to the air around her, dripping down her throat and heavy on her tongue every time she inhales.

Crunch!

Emmie looks down and frowns at the bright blue that peeks out from beneath her heel. She lifts her foot, worried that she's accidentally walked through a fallen bird's nest, but breathes a sigh of relief when she realizes that petals—not eggshells—are stuck to the bottom of her shoe. She doesn't remember seeing any flowers earlier. As she moves carefully through the patch of wildflowers, she can't help but wonder how many roots, rocks, and dangerous obstacles she's narrowly missed thanks to her carelessness.

She shines the light around her, checking to make sure the path forward is clear. In front of her lie a few patches of bright pink and purple flowers, and she steps carefully to avoid walking on them. Unfortunately, this soon becomes impossible: the flowers grow denser the further Emmie travels through the trees, and she's forced to cut a path through the delicate flower beds, crushing stems and petals under her feet.

Isn't it too early in the spring for flowers to be blooming like this?

She understands now why the town didn't want people venturing into the greenspace, and she silently prays that no one will see her or the damage she's caused.

Emmie shines the light ahead of her. The rays illuminate the massive gnarled trunk of a white ash, its branches thick and wide reaching. She freezes in her tracks, chest tight and muscles tense.

A face is watching her from the bark.

Emmie tries to catch her breath and find her balance, her legs suddenly weak, pulse thundering in her ears. Her vision begins to blur at the edges and she can't tell if it's her head, or the forest, that's spinning. She reaches out a hand to try steadying herself against a nearby tree, but quickly pulls it back. What if all the trees have faces, and those faces have been watching her this entire time? The thought makes her nauseous and she braces her hands on her knees and tries to breathe slowly through her mouth, suddenly wishing she was back at the bus shelter with the cold wind and rain on her skin.

I knew this was a bad idea.

She stares at the ground, waiting in fear; when nothing happens, Emmie finds herself wondering if the shadows were playing tricks on her and that she imagined a face where there was none. She musters the courage to look up at the tree again, her heart beating faster when she sees that the face is still there.

It's a woman's face, the lines of her soft lips and small nose lost in the harsh angles of the rough bark. Her eyes are closed, like she's sleeping, and her hair tumbles in waves around her shoulders and cascades down her petite frame. At first, Emmie thinks the woman has been carved onto the trunk of the tree, elaborate art left behind for someone to discover, like statues of Nessie and the Ogopogo left at the bottom of lakes. But as she inches closer, she realizes the woman's figure isn't etched into the top of the wood but is part of it, bark growing uniformly along the soft curves of the woman's face and body.

Emmie reaches out a hand, surprised to find how close she's moved to the figure, and gently runs it down the side of the woman's arm. Despite the bark that coats the woman's skin (is *her skin?*) Emmie's surprised to discover that she's soft and warm to the touch.

Her heart beats fast as she runs the tips of her fingers across the woman's jaw, admiring her full lips. Without thinking, she leans forward and presses her lips against the woman's, surprised that they taste like vanilla and tangerines, and not dirt or moss. She feels the woman's lips move against hers and she pulls back, surprised.

The woman's eyes are now open and they watch her intently. She leans forward, the bark parting and falling away from her pale green face as she pushes herself out of the tree, smiling. Terrified at the tree woman's sudden sentience, Emmie backs away as fast as her legs will take her.

She turns to run, but drops her phone in the pile of wildflowers, the bright flashlight quickly swallowed up by the darkness. She cries out, dropping to her hands and knees, frantically feeling through the petals and thorns for her cell as the naked woman continues to pull herself out of the tree. The sharp foliage bites into the skin of Emmie's hands, palms ripping open on the harsh ground, as she scrabbles to find the light that will guide her out of the woods.

As the woman gets closer, Emmie's fingers finally brush against the smooth plastic of her phone's case hidden among the soft petals. She grabs it and pushes herself to her feet, only to find the woman directly in front of her. Before Emmie has time to think, the woman has laced her fingers in Emmie's hair, and she pulls her close, kissing her deeply. Emmie finds herself kissing back, her lips parting for the woman's tongue, before she comes to her senses and frees herself from the kiss.

She gives the being one last look, her eyes lingering on the woman's full mouth, before she spurs herself onward in the direction that she hopes safety awaits. She runs as fast as her legs will take her, her shoes kicking up petals and ripping through flower beds as she goes. She wants to look back and see if the woman is following her, but she can't risk taking her eyes off the forest floor. Before long, the bright colours fade, and soon Emmie finds herself tripping on muddy roots once again.

Emmie weaves her way through the trees, beginning to hear the rain once more, the canopy of leaves finally thinning out. The droplets roll down her back, chilling her skin, and she finds herself thankful to be able to feel the bracing cold of the night. She soon spots the warm glow of a streetlamp through the woods, and it's not long before she emerges onto her empty street.

Her house is a little further down the road and she jogs towards it, the adrenaline from the night's adventures starting to wear off.

As she closes the door behind her, she's unable to help taking a final glance towards the trees, where she can see a pair of eyes watching her from the darkness.

***

Emmie stares at the ceiling, willing herself to be tired again.

She was dead on her feet when she got back from the woods, and as much as she wanted to collapse in her bed, she'd forced herself to grab a shower to clean the blood and dirt off of her. She'd carefully removed any stray thorns still stuck in her hands, and treated any cuts or scrapes she'd picked up along the forest trail with Polysporin before bandaging them up. When she was finally done treating her minor wounds, she'd brushed her damp hair, pulled on an oversized t-shirt, and crawled into her bed with the hopes of getting a full night's sleep.

Although she'd been tired as she was getting under her down comforter, she feels wide awake now.

She closes her eyes, focusing on the blacks of her eyelids and the quiet of her breathing.

In.

Out.

In.

And out.

She tries to inhale slowly through her nose and exhale even slower through her mouth, doing her best to empty her mind of all thoughts.

She focuses on the soft patter of the rain droplets as they break against her bedroom windows. She's soon distracted by the soft whirring of the fan in the corner of her room that she keeps pointed away from her, because she enjoys the noise the blades make, but finds it too cold to want the breeze on her skin. She absentmindedly grabs for her comforter, pulling it up so that it covers her shoulders and cocoons her body. She breathes deep, enjoying the smell of the blanket and the vanilla and lilac fabric softener that still clings to it.

Vanilla and… tangerines.

Her heart beats faster as she remembers the taste on her tongue. The way the citrus stung her nose and how the rich sweetness dripped down her throat.

Her mouth...

Emmie runs a finger along her bottom lip, remembering how soft the woman felt against her skin. She blushes as she remembers the curves of the woman's naked body, the way her hips dipped, the swell of her breasts. She remembers the woman's dark eyes watching her. Although the being fills her with fear, she realizes that she also fills her with wanting.

With her eyes closed, Emmie imagines the woman's hands as she feels herself through her clothes. She imagines the woman's hands are soft like silk as they caress her nipples and trace their way down her body. She bites her lip, trying to keep quiet, as she moves her hands down to her thighs and imagines what the woman in the tree would feel like if she were between her legs instead. She touches herself, slowly working herself open and then to climax, the taste of the woman on her lips as she comes.

Breathless and exhausted once more, Emmie falls asleep.

***

Emmie wakes up before her alarm goes off. The storm appears to be over, and the sun is streaming in through the thin sheers she uses as curtains. She yawns loudly as she blinks the sleep out of her eyes, the need for coffee urging her out of bed despite how comfortable she is resting in the centre of her crisp white sheets.

As she fills the kettle, she mentally kicks herself for forgetting to pick up drip coffee on the way home last night and forcing herself to settle for instant this morning.

At least I still have some of the good creamer left.

Once the kettle pops, she scoops some sugar and coffee into her favourite mug—a sunflower yellow cup she chipped, and then bought out of guilt, at a craft show almost a decade earlier—before mixing it with the hot water and topping it off with the almond creamer. She checks the temperature outside—18°C, but it feels warmer with the humidity—before pulling the belt on her housecoat tighter, slipping on a pair of flip-flops, and heading onto her porch to enjoy her drink.

She doesn't normally have her morning coffee out on the porch until late spring or early summer, when the weather is still just cold enough to not need the fan on but warm enough for her to not need the duvet. But today, she finds herself wanting to keep an eye on the woods across from her home, half worried and half hopeful that the woman in the trees will come looking for her. She scans the treeline, searching for anything that could be mistaken as a pair of eyes watching her from the shadows, but she only finds disappointment.

What the fuck is wrong with me?

She shakes her head and turns to go back inside when she's stopped by a familiar scent in the air: vanilla and tangerines.

She looks to the greenspace once more, desperately searching for the woman's delicate form among the rough branches, but still she finds nothing. With a sigh, she heads back inside and gets ready for the day.

***

Emmie bites her lip as the phone rings, hoping she doesn't sound as guilty as she feels. She's not normally one to call in sick, let alone play hooky, but she has something more important to do today than be cooped up in a cubicle. It's something she hasn't been able to stop thinking about since she got in last night, since she felt herself in bed, since the smell of vanilla and tangerines followed her out onto the porch.

She needs to find the woman in the tree.

For a moment she thinks her call is going to go right to voicemail, but just as she begins to silently celebrate, Deborah picks up.

"Hello?"

"Oh, uh, hey Deb. I'm so sorry, but I'm not going to be coming in today."

"What do you mean you're not coming in today? You know the department's short staffed."

"I'm *really* sorry," Emmie lies to her boss, trying her best to sound like she has a stuffy nose without laying it on too thick, "but I feel horrible this morning. I think I'm coming down with something."

"Look, unless you're dead or dying, I better see you at the office today. Do you know how—"

"I'm sorry, Deb, but I'm calling in sick. Hopefully, I'll see you tomorrow."

Before her boss can reply, she ends the call and slips her phone into the back pocket of her jeans. She puts on a pair of thick socks before pulling on her Chelsea duck boots, not wanting her shoes to get soaked through with mud like they did the night before, and layers on her thin windbreaker over her turtleneck. She grabs her flashlight from the entranceway table and checks to make sure it still works, before exiting her house and locking the door behind her.

Emmie tries to remember the exact spot she burst through the trees during her frantic run home last night, but it's pointless. Instead, she eyes the other houses on the street, making sure no one is watching her. She suspects that most of her neighbours are either already at work or are on their way, but she knows that nosey stay-at-home parents don't just inhabit the suburbs, and the last thing she wants is one of them ratting her out to the cops for trespassing.

When she's sure the coast is clear, she ducks between two of the trees and quickly pushes her way through the thick branches and into the woods. Although the sun is shining brightly, thick leaves block it out in patches and make it difficult for her to see. She turns on her flashlight and points it at the damp ground as she treads carefully, the earth slicked with the rainwater that filtered its way through the canopy overhead and into the soil.

Emmie breaks out into a sweat as she navigates the greenspace, the mud clinging to her shoes and making the walk harder and slower than it needs to be. She takes off her windbreaker and ties it around her waist, already exhausted. Part of her, the part of her that's afraid of the woods and the creatures that lurk within it, screams for Emmie to turn back while she can. The other part of her, the part that's desperate for another taste of the being in the white ash tree, begs for her to keep going forward.

While she's tempted to let the exhaustion win out, it's the deep wanting inside of her that spurs her onward.

As she moves slowly through the trees, she catches a flash of colour out of the corner of her eye. Her heart beats faster and she picks up the pace, following the bright red that paints the forest floor and leads Emmie to a cluster of teal and lilac, then sunflower yellow and dusty rose, followed by a patchwork of royal blue and orange. She's surprised to see hibiscus and bee balm blooming in the shade of the trees and the spring air.

Soon, the ground is packed so tightly with petals that Emmie has no choice but to crush them beneath her boots as she wades through. In the centre of the cluster is the white ash, the woman's sleeping face appearing just like it was last night.

Although her heart beats in her throat, Emmie forces herself forward. She cups the woman's face and leans in, her mouth finding the being's through the bark. Like last time, her lips are soft and gentle and taste like vanilla and tangerine. The woman kisses Emmie back as she emerges from the tree, guiding Emmie away from the roots of the ash and into the centre of the clustered wildflowers.

"Who are you?" Emmie asks her breathlessly. "*What* are you?"

The woman smiles back at her, but doesn't answer. Instead, her hands pull at Emmie's clothing and peel it slowly from her body. The woman licks and kisses Emmie's exposed skin, her mouth working its way across her flesh and her hands lacing themselves through her hair.

"What's your name?" Emmie tries again, blushing as the woman undoes her bra and traces her fingers lightly across her nipples, her mouth not far behind.

Emmie moans and laces her hands through the woman's long hair, letting herself be guided onto her back. The being smiles at her as she unties the windbreaker from around Emmie's hips and unbuckles the button on her jeans. Her hands trace the curves of Emmie's belly and hips as she plants kisses on her skin. She arches her hips and the woman helps slide her out of the last of her clothing, leaving Emmie exposed and flushed pink.

"You're beautiful," the woman finally says, her voice soft like a summer's breeze. "Like roses."

Emmie opens her mouth to say something, but lets out a soft gasp instead. The woman runs her hands down Emmie's body and between her thighs, slowly working her open before leaning down and drinking deep.

Emmie writhes beneath her, the heat that's pooled between her legs growing hotter, the pressure building deep within her skin. She arches her back and opens her eyes, admiring the beauty of the flowers around her.

Her heart hammers painfully against her ribs as she sees another pair of eyes looking back at her from the flowerbed.

"Wait! Someone's looking!" Emmie says, trying to sit up.

The heat between her thighs is almost painful now, and the tendrils of warmth work their way through her body.

At first, Emmie is afraid that someone has followed her into the woods and is spying on her. But as she looks at the eyes, she realizes that they're not set in a face, but rather they're stuck in the ground itself. She looks around, terrified, and spots another pair watching her from beneath a bed of honeysuckles. With horror, Emmie realizes the right eye is crushed and bloody, her footprint still visible in the mud.

Emmie opens her mouth to say something to the woman, to tell her that something is terribly wrong, but she can't. She looks around, panicked, finding eyes lurking in the flowers everywhere she turns. She looks down at the woman and realizes that the being is no longer between her thighs, even as the heat and pressure inside her become unbearable. She tries to scream, tries to move, tries to do *anything* but finds herself rooted to the spot as pain works its way through her body.

There's a ripping noise, wet and sudden, and black spots appear at the corner of her vision. She watches with horror as her skin splits and stretches in an explosion of fuschia and flower petals. Emmie's eyes roll back, the wet dirt sticking painfully to the whites of her eyes as her body blooms into a thousand flowers, blanketing the forest floor like so many people have before her.

The woman smiles and bends down, picking a flower and tucking it behind her ear.

"Not roses," the woman says as she climbs back into her tree, her skin rippling like the bark of the white ash. "Like peonies."

Wolves Within,

By

Zachary Rosenberg

God's judgment no longer meant anything to Veronika, not since she had met Adinah.

As she did almost every night now, Veronika stole out from the sanctum of the church into the night, her body clad in a rough traveling close instead of the habit of holy orders. Though she wore her cross, it was concealed within the confines of her garments. The first steps from the church were always the hardest, the overwhelming fear that Father Janos might catch her almost making her halt her step.

But as she ever did, Veronika crossed the threshold and slipped out into the cool darkness. Her heart pounded with anticipation in her breast as she pictured Adinah in her mind. She knew the direction from one section of town to the next, a place forbidden to most of the devout.

Father Janos preached against them sometimes, and so Veronika had grown up believing in the worst of them. Those people, neighbors yet unwelcome throughout all of the eastern kingdoms who nevertheless helped to make the town what it was. If not for Adinah, Veronika might have never understood them, even though their ways were not hers. Even with her dissatisfaction with her own faith, she did not entirely understand their neighbors.

The tiny ember of longing within Veronika's chest threatened to fan out into a scorching flame, her breath misting visibly about her in the night air as the moon peered down above them like an eye comprised of silver frost. She had made it, reached the woods so near to Adinah's people: those known as the Jews.

For a moment Veronika feared Adinah might not show, but then she heard her lover's voice murmuring her name. The nun turned as the Hebrew woman melted from the shadows, as though the darkness peeled itself back from shame in covering Adinah's form and figure. Her hair hung about her shoulders, unbound and dark. Her eyes were a brilliant gray, reflecting the gelid moonlight. Adinah took a step close, her anticipation visible in the mist escaping her own lips.

"Veronika." a pale hand brushed forth, warm and delicate across the nun's face. Past the drawn hood and against the pale flesh, thumb brushing against locks of shorn gold. How Veronika envied Adinah's long hair, the flowing dark locks of her. How she embraced the beauty contained in her body, the sparks of rebellion in her eyes. "You made it."

"I told you I would." Veronika let the church and its teachings fall from her like pebbles to mark only the road traversed behind her. She forgot Father Janos and all rumors of the woods. The church was a cold and sterile place, but just the sight of the Jewish woman made her blood run like molten fire.

Unable to contain herself, Veronika leaned forth and pressed her lips to Adinah's own. Her lover caught her, arms snaking about her like a cage. She tugged Veronika forth, kissing her with an uncontained ardor. Adinah's own people would not have approve, but her body gave every sign that she cared as much for that as Veronika herself.

The endless prayers and recitations had left Veronika ravenous. Her hands sought the other woman under her cloak. Shaking legs gave way and they bore one another back with the cloaks and heat of their bodies shields against the cold. They used their mouths to muffle the noises, yearning and arching against one another.

This was ever the way of it: quick meetings, swift slashes of desire in the dead of night and with nobody else to witness them. Nothing save the judging eye above and the distant howls of wolves greeted them. Veronika stopped thinking of the autumn chill, of sin, and damnation. She allowed herself to drown in Adinah, basking in repressed lust and passion.

And when pleasure had crested, they repressed their cries with lips together, slackening and panting joyously.

Exchanging kisses, they brought themselves up, Veronika knowing she would need to hide and wash the concealed cloak to keep suspicions away. She could always explain it as a symptom of her sojourns into town and aid of others; Sister Veronika, beloved healer.

Adinah curled against her, a sigh escaping her. "I missed you, these last days," she murmured. Veronika knew the longing she felt was one half of a vast whole, a shared and pained separation that both endured for the sake of these loving moments. "I have something for you."

Something else Veronika always anticipated. Though the night was dark, through shards of moonlight did the nun see the Hebrew woman withdraw something from the confines of a small pack. A small and leatherbound volume. Veronika's mouth opened in joyous revelation at the sight of the book.

"We can continue from whence we left off," Adinah remarked. The magic of passion was one lesson from the Jewish woman. The other was the magic of letters, books. Nuns were encouraged to study and Veronika's knowledge was basic, but limited only to the few provided books in the temple. She knew her bible by heart through Latin, but Adinah had taught her Hebrew and Polish. Had introduced her to other books as well. Her father was a man of oddities, a mystic who valued literacy even in women.

A howl startled Veronika from her revelry and she glanced upward, following the mournful keening through the forests. "Worry now," Adinah murmured. "The wolves never come this close to the village."

"That sounded close," Veronika whispered. The woods were said to be deep, filled with all manner of terrors and legend. Few in this village entered after dark and only for love did Veronika find herself coming so close each time. "Like they're growing bolder."

"What have we to fear?" Adinah lifted an eyebrow, as if offering a peek into some furtive little secret that only she knew. "As I said, we are protected. Even at night, I hear the river. Anyone in danger need only take refuge on one side. You know the tale."

"Father Janos said the same. But he warned us to beware of wolves in the night." Though in that case, Veronika had seen the clergyman's brow crinkle as he had spoken of the Jews, a clear distaste in his voice.

"Second thoughts now, Veronika?" Adinah's body pressed close and chased away all doubts, just like the first time they had locked eyes across the village.

"None." Two centuries since Adinah's people had arrived throughout Poland, tolerated grudgingly and sometimes subjected to "purges." Veronika had never seen one and never wanted to. She knew she was departing from all teachings of the holy church, putting her soul at risk.

But the next kiss of Adinah's lips told her it was worth it.

***

Memories of Adinah had a tendency to interfere with Veronika's morning prayers and devotions. The village was a small one, though the church was the most elaborate building in town. Father Janos was the one ordained priest with a small smattering of nuns to help administer rites and healing to the people. Jews were rarely spoken of, even by those who did business with their side of town.

"Sister Veronika." The mellow and warm voice announced Father Janos. Veronika turned from her bible to face him. The priest had a kind, wide face, fatherly and comforting. "You appeared tired at breakfast this morning."

The nun plastered a smile on her face. "I merely had a lengthy time administering to the people of the village yesterday, Father." Long practice helped her keep her voice demure and submissive, her eyes downcast. "There is so much to do. So many never run out of problems."

"Indeed," the priest sighed with a heavy shake of his head. "Many problems." He sounded like he was echoing her. "And have you not heard of the events of this morning?"

Veronika shook her head with a genuine puzzlement. "Of this morning, Father?"

"There was a wolf attack. A farmer's lamb has been killed. Several along the farms at the border." A grim look crossed Father Janos's face. "Tensions are running thick, Sister Veronika." He rubbed at a ruddy chin with two fingers. "The folk here grow restless."

"But whatever for? Surely hunters can deal with wolves, Father?"

"We've only heard them, never seen any. Since the pawprints appeared weeks ago. I've had such horrific dreams since I saw them." The priest clicked his tongue. "But that is not the issue. The people have noticed that the only loss and prowling happens near the Christian territories. Jewish crops and livestock are untouched and the Jews go about their business without fear."

Veronika thought of Adinah, heart fluttering beneath the robes that marked her devotion to the Savior. She kept her face neutral with effort, breath escaping her lips while she steepled her fingers before her in prayer. "Surely there is nothing dangerous beyond a few stray wolves, Father?"

"Who can say?" Janos stepped closer, his eyes roaming across Veronika briefly. "You are a beloved child of the Lord, Sister Veronika. Do not jeopardize your standing in our community. I have feared in the past you have sympathies to the Jews."

"Father," began Veronika. Surprised forced the words from her mouth and though she had carefully prepared responses in the past, this left her almost wholly unarmed. "What would make you say such a thing?"

"The way you peer at them in daylight. The way you avoid discussion when they come up. They are a wicked people, Veronika. Sinful. The blood of our Savior stains them. Who knows what dark pacts they have made with ancient beings of the wood and even the unnameable?" The priest frowned grimly. "The Crusaders knew the way to deal with them, but they are useful and so we tolerate them for now. But if the worst is as I suspect, then the people of our village will undoubtedly strike back. We outnumber them by far."

Veronika's heart fluttered so hard she feared the priest might hear it. She thought again of Adinah, a yearning terror rending its way through her insides. Snaking claws of icy dread slid throughout her body and only with effort did she force the smile. "I am sure it won't come to that, Father. Anyone can be saved."

"Anyone." Janos reached and placed his hand to her shoulder, leaning forth so she could smell the breakfast porridge on the breath that drifted to her face. His eyes locked on her own. "But there must be repentance first, Sister Veronika. Do not forget that."

His hand tightened on her shoulder before he released her. Veronika stepped back, a deepening confusion filling her, an unease creeping through her brain. "I appreciate your kind advice, good Father. I assure you, I have nothing to do with anyone condemned by the Lord, nor heathens."

"See that remains true, good Sister. For God is watching."

***

As far as Veronika was concerned, she'd kept her word. Entwined in Adinah's arms, she knew that nothing about this woman could be condemned by a loving God above. Truly, Adinah did not believe that Christ was her savior, the prayers she murmured were sometimes strange to Veronika's ears. But she bore the touch of the divine with each caress.

Veronika had asked only once if Adinah would ever consider baptism, more as curiosity than demand. Adinah's stringent refusal had ensured that the topic had never been broached again. The more time they spent together, the more surprised Veronika was to find that she did not mind so much.

The howl made her press closer to Adinah, feeling the other woman's arms tighten about her. "Don't be afraid, Veronika. My father has ensured we're protected." Adinah withdrew something from her robes, a carving in the shape of a lion. The smile hung fearless on the Jewish woman's face. "My Lion of Judah. He's a mystic, after all. He suspects about us, though he's never asked." She brushed her lips to Veronika's cheek. "He's told me I'm protected. My people have guardians of our own, to keep the wolves away."

The howl sounded again, closer. Veronika stirred, jumping slightly. "I'm sorry. It sounded so near."

"It's alright. I told you, we're protected. Our people have had to fight many times before." Adinah smiled, bold and fearless by the light of the moon.

Something screamed through the night, high-pitched and pained. Like a lamb, or a child. Veronika started up, and now Adinah did leap up with her.

"I heard it, too." Adinah pursed her lips.

"Should we see what it was?" Veronika ventured. The urge to help others welled up in her breast, though Adinah's hand tightened on hers.

"I love you for saying it. But you'd be defenseless against a beast in the dark, wolf or no." Adinah's eyes narrowed. "I am not ready to risk if my protection applies to you."

The notion that someone might be suffering, hurt or even killed tore at Veronika with as much intensity as the teeth of the wolves. She stared in the direction of the woods. "Adinah, I cannot know someone is hurt and do nothing."

Adinah hesitated only once before tightening her cloak. "Very well," she said. "You couldn't be less than who you are if you said otherwise." She kissed Veronika once. "Let's go."

The nun wondered once if this were a test from God Almighty. She had already violated her sacred oaths, but what God could condemn such passion and beauty? Perhaps it was a test, something to overcome for both of them. A sign of divine approval.

They walked together, though the trees swayed in the evening breeze, the whistling wind murmuring through dry leaves. There, in the woods, something shifted and moved. Something large and dark. Veronika's gaze was drawn to it, the dim outline receding through the wooden spires.

It turned back and Veronika caught a glimpse of silver in its mouth, the eyes a burning amber that contrasted the tender argent of the moonlight. Little black droplets fell from the silver teeth, Veronika grasping tighter to Adinah.

She turned to ask her lover a question, but Adinah was staring downward, trembling and pale. A look of grim foreboding on her face. Veronika followed her gaze, eyes going wide as she beheld the ravaged form of a child upon the ground.

***

"And how did you know of this ghastly deed, Veronika?" Father Janos sat before the nun, her habit donned, her hands trembling before her. She and Adinah had left one another only after Adinah had led her to the church in the cloak of night, promising to tell her own people. They were protected, she cautioned Veronika. Do not worry about her flight. They would meet again tomorrow.

"The boy was taken from his home, a farmer's son. Found just where you told me once you roused me." The priest looked tired, sickened. Beneath his eyes were dark rings, his teeth showing as his breath rasped against them.

"I was....out," Veronika murmured. "A walk at night. I know it was forbidden, Father Janos, but I merely wished to feel the air against me, that's all."

"You risked your life with prowling beasts about for a walk at night? Sister, must I order you to confession for your sins? This seems unbelievable. The stench of sin clings to you. Was it a man from the village? You'd not be the first nun to violate your oaths in such a manner."

"I met no man, Father!" This, at least, was no lie. "Please believe me." Veronika clasped her hands. "I saw it retreat through the trees. It must have seen me as well."

"Indeed, and it is fortunate it did not attack you. But this is only the latest, and the people cry for retribution." Father Janos's fist tightened before him. "I have spoken with them, Sister. Our course is clear. The presence of those unclean heathens near us has brought this wretchedness upon us. Do you not know the stories? They betrayed the Savior to his death. They take Christian children and rend them apart, use their blood for unholy purposes. The same has happened all through Europe and it has happened here!"

Veronika could scarce believe her ears. "Father Janos, what are you saying? You can't mean to say the Jews were responsible for this!"

"I do. With God as my witness!" The priest rose to his feet, a thundering shepherd before a flock. "And by God, I will rally our people. The only way to deal with such an infection is to cut out the source."

Adinah and her people. The meaning set in to Veronika, the pure horror setting her mind afire. The Jews would be at risk, massacred in an outpouring of violence. The wolves would be undeterred, the bloodshed might even embolden them. And if it was indeed dark magic, the true culprits would escape all justice. "Father, you cannot be serious! These are innocent people!"

"Innocent people do not refuse salvation. You know your bible, Veronika. They demanded the blood of the Savior be upon them and their children. We simply call in the debt when they transgress, as they have now. You will remain in the church. I will make preparations, speak to the villagers. That is an order. The Jews must know nothing."

Janos rose and walked for the door, Veronika's sweat freezing upon her face. Adinah was at risk, her father and people at risk. She swallowed heavily, already preparing her next moves. She had to warn them.

She waited, cloistered in the temple, taking little food or drink. All she could think of was the setting sun, her waiting lover. At last, when the sun had departed, Veronika found it in herself to flee the church, to her and Adinah's meeting place.

She found Adinah waiting, cloaked and smiling. "Veronika," she started, the nun embracing her with a fervor of passion.

"You have to take your people. Flee. Father Janos means to set the people of the village against you. He told me you were responsible this afternoon," Veronika babbled out. Her eyes were wide, horrified. Adinah pulled back, confusion on her face.

"We've done nothing. We can't just pick up everything and flee overnight, Veronika! Even if my father listens to me, there are dozens of families, the Rabbi, who won't. You're being absurd, surely we are in no danger."

"Father Janos said you were sinners, that you would need to be blamed!" Veronika's tears poured down her face, her lip trembling as the words flowed from her. "Adinah, please. You have to run. You and your father, if nobody else. Father Janos barely seemed surprised when I told him of the child, as though-"

"As though he suspected it was us all along?" A strange serenity approached Adinah's face. She sighed deeply. "I see. So he knew."

"Adinah?" Veronika was certain she must be mishearing. "What do you mean?"

Adinah hugged Veronika close and peered over her shoulder. "You should come out now. You hide yourself well, but your game is at an end."

For a moment, there was nothing. And then Veronika heard a form slide and shift through the woods, heavy footsteps approaching. The man who pulled himself from between that fortress of trees was familiar to her as her own face.

"Veronika," Father Janos growled. "What have you done?"

It was as if someone had removed her tongue and nailed it to her heart. Veronika stared at her priest, a burgeoning horror on her face. "Father, I can explain," she began.

"I told you the scent of sin clings to you. Oh, child, what have you done? To despoil yourself with one of them?" His eyes narrowed, a harsh cast to his face. "Did your eyes never see me before you?"

Adinah stepped before them, a shield from Janos's eyes. "My people are innocent of any ill doing, priest."

"Innocent?" The gruff snarl clawed from the back of the priest's throat. "Innocent?" He thundered it now, a roaring bellow as his eyes blazed beneath a wild tangle of hair. The priest seemed to grow larger, broader, his face darker in the shadows of the trees. His lips stretched back from his teeth. "On your hands is the blood of Christ, the blood of children. You have corrupted even *me*. And this, *this*. To find your sin before me. When I drank from the wolf print, never did I envision, always did I tell me my senses lied. But they will know you for what you are, this entire nation will see you unmasked."

His body grew, his hands large and the nails lengthening. His face grew longer and how large his teeth were.

The priest's hands pulled at the cloak, tearing at the cloth to reveal a muscled body, covered in thick fur. Before them stood the wolf, eyes blazing like pits of molten moonlight and saliva clinging to its lips.

Veronika stepped back, aware she saw the devil's work. Adinah's hand clutched at her, her lover ushering the nun back. "The woods, Veronika. Run!" She urged. Run, for it was their only chance.

Veronika stood face to face with devilry, death glaring at her. But in that moment, it was not death that terrified her most. It was the notion that were she damned or saved, it would mean separation from the woman at her side forever.

She ignored Adinah's advice, making to run for the town. But the beast that had been Father Janos, or still was, moved suddenly to block the way. Crouching low as a predator, snarling with a low fervor that promised death or torment, the beast advanced slowly as if meaning to savor the hunt.

"Veronika, we're protected. The woods!" Adinah shouted. Veronika didn't know the meaning of her lover's words, but on instinct, she obeyed. Even though the fear of entering the woods under cover of woods almost stole her breath. She heard the steady gait of the predator behind her, enacting a dance as old as time itself: predator and prey.

Adinah clutched to her hand, Veronika unwilling to let go for a moment. With the power of the wolf, surely the beast could overtake them in but an instant, yet no nail nor claw ripped through Veronika's flesh.

It was toying with them. That could be the only explanation. The creature that had been her priest was chasing them, though she could not hear its footfalls. There, in the dim grooves through the trees, Veronika believed she could hear the stride of the beast. There, in the bite of the wind, she heard its snarl.

"Adinah," she managed, panting.

"The woods," Adinah whispered as they followed on. "Here, quickly." Veronika did not understand, and yet they let the trees close in upon them.

Just before she saw the shape ahead. Rising to its full height and leering with a mixture of hunger and lust. The wolf opened its mouth, running a tongue blackened by shadow against teeth that yet shone silver.

Veronika skidded to a stop, holding tighter to Adinah's hand. She tried to pray, but there were no prayers in Latin that seemed sufficient. Instead, she thought of what Adinah had taught her, hearing Adinah's own whispers that seemed more invocation than pleas for deliverance.

Father Janos took a step forth, lifting a taloned paw. The snarl grew hungrier, ravenous.

Something sounded in the woods. A twig cracked. The shadows seemed to darken and the wolf paused. It sniffed at the air rapidly, Adinah tugging Veronika close.

"I told you, beloved. There was no reason to fear. Not with me." Adinah brushed a hand across Veronika's back. "My father suspected a great deal. And there are older things in these woods than wolves. Hungrier as well." Her lips gained the bare trace of a smile. "Ancient things, who understand what it is like to be hunted. Things with sympathy for us. Whose dominion extends through the woods and who guard those who are different."

She pulled Veronika even closer, arms about her. Though Janos advanced further, the shadows grew deeper, and the wind sounded like whispers. Ancient and sibilant tongues in a language older than humankind itself.

The wolf snarled, but now there seemed to be fear in it. The whispers became laughter and the shadows moved. A flutter of wind and deep furrows opened in the wolf's flank. He snarled, eyes wide as dark crimson leaked out from the fur.

The shadows quivered again and more cuts opened. Janos howled in disbelief, whirling to cut at the air, but he was far from Veronika and seemed to have no purchase on shadows and air. Veronika looked at Adinah's quiet satisfaction, her lover's hand cupping her cheek.

The wolf screamed, more man than beast now. Adinah kissed Veronika's head. "There are secrets we don't share easy. My people have been chased from many homes, oppressed for years, my love. I couldn't so easily say all my family knows. I was afraid of losing you already."

But Veronika felt no horror, nor shame. Nothing but gratitude. Janos began to run, to turn and stumble as the blows continued, the laughter ringing out about them. "I'm a poor Catholic," she admitted, the surge of liberation chasing away the horror. "I'd sooner forsake my robes than you. I've already shaken off my vows."

This was not witchcraft, but salvation.

Janos ran, and Adinah led her lover from the trees, holding to her hand tightly as the shadows cavorted and danced all about them. Veronika closed her eyes, letting Adinah lead her. Just before a great cry went up, a dozen voices shouting as one. There went a great howl, but it was pained and desperate. Then it cut off, strangled and lost.

Veronika ran away now, peering from between the trees as they reached the end of the woods. Peering through the trees, she saw the people of the village. They stood armed, with farming tools and knives. On the ground lay the wolf, torn and rent. Its body shrank, becoming human. A man cried out the name:

"Janos!"

"The priest was the beast!" Another cried. Veronika turned back to Adinah, the two safely concealed. Her lover sighed in what sounded relief.

"And my people are safe. And so are we." She took Veronika's hands. "We should sneak back, return you to the church. Tis best you not be missed long."

Veronika could not argue, except only that the church did not feel like home so much anymore. She held tighter to Adinah, considering something even madder now. She should have been horrified, a good catholic would be by such sorcery.

But, she had admitted, she was not such a good Catholic after all. "How does one…become a Jew, Adinah?"

"It's a question for a Rabbi. Or my father," Adinah whispered. "Careful study. Conversion. Nothing so simple as Christianity. Are you interested?"

It had been Adinah and that mysticism that had delivered them. That mysticism, Veronika already knew, was not Judaism itself. But the nun was interested. And she smiled as they withdrew back into the protective embrace of the woods and its strange denizens.

"I think we have all the time in the world, my love."

And she felt delightfully free just saying it. Just like a wolf racing across the land.

The Loss

By

Michael R. Collins

I first heard about The Loss from Tee. She told me about it with all the air and practicality of one who expected me to believe it existed. The delight she took in explaining how it fed upon those who were down and depressed was endearing. "Grief." She said, her eyes wide, "I relishes grief the most." I didn't think too much of it at the time because she was always telling me weird folk stories. Like The Flying Vagina Of The Goddess Kapo or all the shit Kokopelli got up to. To be fair though, this was also back when she snorted her Adderall and before she started sleeping with Catherine the Prep.

Catherine the Prep was a pretty twenty-something who liked slumming and sleeping her way through the clubs. Apparently, being a lesbian wasn't enough to piss off her rich parents, so she had to bring home the tweaked-out club kids. Tee wasn't strung out like the others, but she had the bad habit of seeing the best in people who were using her.

They are both gone now. I know why and by who. I'll be damned if I let the same thing happen to me.

I didn't see The Loss at first. No one does, in the beginning. The sneaky bastard comes at you while you're distracted. It sidles up next to you, matching your footsteps and moving when you do, pretending to be a shadow in the corner of your vision. Only after it's too late, do you realize the shadow is something horrifying and real.

Tee's last text to me was '*I don't think I can hang on much longer*' My stomach twisted into knots because she was never into self-harm. It was one of those rock-solid ideas that you could stake your life on. For all the old dark tales she loved to tell, she was the brightest light. But after what happened to Catherine, I assumed she might be desperate enough.

Her last text haunts me because only after reading it did I take any action. I stayed away and I shouldn't have. I'm not sure it would have done any good, but maybe the guilt would weigh less on my shoulders. Fear and selfishness kept me away from her door. Instead of helping her fight The Loss's assaults on her, I hid like a coward, rewarded for my spinelessness with losing my dear friend and contracting The Loss.

To use the word 'contract' insinuates a nasty virus or cold. The Loss isn't a biological agent but spreads just as easily. Tee didn't mean to transmit it to me. She always wanted to soothe people's wounds, so her pushing me away was a kindness. Or so I tell myself.

Why The Loss came into our lives, I can't say for sure. Maybe proximity, or even happenstance. The why and how doesn't matter. There has been time for me to study and I know it's inevitable. Others might shrug it off, often not knowing the thing is there, or possibly it's the epidemic we choose not to talk about. All I know for sure is it is looking at me right now, looming over me like a hateful enemy.

Like a smothering parent.

Like an intimate lover.

As it does, I begin to dwell again.

"Jeremiah!" Tee yelled over the blasting beats. She wrapped her arms around my neck and gave me a peck on the cheek. This was the last night I saw her smile. She wasn't happy, but I was too wrapped up in myself to notice the bags under her eyes and the scaffolding holding her smile up.

"Let the party begin." I joked. 'Party Animal' was not a moniker naturally associated with me, but I did love to dance. The clubs and small apartment dinners I frequented helped kill the loneliness. Too tall, not skinny enough, a little older than the rest, and posing no threat; I'm the responsible friend. Not that I minded. I had fun, and when the fun stopped, I left.

"So." Tee said as a statement all on its own. A preamble to a decree I had no freedom in or out of. Her skin radiated blue and white in the glow of the lights from her body powder. Her kinky hair a perfectly wild halo. She reminded me of some ravepunk fairy about to ruin your night in the best of ways. "I've decided you are getting laid tonight. The last time was with Giselle, ages ago, and that didn't end well." Actually, Giselle and I ended things well enough. We slept together for a couple of weeks and then wandered off in our separate directions.

"Who am I to argue?" I laughed it off, hating when she did this, but letting it happen because why not?

"Over at the corner of the bar is Dar. She is cute, has green hair, and seems very sweet." She jammed a finger at a tall skinny woman with a shock of emerald hair and a rose tattooed on her neck. Tee swung her finger around to a table on our right. "And there, talking with Catharine is Gerard. He is dark, moody, and looks like he'll make your toes curl."

Only in retrospect do I realize my first glimpse of The Loss happened as I watched Gerard talking with Catherine. What I assumed to be a quirk of light and shadow was the damned thing. My attention taken with Gerard's dark eyes and dark skin, I paid the anomaly little mind.

Later that night, I brought Dar home, and she was indeed sweet. We had fun and while our sweat cooled in the early morning hours, Catherine was being assaulted by a darkness none of us expected. And in case you're wondering, yes, I took a chance on Gerard a few nights later. He was as advertised.

A few days later, Tee pounded on my apartment door far too early in the morning. Wiping the crust from my eyes, I pulled it open. She had been crying for hours. With her face red and puffy and her voice broken from sobbing, she told me the news. Catherine was dead.

She hit a telephone pole at one hundred and ten miles an hour, a couple miles from her parents' sprawling house in the country. Her little Audi Quattro folding into itself like paper. I don't know if they even bothered with an autopsy, but everyone assumed she was drunk. Tee was devastated.

She sobbed into my chest, drenching my shirt as I held her. I pushed away my own shock so I could be strong for her. I had mixed feelings about Catherine, but this was miserable. Even if she wasn't a good fit for Tee.

The rest of the day, we talked, cried, and drank all my green tea. Occasionally Tee would look over her shoulder, or stop talking as if tracking something across the room. I assumed her behavior was grief.

The day wore on and she ran out of tears. In mid-sentence, Tee sprang up like she'd been poked her in the ass. "We should get out. Let's go eat." She barely gave me time to slip shoes and a clean t-shirt on, before pulling me out the door. The sudden immediacy caught me by surprise, but like usual, I went along with her whims.

As I grabbed my keys and wallet, I looked at her standing in the hallway waiting for me. Behind her loomed a shadow of a person, or person shaped thing. It stood over her by at least two feet with a smooth face, amorphous and emotionless. Shadows cloaked the tall form like living things.

My eyes must have grown wide for the split second I saw it. In a blink, it disappeared from my sight. Tee must have seen my expression, because sorrow washed over her again. "Just concentrate on the good thoughts. Not the bad ones. Only the good ones" She grasped my hand and led me out to search for comfort food.

Tee regressed after that. I checked on her through text or phone conversations. I'm not a brave man and what I observed scared the living shit out of me. She told me she was okay, really she was, and I shouldn't worry. The lie was for both of our benefits. She wasn't okay. Not even a little bit.

I visited her only once. Guilt and concern teamed up and grew stronger than my terror. The Loss now brazen enough to not hide at all, hovered near her and stayed within my sight at all times. We both pretended it wasn't there. If she acted as if this phantom didn't exist, then the doubting of my sanity acted as a cushion to the horror.

Only in the safety of text messages did we talk about it.

'I'm scared, Jer,' she texted me late one night. *'It won't let me go.'*

'The Loss is just a story, right? I mean, one of your weird little folk tales.' My denial game was strong. *'It can't be real!'*

'You saw it too! I'm certain you did! If you didn't see, then you're saying I'm going crazy for nothing.'

'You're not crazy. But what does it want? What is it doing to you? I'm scared for you.'

When she didn't text me back immediately, I panicked. I drew up my courage and readied to go to her apartment and face her tormentor. My phone pinged as I reached for my keys with a shaking hand. She texted back.

'I feel so empty, Jer. Inside of me is a wasteland full of blowing sand and bleached bones. The sun burns cold. The only emotion I have left are despondency and mourning. There is no light or joy. It took all my happiness, Jer! What's worse is I'm slipping into apathy. That scares me the most.

'The Loss is sucking everything out of me, feeding on me. What warmth I had is gone. Remember when I told you to concentrate on the

good thoughts? That is a trick. I thought it was a defense. Turns out it was a buffet.

'All I have is sorrow. When Catherine died, IT found me. And I'm afraid it'll go to you next. I'm so sorry.'

After this conversation, we kept our distance. Terror and confusion held hands with me as I tried to act like a normal adult. I went to work, I came home, and functioned in a daze. On the nights I didn't drink myself to sleep, I sat in a wide-eyed trance in front of the flickering television. Guilt grew. I should be helping my friend, but I couldn't even be bothered to check on her. How was I supposed to help her, though? Do I call an exorcist? The police? Ghostbusters? A voodoo priestess?

As scared as I was for Tee, I was scared for myself more. When she finally called me, her voice droned on with a tired and ragged vacancy. We talked about everything except the issue at hand, dancing around the topic like Fred Astaire and Ginger Rogers. Afterwards, I felt worse for it. As I gathered my courage to go to her, Dar called. She wanted to see me. I spent the night with her instead of my best friend. Desperation drove my lovemaking to a frenzy and as I slunk out her door the next morning, Dar admitted that the passion was nice, but the haunted look in my eyes disturbed her. I knew I wouldn't see her anymore.

Three days later, I received the final text. *'I don't think I can hang on much longer.'*

I raced to Tee's apartment. Using my key, let myself in. Tee lay on her couch, in the same clothes as our last visit. Her body emaciated and jagged from dehydration and malnutrition. From the soiled state of her clothes, she hadn't even bothered to get up to use the bathroom.

The Loss stood behind the couch, looking more substantial than before. The formless face exuded pride. "What have you done to her?" I yelled, running to Tee. She held up a weak hand. I took it, unsettled by her chilled skin.

"Too late, Jeremiah. I'll die soon. I deserve it." She whispered.

"No, it's never too late. Let me get you to a hospital." I brushed a greasy strand of hair from her cheek.

"What does it matter, anyway?" She turned away from me.

"Everything matters. You matter. I matter. Dammit Tee, you're going out like a punk ass!" I scolded her.

A small smile cracked her lips. "That's my boy. You may beat this yet." Behind us, the dark shape shifted and shuddered. The creature grew, spreading out in defiance. Tee was rebounding.

"Let's get out of here. We'll split a patty melt and fries and hit the club." I said, trying to give her something to grasp onto. Her smile grew stronger. She raised her arms for me to lift her. As I bent down to gather her up, The Loss flowed over the couch at me.

I turned to fight it, my resolve faltering as it shed the cloak of shadows, revealing a black form of sharp edges. The vague face tight with rage and clawed fists readied to strike. Tee touched me as I stood between the two of them.

"Fuck off! I'm getting her out of here and making sure you can't hurt her anymore!" I've never been bold, but despite my fear, I took a stand.

"No," Tee's hand dug into my side. "Jer, don't. Sometimes the Loss isn't always the Loss."

The clawed hands slammed into me. Burning pain spread across my chest. I flew backwards in an awkward tumble.

"It's more than one thing," Tee croaked as I scrambled to my feet. "Sometimes Loss turns into Wrath."

I watched the thing scrutinize me, waiting for my next move. My chest still burned from the contact. After a moment, the jagged form deflated into its normal wispy state. It no longer viewed me as a threat.

From the couch came a hiccupping sob. "I'm so sorry, Jer. I am so sorry." The Loss turned to Tee and reached down to touch her. With a scream I rushed it, but as soon as a claw tenderly caressed her cheek, I was too late. The Loss became insubstantial once more as I ran through it, overcome with the chill and a depression that nearly stopped the beating of my heart. I fell to the floor again, calling out Tee's name.

Only stillness lay on the couch. Tee's eyes stared at the ceiling and her chest did not rise. The Loss won. I crawled to her and held her. For the moment, it was only her and I in the room, alone for the last time.

At the funeral, I saw it again, standing in the back of the small crowd not as a mourner, but a catalyst for mourning. I didn't bother trying to guess who it might be here for. It wasn't here to choose a new victim to feed off of, it already had one.

As soon as the funeral ended, I made obligatory goodbyes, hoping for a hasty exit. Gerard stopped me and wanted to talk. He was sweet and appreciated my pain, offering to spend time with me. At first I thought he wanted to offer me comfort with his dick, but I realized The Loss, now hovering over my shoulder, was already turning my mind sour with misery. Politely declining, I lied to him with a promise of coffee in the future.

I haven't left my apartment since the funeral. Calling in delivery and forcing myself to take in the basic necessities, I continue to fight. The Loss is always here, silent and patient. I shouldn't say silent. Tee forgot to mention how it likes to whisper in your head. It's smart, this thing. Dredging up all my past indiscretions and remorse to chip at my ego and self-confidence. Once my defenses were down, the insidious shit dived deep and feasted on all that came up.

Between the assaults, I've studied my enemy. The moments of clarity are few and far between anymore, but I utilize them when they come around. I am going to defeat The Loss, for myself and for Tee. To do so, I need a strategy.

I'm certain The Loss caused Catherine to drive into that pole, knowing it would be easier to get a hold on Tee. Whether The Loss was feeding off Catherine too, or simply pressed the accelerator to the floor for her, is immaterial. The Loss causes anguish when it gets hungry. It creates its own meals.

For all that Tee was right about, she was wrong on one point. She told me thinking the good thoughts were a trick so the thing could feed more. In reality, this is the best defense, but you have to bolster them early, use them as armor. The moment you doubt the goodness, then the defense crumbles. Tee gave up. She allowed herself to be fed upon until she let it all go and die alone. She saw it as a win-win.

Alone is what it wants. Alone is how it grows.

The hour is late. Sometime past two in the morning. I'm sitting on my floor, naked, with plastic crinkling underneath my bare ass. As I sit here, feeling the winds of nothingness howling within me, I understand true emptiness. This sort of vacancy is an absence, and the absence is pain. A dull agony, subtle and soft, that is easy to get used to. But it's also a cancer that grows. Inside me is a growing void. That was Tee's true cause of death. The void in her grew, while The Loss gobbled up all the light in her. In the end she died a husk, her body full of emptiness.

I recognize the truth, though. I'm far too gone for that. I stopped eating days ago, thinking like she did, but in a moment of rationality, it came to me. There is a way to save myself.

The pain of the void eating away my insides, allowing my tormentor to nourish itself, is too much to bear. Any action I take now is triage, a final desperate measure. The Loss has fed on my warmth, joy, sorrow, anger, and despondency. Soon I too will be a husk, the void it created inside me being all that remains.

In front of me, The Loss hovers. It thinks it senses triumph, but I'm about to present it with disappointment. To my right is a kitchen knife. As I pick it up, The Loss shudders, assuming it is about to taste a suicide.

The Loss has left me so numb that when I pick up the knife and run the razor-sharp blade across my abdomen, I feel the deep bite of the blade only as a nibble. My taut skin splits open and the muscles give way. Blood bubbles down my crotch. With a shaking hand, I push past my own guts. I will pluck out the void The Loss created inside me. The emptiness of emotions and self *must* be removed. I imagine it to be an orb of black vacuum. Once I extract it, there will be room for everything to come back. I will feel something again. It won't be able to feed off of me anymore. This has to be the way.

The pain rises as I search, feeling for the ball of nothing. I only touch the slimy ropes of pulsing entrails.

I can't find it!

Where is it?!

The Loss comes closer, gloating.

I pull intestines out of the way. The desolation has to be here!

The pain increases and clears my mind, giving me a sudden moment of lucidity. Real clarity to see through the delusion that led me to believe that I contained a physical wasteland inside of my body. The wasteland isn't a material object. It is only intangible emotions.

I look up at The Loss and then at my insides spilled out onto my lap. It used my own delirious despair against me, allowing me to think triumph was near. The Loss wins again.

If only I had been there for Tee.

If only I allowed others to be there for me.

If only I-

The Acquisition

By

Lindz McLeod

Fiona pulled up outside 33 Thorn Street, parked, and peered through the passenger-side window. The house was nice enough from the outside; a little dingy, maybe, and the shutters were cracked and peeling, but otherwise it looked much like everything else in this part of the city. A two-storey detached townhouse, reasonably priced—basically a unicorn. A stiff breeze buffeted the vehicle, rocking it from side to side. One of the upstairs shutters banged closed, making it look like the house was winking at her.

Close up, the walls of the house were made of grey brick—the sort that might, in the right kind of moonlight, look almost blue. Not quite her style, but then again, she really did need to move somewhere bigger than her current, cramped apartment. It had suited her for a while, but the pandemic lockdowns had left her feeling claustrophobic. Three bedrooms, the website had enthused. Two bathrooms. A well-lit, spacious family room. They'd gone on about the chimney stack too, though she didn't really approve of fireplaces these days; air pollution was bad enough already without adding to the problem. The topmost step leading up to the porch was loose, causing her to wobble precariously. Safety hazard: red flag number one.

Fiona knocked on the door, then checked her watch. She was late, certainly, but still within the designated viewing time. Casting a glance over her shoulder, she noted the lack of cars in the street and the lack of voices from inside the house. Maybe she'd got the time wrong. She'd just pulled out her phone to check when the door swung open, revealing a middle-aged man with shiny, dark hair which had been combed back like a neatly ploughed field. A smoky cloud of cologne accompanied him. Fiona bit back a cough.

"Come in, come in," he enthused, ushering her inside. "So glad you could make it. Let me show you around." He made a sharp right turn. "This is the family room. So spacious, right? Great windows, right? And all these amazing period features. You don't see them every day."

"Oh really? Which period?" Fiona asked, repressing another cough. The room had looked nice enough in the pictures—bay windows, polished hardwood flooring, French blue walls—but now that she was actually here, the stains on the plaster ceiling and walls were evident. There were deep gouges on the floor, only partially hidden by a threadbare rug. The smell, too, was pungent. Black rot, maybe; otherwise known as house cancer.

He blinked. "You British?"

"English." He hadn't actually answered her question, she noted; red flag number two.

"Uh." He blinked again. "That's great. That's so great. I love your accent."

If she'd had a pound for every time she'd heard that since moving to America, Fiona thought, then she probably could have bought this house in cash, exchange rate notwithstanding. She shifted, feeling another loose board under her left foot. "Have there been many offers yet?"

"Oh yeah, we've had viewings all day. It's a real popular place, you know. Great location. Good schools in the area too, if that's something you're interested in."

Fiona made a noncommittal noise and retreated into the hallway. The realtor followed, scuttling past her into the kitchen. "Period features," he announced again, waving vaguely in the direction of the corniced ceiling and away from the scorch marks above the stove. "It's really a steal. Hell, I wish I could buy it myself!"

He walked her through the myriad features of the hallway and downstairs bathroom—smaller than she'd thought, with a window frame that looked soft and half-rotten with damp—before moving upstairs. The air was tepid, unmoving, as if no one had opened a window in quite some time. The realtor's collar was damp with sweat as he dashed ahead and flung the door to the master bedroom open. Fiona examined it carefully, trying to picture her own furniture arranged artfully along the walls. Her desk here under the window, maybe, where the light fell in golden squares. She

pushed aside the curtain, heavy velvet dragging against her fingertips, and peered out into the garden. Haphazard flower beds lined each side, while a tall apple tree stood alone at the bottom, branches bowed like a prisoner awaiting execution.

The realtor watched her. Sweat beaded on his forehead, making his dark hair glisten even more. "Great period features," he repeated, a little louder, though he wasn't looking at her. Instead, he was staring upwards at the ceiling. "Don't you think? A beautiful, unique style?"

Which period? she wondered, irritation pulsing through her temples. Victorian? Georgian? Pleistocene? "Thanks." She edged back towards the door. "I have to think about it, but it's a great place."

For a moment he hesitated in the doorway, blocking her path, but then moved aside; red flag numbers three through five thousand. Reaching into her pocket, she gripped her car key between her knuckles and held it firm. When she reached the bottom stair safely, she heard the realtor sigh behind her—not in exasperation, like she might have expected, but something more akin to relief.

After work the next day, Fiona drove to another house, vowing to flee the moment things got weird. This one was across town—a little smaller, a little more pricy, but she'd liked the look of it. The curvy woman who met her at the door was dressed in a well-fitting grey suit. "Two bedrooms, two baths," she said, leaning against the doorway. A rainbow lanyard hung around her neck, displaying her name and title: Debbie Fischer, Realtor. No wedding ring, she noticed, though that didn't necessarily mean anything. "Feel free to look around. Take your time. I'm happy to answer any questions."

It took Fiona all of ten minutes to fall in love with 78 Beech Drive. The modern kitchen was exactly to her liking, with its new electric stovetop and tasteful marble counters. The dining room was a perfect size, perfect for entertaining a select few guests. Even the bedrooms were ideal, overlooking a patch of woodland. The sweet scent of mint drifted lazily towards her. Rewilded land, the advertisement had said, because we're deeply concerned with sustainable living. Fiona stepped out onto the porch, called up her broker, and arranged an offer on the spot.

As she pocketed her phone, something flickered in the distance. Craning around, she stared at the end of the street. For a second, she'd thought that one of the houses had jerked forward. She frowned. Earthquakes did happen in this part of the country, though they were usually minor. Wouldn't she have felt the ground shaking? Perhaps it was a sinkhole. She squinted at the house. Now that she looked at it more closely, it bore a remarkable resemblance to 33 Thorn Street. The rest of the houses in this row were darker, leaner, and none of them had chimneys.

The realtor stepped outside, locking the door behind her. "I've just made an offer," Fiona said, handing a business card over. "Call me if you want to go out sometime. No pressure."

Debbie grinned. "Absolutely. Do you want to come back to my place? We could celebrate your new purchase."

Flattered, Fiona blushed. "Are you always this blunt?"

"I don't know." She leaned in, close enough for Fiona to smell her perfume; wild, oceanic, salty. "Are you always this cute?"

"I suppose I must be." She could feel the flush spreading down her neck, warming her skin. "Let's go."

The following week, Debbie took her to dinner at a candle-lit restaurant set high on a hill. The waitress seated them in the window, where they could enjoy the view of the city laid out before them like an unrolled treasure map. During their starter course—a single braised woodpigeon breast perched on a thick smear of roast carrot mash—something flickered in Fiona's periphery. She paid it no attention, focusing instead on Debbie's tales of real estate horror, until it happened again. She glanced out of the window at the setting sun, painting the western sides of the buildings in brilliant scarlet. Everything looked normal. Tall, slender buildings which housed offices and production companies, were dotted amongst large squat hospitals and schools. Yet among these things which should be rooted to the landscape with feet of concrete and steel and clay and whatever foundations were made of, Fiona had thought she'd seen something moving in the darkness. Something the size of a two-storey house.

"Are you okay?" Debbie said, pausing with a sliver of wood pigeon on her fork.

"Sorry. I thought I—" She shook her head. "Nothing. Please go on."

"Okay so, this guy says to Mike, I can't believe—"

There it was again; a flicker of movement deep in the city. Fiona kept her eyes fixed on Debbie, all appetite gone. It's just the stress and strain of work, she told herself. A trick of the light. That's all. Nothing the size of a house is stalking you. It's ridiculous to even entertain the idea.

She poured herself another glass of Malbec, and let the wine do most of the work. By the time their main course had arrived—beef wellington on a pyre of tender green beans—she was feeling a lot better.

"I sometimes cycle the route between here and Dalton." Debbie tapped the stem of her wine glass with a single, crimson nail. "It's a great workout and an even better view. Do you bike at all?"

"Only at the gym," Fiona admitted. "I'm not really a fan, to be honest." Debbie didn't seem to notice her discomfort.

"You'd love it if you tried it with me." She leaned across the table and took Fiona's hand. Her fingers were cold.

"Yeah, maybe." She shifted on her chair. Why were all her dates like this about their hobbies?

"I'll take you there soon." Debbie's eyes glazed over. "You know, there's a beautiful lake. We could take a picnic!"

Fiona smiled and nodded through dessert, listening to Debbie bang on about all the benefits of cycling. Annoying, sure. Self-absorbed, certainly. But at least she was hot, and she'd read most of the classics. Sometimes you had to make sacrifices.

When they left the restaurant, Debbie stuffed her wallet back into her pocket and sniffed. "Jeez! They must have hit a pipe somewhere."

Fiona wrinkled her nose. It did smell awful—smoky and sour, like a Dickensian parlor. She glanced up at the sky, where the moon was being strangled by thick clouds. Behind the immediate row of buildings, a single chimney stack belched noxious plumes into the air.

Figuring she should get a head-start on upping her fitness level, Fiona cycled home from work the next day. It was harder than she remembered, with the added stress of negotiating road traffic, and by the time she arrived home every nerve and fibre of her body twanged with agonizing adrenaline. Sighing, she loaded the bike into the back of her car, intending to return it to the rental place in the morning. She was in the middle of calculating how many miles the route Debbie had suggested was likely to be, when something moved at the end of her street.

She closed the car door, keys gripped tightly in her hand, and squinted. The end of her street had previously held only one apartment building, surrounded by a half-moon lawn. Yet now there was a second dark shape, crouched beside it like a great, squat beast. Fiona scuttled towards the front door, unlocked it, and threw herself inside. Running up the stairs, she stopped on the second floor landing and peered through the window. The shape was still there. She pressed her face against the glass, straining to see in the dim light. The shape had a single chimney stack, just like 33 Thorn Street. This can't be happening, she thought. People don't get haunted by houses. She hesitated, her breath fogging up the glass. Well—

They did, didn't they? Except, people were usually—in her admittedly limited experience of the subject—inside the house at the time. She'd never heard of anyone being haunted by a house like this, following her around like a stray dog. Like a stalker ex. A cold thrill fizzled down her spine. What could a house possibly want from her? Images ran riot in her mind; loose, rotten floorboards breaking into rows of splintered teeth. A scorching blaze, escaping the safe confines of a fireplace. A door, closing on the outside world forever, leaving her in darkness.

That night she barely slept at all. Instead, she cowered in the darkness of her tiny bedroom, pressed against the wall and watching through a tiny slit in the curtains. The house stayed in the same spot for hours. Eventually, she managed to convince herself that she'd imagined the entire thing and was in all likelihood actually having some sort of mental health crisis. Of course a house couldn't move. Not by itself, anyway.

The moment she relaxed, the house inched closer, dragging itself over the tarmac, leaving a trail of dust behind it like a dry, oversized snail. The ground rumbled, causing ornaments to shiver on her

shelves and tremble their way towards a fatal fall. Half-grating, half-screeching, the house edged closer. Fiona shrank back, horrified. The street below was empty and silent, so there was no way to tell whether anyone else could verify that a house—undeniably a house, and undeniably 33 Thorn Street—was haunting her. No car alarms had gone off. No concerned faces had appeared at windows. The world slept on, ignorant to her panic. She was entirely alone.

The house rotated slowly until it faced her building. The right upstairs shutter closed, as if it was winking, the same way it had when she'd first come to view it, before it retreated to the end of the street again and disappeared. Fiona squashed her face against the glass, and eventually risked opening her window and leaning out. In the amber glow of the streetlights, she could see nothing beyond the pale building.

33 Thorn Street had vanished. Drawing the curtains tightly, she sat in the dark, trembling. This was nothing more than a strange dream. A mirage. A house couldn't get up and wander about the city. It was simply impossible. She left for work that morning, frazzled and exhausted, and cruised slowly past the end of the street. The pale building looked perfectly normal, and so did its half-moon lawn. Not a single blade of glass was out of place. Not a single flower petal was crushed or bent. Her body, which had been rigid with fear for the last few hours, sagged in relief.

She drove to her office downtown, casting wary glances in her rearviewmirror the whole way. The day had dawned beautiful and bright, the kind of blue-sky spring morning that caused birds to break into delightful song. The streets were lined with cherry blossom trees in full, riotous bloom, brushing the tops of buses and trucks with soft kisses. The air was temperate, bordering on warm; the kind of day that called for the first sunscreen application of the year. Fiona was too exhausted to appreciate any of it. She called her broker before she'd even exited the car, and pushed him to seal the deal as quickly as possible.

"Of course," the broker said. "The paperwork does tend to take a few days, but I'm sure we'll—"

"If there's anything you can do to speed it up, please do it," Fiona ordered. Once she had the keys to her new house, then surely this bizarre hallucination would end. It was a delusion, plain and simply, brought on by the stress of a large purchase. It could happen to anyone. It probably did.

The broker tapped his keyboard. "I'll see what I can do, Ms Williams."

"Thank you." She hung up and got out of the car. Across the street, behind a large convenience store, a grey-bricked chimney stack was clearly visible.

She spent the next couple of days in a fog of fatigue, barely able to comprehend either her work projects or casual conversation. At night, 33 Thorn Street lurked outside her apartment building, getting closer and closer. During the day, it stalked her through the city streets, leering at her with half-closed shutters, flashing her a glimpse of its open front door. Unable to bear it any longer, and aware that her broker was sick of her calling every few hours to see what progress had been made, she called Debbie on Thursday morning. "Any chance you can speed things up for me? I'd be so grateful." She peered through the blinds. 33 Thorn Street sat in the car park like a smug cat, curled between two Jeeps.

Debbie practically purred down the phone. "I might be able to manage something."

A tall man wearing a puffy gilet loaded a cardboard box into the back of one of the Jeeps and then got in, apparently unaware that a two-storey townhouse was sitting only feet away. "Thank you so much," Fiona said, trying to sound breezy. "I'm just so keen to get out of my old place, you know? New home, clean slate."

"You'll hear from me by close of play on Friday, I swear," Debbie promised.

By the time 6pm rolled around on Friday, Fiona was pacing her small office, chewing on fingernails which were already little more than stubs. She stopped occasionally to peer through the blinds into the car park. Several harsh yellow floodlights illuminated the area, though these were largely blocked out by the bulk of 33 Thorn Street, which was even closer than before—close enough for her to smell black rot wafting through the window of her office, and even to see the grain of the wooden steps leading up to the porch. Her phone finally beeped, displaying a text from Debbie. All wrapped up! I could even give you the keys now if you want.

Fiona closed her eyes and sent a silent thank you heavenwards. She drove to the suggested bar downtown, unable to keep from glancing over her shoulder. The bar was in a basement, the windows criss-crossed with iron bars, and for the first time all day, she began to feel like herself again.

"You seem stressed, honey," Debbie murmured, hand squeezing Fiona's thigh. "Hard week?"

"You have no idea." She forced a smile. "All the better for seeing you, though."

"I'll drink to that."

Alcohol was almost as good as home ownership, in Fiona's opinion. She and Debbie flirted over a few rounds of shots and chasers, before taking a cab to her new address. Giggling uproariously, they had to help each other navigate the stairs up to the front door. The topmost step shifted under Fiona's boot. That's weird, she thought. 78 Beech Drive's steps hadn't—

She looked at the front door, then at the grey bricks surrounding it. This wasn't 78 Beech Drive. It was 33 Thorn Street. "What the hell?"

"Oh my god, we're on the wrong side of the street," Debbie cooed. "Wow, we must be so drunk. Come on, it's over there."

She tugged at Fiona's hand, but Fiona didn't move. Something was standing in the living room window of 33 Thorn Street—a crude approximation of Debbie. It was barely human; just an oval of white flesh, like a bowling pin, freckled with dark spots in the places where facial orifices usually were. The thing that wasn't Debbie raised a hand and waved. Fiona scrambled backwards, dragging Real Debbie across the street and into 78 Beech Drive, slamming the door behind them.

"What are you doing?" Real Debbie asked, frowning.

Fiona shushed her. Through the peephole, she could see 33 Thorn Street just sitting there. The Debbie thing in the window was still waving, and now it had been joined by a tanned, lumpen Fiona thing, with wavy brown hair.

"Seriously, you're being really weird. What are you looking at?"

"There's something out there," Fiona hissed. "Just shut up, please, and—"

Debbie pushed her out of the way and grabbed the door handle. Yanking it open, she stopped dead.

33 Thorn Street's grey-bricked facade was pressed against the front door. Fiona screamed and stumbled backwards. Debbie stood frozen, slack-jawed. The front door of 33 Thorn Street yawned open, revealing a dark hallway. Two pale shapes emerged and stood side by side; two things, which still looked more like bowling pins than people but had developed lopsided eyes. The Fiona thing lunged at Debbie, shoving her back into 78 Beech

Drive. Debbie screamed, clawing at its face. Fiona grabbed the sleeve of Debbie's jacket, tried to yank her free, but the Fiona thing smacked her away with lumpen, handless arms that felt like they were made of solid clay.

Fiona hit the wall and slid down, panting. Before she could rise, the Debbie thing had grabbed hold of her leg and was tugging her inexorably through the doorway into 33 Thorn Street. She kicked wildly, catching the Debbie thing in the face with the heel of her boot, but it made no difference. Once inside 33 Thorn Street, the door slammed shut. The lock clicked. Fiona wailed and curled into a ball, awaiting her fate.

Nothing happened.

She uncurled tentatively, whimpering in terror. The Debbie thing had disappeared. Fiona scrambled to her feet, yanked on the front door with all her might. It didn't budge. She scrabbled at the lock only to find it had melted. There was no way she could get out. She dashed into the family room, thinking that she might be able to break the window and crawl out, but real Debbie was visible through the window of 78 Beech Drive and she was—

Laughing.

Fiona stared, unable to believe her eyes. Real Debbie was clutching an ice pack to her head and laughing, while the Fiona thing made bicycling motions, paddling the air with its new, lumpen hands. Its mouth was little more than a diagonal wound in the pale flesh of its face, but real Debbie didn't seem to mind. "Hey!" Fiona shouted, banging on the glass. "What the hell? Stay away from her!"

Neither took the slightest notice. The Fiona thing stepped closer to Debbie, who batted her eyelashes, and pressed its speckled, smooth face against her mouth.

A floorboard creaked behind Fiona. She spun, raising her fists against any attack that might come. The Debbie thing stood awkwardly in the doorway, gold something. It was meant to be a bottle of champagne, Fiona realised, recognizing the approximate shape, although it looked like it had been blown by Dali in a drunken pique. She lowered her fists, waiting for the Debbie thing to lunge at her, but it simply stood there, slash-mouth curving in a loose approximation of a smile. "Period features?" it slurred. "Period features."

The room around them was changing. Gone were the French blue walls and scratched hardwood flooring, and in their place was the modern grey laminate of 78 Beech Drive, the pale jacquard wallpaper. 33 Thorn Street was adapting to her tastes, doing its best to compromise. That was what a relationship was, wasn't it? Sacrifices on both parts, to ensure happiness for all?

The Debbie thing thrust the champagne bottle at her, cooing hopefully. Fiona cast a look over her shoulder at the embracing couple in 78

Beech Drive. "Fine," she said, sighing. "You don't like bikes, do you?"

"Period features," the Debbie thing agreed, shaking its head.

Fiona held the green blob aloft, watching as it morphed into a champagne bottle. The weird, pixelly hold label became a clear, recognizable brand name. Across the street, Debbie and the Fiona thing were slow-dancing to the strains of Imogen Heap.

To our new home, she thought, half-dizzy, half-giddy.

Zero Sum

By

J. Daniel Stone

"Think for yourself…question authority," Ceylon said as he tipped the bottle of Wild Turkey into his black hole mouth.

We were already drunk and listless, recalling the rush of our five-finger discount. The Honda Prelude soared up I-95, wheels sizzling, and behind me the road spun like a film reel. In front, it was a wavering tapestry of insects and headlights.

"I hope she makes it."

"She'll be fine," I said.

I took another swig, cringed from the liquor's menacing aftertaste, but suddenly overcome with the spirit of Lestat de Lioncourt and the misery of hurricane ghosts. I recalled the odor of carrion flowers and kudzu fingering itself through abandoned houses; the smell of waffles that dripped into the back of my throat like warm butter. Ceylon raised a questionable eyebrow, dark lips pursing.

"The moon's bright. Wanna stop?"

"No."

"Don't make me throw you back in the gutter where I found you."

The engine whined…whinnied, and for a split second I thought I'd left a bottle of beer underneath the hood when we had made that pit stop in Raleigh. Plumes were shooting out of the A/C vents, the smoke twice as choking as our Parliaments. Then the car jerked, sending me forward so that the Wild Turkey flew out the window.

"Damn it," Ceylon said.

"Damn *you*," I added.

Judging by his sinister smile and the dark stain on his tongue, Ceylon had already transcended the state of pain and reason. But that didn't sway his trajectory. The Prelude's four little wheels moved even faster. I trusted the car to get us to NYC safely, and before I knew it we were pulled free from the swelter of the South and on our way into DC.

"I almost forgot how cold it is up here."

The ghostgreen glow of the dashboard light crawled on Ceylon's skin, suffused his lips and changed the color of his eyes. It saturated me with the feeling of being safe. I sifted through my CD case and grabbed one at random, putting up the volume as loud as it could go. For the next four hours Otep and The Cure vomited out of the speakers before we saw the glass and iron spires of New York City.

"The place we met," I said out loud.

We penetrated Manhattan via the George Washington Bridge. Not much had changed. The river still smelled like boat fuel and the buildings remained ominous across the vista. The battered roads had been taken over by construction projects that only caused more congestion. But as it is for anyone who travels away from their home, returning was bittersweet.

Space was limited; freedom was imminent, and violence was accepted.

Ceylon found parking on west 16th street. We pulled our bags out of the trunk and said good night to the Honda Prelude. But that's not all we said goodnight to. The boy we picked up in Atlanta was barely breathing, a transient of nineteen, too horny to listen to his gut and bypass the lurking car. But he had cash in his wallet—and Ceylon was a certified slave to the almighty dollar—so we had to have him.

"Another runaway...gone."

I saw the boy's flaxen hair and pink lips, a spot of blood dried on his chin. He'd drunk himself into a stupor while Ceylon had his way with him, biting and tugging and scratching, taking in all the delicious flavors of youth and carelessness. I was on duty with another trick at the time, and so I couldn't really tell what was going on in the back seat. At some point I did hear a scream that eventually turned into pleasant moaning.

All the while the car was in gear—

—speeding with no one behind the wheel.

"Think he'll live?" I said.

"Since when do you care?"

The street was not as busy as expected, and so Ceylon removed the boy from the car, pulling him into an alleyway by his hair and setting a few pieces of cardboard over his body so that he blended in with the rest of the bums. I hit the beeper to lock the doors, could almost hear the Prelude's sigh of relief being that we would ask no more of it tonight. A thought came into my head. It had witnessed our antics, our debauchery, remaining resilient through rugged highways and seedy back roads, through mud and ice and sand. It was a strong little car. It had charisma, courage…something I certainly lacked.

"We sleep here," Ceylon said.

The hostel was deserted, but not unwelcoming. The walls were dark, and the hallways smelled of a watered-down cleaning agent. As usual Ceylon had his own plans. We'd not pay for this dwelling. A kleptomaniac by trade, Ceylon lifted a key from the wall, taking the stairs fast until we settled into a room no bigger than a closet. It wasn't long before we rained havoc, our shit spilled everywhere, candles and incense, CDs and books in no fucking order. I looked up and saw Ceylon's madness already smudged in red on the ceiling: *DeFiAnCe in RiOts*, the prose of living life on the edge.

"Nobody'll find us here...not for a while."

"Until you fuck up," I said.

"Why can't you accept me the way I accept you?" Ceylon was angry. He ripped my t-shirt down the center, twisted one of my nipples until he drew blood.

"I hate it when you do that. I can't afford new clothes."

"But I love it when you get mad."

"Love?"

"Love is..." Ceylon looked in the mirror, sizing himself up. "Never mind!"

Then he made his move. It was the usual carnality and rage, his hand seizing the back of my neck, freezing me in place as his tongue left a trail of fire on my cheek. When we kissed, I tasted engine oil, and I was in full surrender as his hand cupped my testicles.

"You don't understand," Ceylon said. "People refuse to accept the fact that we don't know who we are or where we're going in life. They terrorize themselves."

"I understand that. I've been with plenty of men to know."

"You're a lousy hooker," Ceylon scowled. "You've no idea what's *really* going on. The political, the religious, and educational authorities are forcing their reality down our throats."

I lit a Parliament. "You sound paranoid."

Ceylon turned up the Logitech subwoofer that we always took with us on our road trips. Deep bass flooded my body, trampled through the whorls of my brain. Then Ceylon pulled out a fresh bottle from his bag.

"Gimme some!"

I took the bottle and drank deeply. My face immediately reddened as the liquor burned down to my bladder. But it was doing the trick; I was relaxed, in my most vulnerable state of mind...which turned me feral.

"How long were we away?" I asked.

"About a year."

I spread myself across the bed, pulled Ceylon's heart-shaped face close to my own. He smelled of autumn and burning leaves. I bit his lip and pulled, stripping off a layer as thin as a rose petal. I saw blood star his mouth, then drizzle over his rib cage to finally blend with the intricate tattoos he had gotten years before.

"You taste like the end of summer," I said.

Ceylon was smiling. The blood turned him on, belt buckle already undone so that I could see his seven-inch meat white as a newborn star. I refused to breathe until I worked him into the pleasures and treasures of orgasm, until a warm salty flood coated my throat.

"Do it again," Ceylon said.

"I don't want to hurt you."

"But you hurt them."

Because you told me to.

***

I came to New York City in 2013, settling in the bohemian paradise of the East Village. My luggage consisted of a backpack filled with books, CDs and one change of clothing. Though the buildings were in shambles and the streets more compact than every town north, the city was not as unwelcoming or dirty as it's notoriously known. Spring had turned the air crisp; all the sidewalk trees were in bloom and the sweet brown scent of Arabica coffee was everywhere.

I soon discovered that the streets were not lined with garbage or bums as one is told about this seedy city, but with plants and elaborate signs. All the busy avenues were taken over by Starbucks, banks and retail chains. Storefronts were dressed as luxuriant as the mannequins that filled their windows; the chemical smell of cleanliness was almost sickening. This was not the playground of innovation and deviance that I had read about in so many books.

Because I lacked the necessary skills to keep a minimum wage job, for a while the streets were my home. Long warm days slid into even longer, sweltering nights. I noticed that the people here came in two forms: the version when the sun was up and the version when the sun went down. Business attire and iPhones were traded for cigarettes and liquor in brown paper bags.

I perused the parks and shelters looking for the company of a sordid lot, and it wasn't long before I discovered that beneath all the glitz, glam and cover up, New York City was still as ugly as its reputation. I crossed paths with peddlers, transients and transplants, winos, beggars, hookers and street musicians. None of them had a dime to spare, but all of them were more than willing to give in to human nature no matter how divided they were by their vices and virtues.

At that time I was staying with a transsexual prostitute named Kai. Though she was painfully young the streets had worn her down considerably. Her hair was considerably thin, and her countenance was flawed. The makeup she wore turned her face into a scary raccoon rather than the porcelain beauty she was itching to achieve.

"Men will do anything to get off," Kai told me. "It's coded in their nature. Gay or straight or still questioning, they're all pigs."

Whenever Kai smiled, I saw a huge gap between her teeth. Sometimes, I stuck a finger in it to feel her tongue.

"Do you find our ruthless existence appealing?" I asked.

"Absolutely."

Kai took me under her wing but warned me that once you start hooking there was no way out. If I accepted that self-degradation, it wasn't such a bad way to get paid. Hooking, I admit, was hard at first, but once I put myself out there under Kai's guidance, I became the nascent king of the streets.

"It's easy money," Kai would say. "Just do what they say, even if they hit you."

"Hit?" I asked.

"A black eye won't kill ya. But having no money will."

I found out fast why Kai was missing a few teeth. The first guy who laid his hands on me did it just because he could, a man passing through New York on business whose ego was as big as his wallet. The meet was cordial at first. He was into rough play, tugged my longish hair as his cock slid into me. Once he finished dumping all his gayness into my intestine, he said it was people like me why the world was going to shit. The homosexual agenda, to be precise.

I took my money and called him a boy-fucker. The next think I remembered was his hands clasped around my neck and a bright shock of light before waking up outside of his hotel, my nose bleeding and lip swollen.

"What a flaming piece of shit," Kai said when I got home.

"I got the last word in...I think."

Three weeks later I came home after a difficult trick to find Kai stone-cold dead and a needle sticking out of her arm. Her face was a mask of gore—someone had done her in for the last time. Luckily, her death hadn't left me in vain. I was ripe with wisdom now that I understood that the human body was not just a temple, but a vessel. It could bring us to completion, or it could bury us, but that depended on how we used it. Youth was the key to getting us there.

That night a client sent me an Uber. A Chinese-American man who liked a finger up his ass while getting sucked. His cum was bitter and copious; it burned halfway down my throat. When it was over, he gave me a crisp Ben Franklin, then ushered me to the front door and slammed it in my face.

I barely got my laces tied, tripped and clocked the side of my head against a radiator. When the stars drained away from my vision, I tasted blood on my lip. Through my embarrassment, past the satisfaction of getting paid, animosity reached the surface. I screamed as loud as I could, smashing the window above the radiator with my fist. But he never answered. In my defeated state I wiped the blood from my head and wrote BOY FUCKER on his door.

Fearing that he would report me to the police, I decided that it was time to leave Manhattan and take my trade to Brooklyn. The minute I stepped off the L train I felt a change in the air and judging by the thrift shop fashions I could tell that the people cared less about Ivy League education and salary, focusing their energy on creativity.

I sat on a park bench waiting for anything—a car to pull up, a passerby to ask for a blowjob—until the streetlights swirled like hypnosis. Just before dawn I heard a car horn beeping and someone yelling. I got up and stumbled my way toward it, a two door Honda Prelude that was deliberately parked beneath a broken light. The window rolled down slowly.

"You on duty?" Moonlight filled the boy's face. "Looks like someone had their way with you."

I tsked. "It's nothing. Fifty for a quickie; a solid bill to spend the night."

I smelled youth and carelessness, more than the Parliament smoke that tainted his breath. From what I could see he looked to be the same height as I, average by North American standards. His eyes had a weird purple tint, and his smile was so sharp it could cut into glass. If humans could ever reach that remote concept of perfection, I had found it.

"Why don't you get in?" the boy pulled a wad of cash out of his pocket. "I just want your ear."

With the fear of the police still racing through

me, I took him up on his offer. We rode back into Manhattan, and my first instinct was to take cover, maybe stick my head into his lap, suck him off until I made my wage, but he didn't want that from me, at least not at first.

"I'm not interested in your rudimentary services."

"What?"

The boy lit a cigarette. "If you listened instead of talking so much, I'll get to the point."

"As long as it comes with money, talk away."

"My name is Ceylon," and he put his hand out to meet mine.

"Efrain."

That was when I noticed that *both* of his hands weren't on the wheel, and that the Prelude was still driving. I knew that technology in cars had advanced to the point of self-braking and self-parking, but self-driving? The idea was preposterous. The road was just too dangerous to allow such a thing. There were more cars these days than ever, and that meant more drivers, more bad judgment calls and thus, more accidents. No machine could handle such a conscientious responsibility.

"You look like you've never seen a car drive

itself," Ceylon said.

"I never have."

"But a boy like you must've been in many cars."

"What's that supposed to mean?"

Ceylon ignored my question. "If the car trusts you, it'll take you into its care."

It turned out that Ceylon was truly after my ear. But there wasn't much to tell him. Life before New York had been erased from my memory, and hooking was about the only thing I did with my time.

"To be so chained to your self-hate is a disease," Ceylon chuckled. "That's not what I want in a friend."

"What are you talking about?"

"Your face says it all. You hate yourself because you don't fit in."

I lit a cigarette, looked away from him.

"We're all on this planet, at this certain time, because we have a unique purpose."

Though he spoke in maze-like patterns, I quickly discovered that Ceylon and I had much in common. We were both dissatisfied with life, numb and dumb to every voice and reason but our own.

We called no place home; no city could excite us enough to stay. Order, rule and regulation were dull concepts. We were both twisted into a silent scream.

"Maybe death is my only commitment in life," I said.

"To age and rot and turn to bones is part our ephemeral beauty."

"But is it liberation?" I asked.

"It doesn't matter. We're all dust in the end."

Ceylon marked me with his stormy eyes, then bit his lip piercing. When he put his skinny arm around me I could see all his ornate ink. Crop circles and hexagrams; poetry and palindromes. I was immediately enamored. A calm rush flooded my senses. Love?

"You're a natural beauty," Ceylon said after taking a pull of his cigarette. "Think of all the things you can do with it."

He was now completely looking away from the road. But the wheel was turning, the gear shifting. When a red light popped up the Prelude stopped, and when it turned green, we began to head north on the West Side Highway.

I shuddered, tried to make sense of what I was seeing, but Ceylon was already taking off my jacket, his calloused fingers running down my sternum. When we kissed, I could feel the beat of his heart on my lips. Suddenly, our clothes were restrictive pieces of cotton. I had to get them off immediately.

"Let's get out of the city," Ceylon said. "I'll take you anywhere you want to go. New Orleans? Chicago? San Francisco? Say it, and we shall ride."

"Just drive," I said.

But to Ceylon or the Prelude, I didn't know.

***

"It's time that you learn the art of resistance," Ceylon said.

We drove away from the restrictions of society like ghosts too quick to be seen, a journey into our own inner darkness: Beauty and the Beast, Jekyll and Hide, Captain Ahab and the White Whale. I waved goodbye to the only city that that made me want to stay—the place where I had made it—but I did not tear up, did not even promise that I'd be back.

Clouds inked the sky the warmer the weather became, and the air thinned so that for the first time ever I could breathe easily. The drive was borderline hypnosis. Between Ceylon's venomous rhetoric and the sound of the road hissing beneath me, I'd almost forgotten that I'd taken a stranger up on his offer without thinking of my own safety. But was that any different from hooking?

"They want us to all be the *same*. To work, consume, to remain stupid...to follow. I could go on forever."

I stuck my head out the window, letting warm air lick my face and hair. "Maybe you're overthinking it."

"No, I'm not." Ceylon lit a long cigarette, gripped my wrist with his spider-fingers. "I would kill myself if I had to wake up every day and go to the same dreadful office and see the same drab people."

"Some people are content. Can't you accept that?"

"They make me sick"

We took shelter on whatever grounds would keep us until the poison of law forced us on the move. There was no point in trying to listen to reason—we were to be nameless and free—as we headed straight down the road to nowhere. Sometimes, on long drives, the air became permeated with the smell dust and bones, the permanent mark of moving through another town, another dusky hole in the center of the earth.

Days spiraled into nights and nights faded to days. The Prelude was our trustworthy guide. Sometimes I wondered if it could read my mind as we always wound up in places I had thought about the night before; I also wondered if it had warmed up to me faster than Ceylon wished. One thing about the Prelude was that it never made me feel unsafe. I'd experienced that bottomless feeling one too many times in New York, but with Ceylon to my left, the car seat warm and the engine singing me to sleep every night, I was in heaven.

But Ceylon would constantly remind that Hell was empty.

"The devil's here and he takes many forms."

"Why is the devil always *he*?"

Some nights we'd stare into the night sky, our backs resting against the windshield of the Prelude, warmed by the engine heat. The countryside moon always felt too close for comfort; I often thought it would fall right on my head, or the stars themselves drip fire down my throat.

"What do you know about the moon?" I asked.

"Not much."

"Bummer," I sighed.

"And what do you know about it?"

"Well, its birth was a violent one," I began. "Proto-Earth collided with another planetoid, and part of the debris that was thrown into orbit is now what we call the earth's dark daughter: the moon."

"Then it would make perfect sense," Ceylon said.

"What do you mean?"

"The evil that's between us."

I didn't respond.

"You're not like them, Efrain. We can do this together."

As soon as we passed DC I was expected to start working again, but not in the same way that I was used to. Ceylon wanted to exploit the frustration that I kept dormant, let it loose like a caged animal. I told him about the guys who beat me up, the ones who did it just because they could, because I was so much smaller than them. This touched Ceylon in ways that I didn't expect. He threw a fit, swearing to multiple gods that if anyone ever laid a finger on me again, they would pay. I assured him that wasn't necessary, but once Ceylon got something into his head there was no stopping him.

"Why did you let them do that to you?"

The Prelude sounded like it had growled in agreement.

"Because I need money to live."

"With me, you don't!"

Then Ceylon went into story mode. Apparently, all I needed in life was my young face and skinny body. Everything else would be eventual. But I told him that things like gas and chips and beer weren't free, and to spite me Ceylon would get me these things from every rest stop we went into with his special five-finger discount. That was when something dawned upon me: we'd yet to fill up the Prelude with gas ever since we left NYC, and we were far enough south now that the tank would have been empty two times over. But I dared not say a thing.

"Why don't you get a real job?" I asked.

"Fuck that!" Ceylon sighed. "I'd rather eat dirt."

The selection of men outside of the city was less than affluent. It took three tricks to make up for the money I would've been able to score in one up north. Sometimes the guys hit me, and sometimes they paid less than half of the agreed charge. I never let Ceylon see me cry; never let him know where to find the guys, because in the end their fists were nothing compared to their own self-hate.

"That's what I like to see," Ceylon said. "Disgust in your eyes."

I didn't even realize he was there. The poor trucker had just pulled up his pants when Ceylon swung the Louisville Slugger and cracked his kneecap. The man hit the pavement fast, and when he howled birds flew out of the trees. Ceylon brought the bat down on the man's other knee, took his wallet and the wedding band off his finger, and then pushed me into the driver's seat.

"Do it," Ceylon said.

My seat was strangely cold, like the car hadn't been turned on in months even though we were just in it. Ceylon fiddled with the keys madly, pulled the shift into drive and then tapped my knee so that my foot pressed the gas pedal. But the car refused to move, even with the engine roaring and the wheels sending smoke all around us, bringing to life the heated argument between Ceylon and the Prelude, as if it was intelligent enough to talk back.

"Fucking brat!" Ceylon yelled. "You move when I tell you to."

"What are you trying to do?"

"Just drive!"

Ceylon punched the dashboard, which sent the car forward, its wheels angled so that they crushed the man's head in one shot. My hands were not on the wheel and my foot had long left the gas pedal. All I could do was turn the music up to drown out the screams as lifeless jelly exploded out of the man's ears. In that moment, I was overcome with a queer relief.

"Brilliant," Ceylon said.

"WHAT DID YOU DO?" I found myself yelling.

"You have the gift," Ceylon said as if nothing had happened.

"I don't have any gift!"

Ceylon ignored me. "This defiant car thinks it's going to get one over on me."

"It has more of a conscience than you ever will."

We drove all night. I fell in and out of sleep, dreaming of brains and splintered bone. When I woke the sun was in my face, the car a hot box. I had no idea where we were, how long I'd been out, but Ceylon was washing the wheels and whistling. I could smell blood and burnt rubber; the echo of the trucker's scream burrowed deep into my head.

"I hocked the wedding band," Ceylon said when he got back into the car. "Two bills, but I had to convince the pawn shop it was really silver."

"I think I'm going to be sick," and I really was, my stomach in knots and my head all foggy.

"It'll pass."

Back in the passenger seat my heart was racing. A few hours later Ceylon stopped at a convenience store in the middle of what seemed like a forest. We could have been in South Carolina or the backwoods of Alabama, any place where the trees had full reign, as their relationship with the sun was healthy and bright. I didn't follow Ceylon in, as I knew what he was about to do. I put the music up in the car, "Zero Sum" by Nine Inch Nails. The lyrics spoke worlds to me, shaming us…doomed from the start. Prophecy fulfilled?

I closed my eyes and swam into the bass and keyboard. Just as the song was ending Ceylon opened the door without talking, threw a bag of Doritos into my lap and put a six-pack of Lagunitas next to my feet. He started the car and backed into the street furiously without saying a word. From the rearview mirror I saw a heavy-set woman rushing out with a gun in her hand, aiming right for us.

"Drive!" I screamed.

The road spilled out before us, a silver and black ribbon. The first bullet shattered the back window; the second punched through the trunk.

The third flew right past my head and out the windshield.

"She fell for the old water bottle in my pocket trick," Ceylon burst out in laughter. "Got us a few hundred bucks and some food."

The Prelude sent us hurtling through a dozen towns and cities. I immediately found something oddly in common with all these places: architectural design was in a civil war. Hand crafted stonework gave way to sandblasted brick, archaic beauty faded before the heat of contemporary trends. It seemed these cities were the start of an antediluvian tale, and Ceylon and I were the main characters.

By the time I was ready for my next trick, my heart was hardened and my soul heavy as stone. I sort of understood why Ceylon did what he did, knowing very well that he'd never do it to me, which made me feel special.

That night I met a guy at a truck stop after chatting on Grindr. He was scared, but too horny to care about his own safety. I straddled his lap and gyrated until he oozed inside me. He gave me a fifty and asked me to leave, his face red and wet, reminding me so much of all those guys who used to hit me.

I ordered him out of the car and pulled out the switchblade Ceylon gave to me. This time I was not going to let someone hit me. I swung left to right, hitting cheek and lips, running it down his chest until my hand was warm with blood. The guy fell to the pavement, blinded by his own tears, and before I could do anything else Ceylon pulled up and honked.

"You're a mess," he said.

"That felt amazing."

Ceylon's eyes widened. "I told you it's liberating to watch them fall."

"Yes, it is," I reached out and grabbed Ceylon's hand, but he pulled it away.

"I hope you're not falling in love with me. I know that look."

"What?"

"Labels will never work for us."

I'd never felt so many feelings in my life. Every time we touched the hairs on my skin would stand, as if he infected me with a great electric charge, but for Ceylon I was just a flesh doll. The more I yearned for him the more walls he put up. What was the harm in wanting to feel normal? What was so wrong with the bliss of ignorance?

"We can't stop. It's in you and me…to be different."

We drove through another five cities or so. Not Ceylon or I, but the car itself. Through my defeat I managed to keep working, but with a new outlook: clientele were meat puppets that deserved no respect. It was then that money started coming in on a steady schedule, sometimes more than we could handle.

"They still sicken me," Ceylon said.

"Even though they pay our bills?"

Ceylon scowled. "We don't got any bills. Even if we did, I'd never pay them."

"You still didn't answer my question."

"The answer is," Ceylon pulled back his dark hair and lit a cigarette. "They'll eventually hurt us"

He was in a state of malcontent, convinced that revolutions were on the rise, but that we were one step ahead as all the problems that divided normal people—religion, race, class, money and sexual orientation—couldn't touch us.

At sunset we spotted a young boy walking north toward the highway. I saw that his face hadn't yet washed itself of its teenage years, and though we never got his name, we did ask if he needed a ride. The look in his eyes was apprehension at first, seeing bullet holes in the car, which made such perfect sense it made me laugh. Ceylon managed to convince him, naturally, that we could bring him safely to his destination for a small fee.

Later, he drugged the beer that he offered the boy, and as soon as he knocked out Ceylon hit him over the head with the Louisville slugger to make sure he stayed asleep. *Watch me*, he said. The Grand Finale. Stripping off his clothes layer by smelly layer, and Ceylon made sure to pocket the wallet and cell phone. I saw the boy's stiff cock, heartbreaking sag of balls, and a pink eye between his ass cheeks as the blade drew a crimson frown ear to ear, then a velvety line down the sternum and through the abdomen.

"You're fucking crazy," I said.

Ceylon didn't respond.

"Don't you think it's wrong?"

"They're the dead and dying. Can't you smell them wasting away?"

I was suddenly taken over by an image of this life repeating itself, and I knew then that Ceylon was bad for me.

"Where are you going to put the body?"

"To the edge of the lake. The gators will do the rest."

We left a red trail with every step we made.

Good thing that there were no authorities in sight. As good as it felt to hurt those who might in the future hurt me, I didn't get off to it like Ceylon did. It made me just feel empty, which I subconsciously realized made all our efforts in living life dangerously pretty pointless.

Not too long after midnight, Ceylon and I were back on the road. I didn't talk; he drank a beer while driving. The night wind was pricked with stars and fireflies, the passing trees settled with moonlight. I dreaded Ceylon's next move as I could see his eyes darting to and fro, sometimes paying attention to the road sometimes not. Did he really have to?

"I wanna go back to the city," Ceylon said. "I'm sick of the road. Plus, I don't know how much longer the Prelude's going to hold out."

True to his word, the engine light was on alongside a bright red exclamation point. I'd no clue what either of them meant, but any idiot can figure out that the car needed service. I could not recall the last time we'd gotten the oil changed, or even a tune up. But I didn't add my two cents, knowing very well that the latter stated were moot points in Ceylon's head.

"Can you drive? I'm sick of it."

I got behind the wheel. The second I did the

engine light turned off and the Prelude went back to smooth sailing. Ceylon didn't know this, but from the moment my foot eased onto the pedal, it was as if the car itself trusted me. The Prelude never hissed, never complained when I hit a bump. It seemed the car was driving happily for the first time, only because I was in the driver's seat.

When dawn bled light into the sky, I fell asleep.

Somehow, the car kept going.

***

Teetering in a part of Brooklyn where buildings slashed the sky black and light was swallowed whole, I stood around patient as a grave waiting to be filled. It was the usual gimmick: me with a cigarette in hand and liquor on my breath, ripped clothes to attract the worst of the city—so long as they paid. Above, the moon was waking the silver ghosts of hookers, their shadows sharp as knives and their eyes bright as the gas lamp stars.

But something was different about this night.

Ceylon had chivied off to a party that was to start at midnight and end at 9am. I remembered looking at the advertisement and rolling my eyes:

silver and black juxtaposed in space, poetry's informal statement. Since I expected to hear nothing from him for a while, I waited for a customer impatiently.

An hour flew by. Not one person was looking to fuck or get sucked. Nobody had money to spare. I began walking west on Myrtle Avenue toward Bushwick Avenue, all the while forcing myself to look at the street rather than the people and things around me. Brooklyn was quiet, ominous, but Manhattan was raging in the bright vista. I thought about Ceylon partying, maybe hurting some unsuspecting boy and finding an inner peace because of it.

Then there was a sound. The hum of an engine, the slight squeal of rusty brakes. In the cover of darkness, I saw the Prelude across the street, waiting, watching, needing. Nobody was behind the wheel, and I knew that was perfectly fine as I put myself in the passenger seat and turned up the music.

The wheel cut left, and we were out of Brooklyn, rushing into Manhattan like blood pumping through my own vessels. I didn't ask the Prelude any questions, because I could feel it inside of me as if we were one vital organ. When I focused again, I saw that we were on The Bowery heading north, ending at Astor Place. The Prelude was slowly skulking the street for something I did not know.

But out of the corner of my eye I saw him.

Doing what he did best.

Ceylon dressed to impress, high top converse sneakers and a shitty denim jacket. In his arms was a pretty little boy, tattooed and hair that hung loose behind his ears. Another victim in his game. The Prelude hissed in protest, and then sped toward Ceylon. The headlights illumined his eyes, blotted out the fine features of his face as the boy ran out of Ceylon's arms for his own safety. The Prelude skidded to a stop just before crushing Ceylon.

"You ballsy little shit!" Ceylon punched the hood.

"Get in." I yelled. "Time to talk."

Cars behind us went into a mad song of horns. Ceylon got into the driver's seat and the Prelude sped up again.

"You and this filthy car!"

"You actually *like* to do this to people," I said bravely.

"Is this an interrogation?"

The rearview mirror cracked when Ceylon hit it, and the car whined as if it could feel pain. My reflection looked grotesque, disjointed. Memories filled my head, good and bad, beautiful and repulsive. The spontaneity we shared had grown tired. I was going nowhere in this ocean of chaos, also known as life.

"Where's all this coming from?" Ceylon said.

"You crave a life that doesn't repeat, and yet you do it so well."

Ceylon gritted his teeth. "Oh, how I wish I could make you despise me!"

"Then why don't you?"

Ceylon spit. "If I left right now, you'd only end up hating yourself. You and this wretched vehicle."

He might have been right, but I knew that I couldn't go on doing this any longer. On the outside I may have played the part of the freak, but Ceylon was the true monster. To be evil is to enforce your own ill will upon someone else's fragility, and Ceylon had done it so well. In that moment his aesthetic beauty faded; the skin that I once worshipped peeled away like our consummate victims. His eyes shriveled and fell out of his skull, his lips…his tongue, were now made of cobweb. What I saw was a shell of someone that I used to know, a great void opening the gateway to his abysmal soul.

In that, I knew we had more in common than

ever.

I would think for myself and question authority.

I put a thought into my head, willed it so hard that the Prelude understood the command in a matter of seconds. We were moving fast up the FDR Drive, the lights passing us crazily, cars moving out of our way. Ceylon looked not the least bit thrilled, cracking a beer open with his teeth and finishing it in two sips.

But the car kept going.

I put the thought into my head again, remembering that all of us, dead or alive, are eternal.

We could always start fresh.

That's when the engine cut off and the tires screeched as the car came to an abrupt stop. Being that Ceylon wasn't wearing his seatbelt, he went flying through the windshield. Little shards of glass hit my face, piled in my lap. For a moment time came to a halt, and I saw my life stretch out before me, a clean slate clean as the open road.

Then the Prelude started up again.

With no intent to stop, not even with Ceylon rolling on the pavement in front of us, his arms and legs twisting at angles that could not be, and his body already painted in blood. As the cars were piled behind us, sirens already whistling in the distance, the Prelude crushed Ceylon's body as it made its way to the 59th Street Bridge. A few minutes after that, rain began to wash us clean.

There was no remorse or fear of loneliness. I knew that one day I'd revert to the dust that came from stars, become compacted and build momentum so that another big bang would be inevitable. A cosmic irony told at my expense.

Ceylon and I would be together soon…if anything at all.

Bad Night at the Office

By

Emma K. Leadley

Hannah yawned, stretching her shoulders before glancing at her watch. It was close to 10pm, far later than she'd intended to work, and everyone else had gone home. Even the cleaners with their squeaky cart and loud vacuums had finished. She logged out under the dim glow of her monitors and glared at her dirty coffee mug. *It can wait*, she muttered, and made her way through the soft-cladded walls of the cubicle maze to the elevator. She tapped her foot, impatient at its seemingly wilful lack of speed, as it whirred slowly into position before the metal doors creaked open.

A buzz from her pocket made Hannah roll her eyes. But it was Steph, so guilt quickly replaced irritation. "Hey babe," she answered. "I'm so sorry. I'm just leaving—Shit!" The elevator doors closed. She sighed. "Are you on your way? Shall I order us takeout to pick up on the way home?"

Hannah waited for the elevator again, thumbing their usual Chinese order into her phone. By the time the doors opened, food was confirmed, and she stepped in. She winced under the bright overhead lights, and stale smells from the day, and on autopilot, pressed her thumb onto the button for reception. It started with an expected shudder and as it moved, she looked at her reflection in the mirrored walls. A tired version of herself stared back: pale and gaunt with dark eyes. *Time for a break,* she muttered to her reflected self.

On the ground floor, the elevator opened up into the reception, soft carpet underfoot and beyond that, tiled floor in the atrium area. In summer it made a nice place to take a break, full of leafy plants and a far cry from the artificial light and air freshened atmosphere of the office. Now, as she strode towards the carpark, the near-full moon rose low in the sky, casting long shadows. Her soft soles barely made a sound and she took a deep breath, enjoying the relative quiet after a long day working on a complex contract.

She rubbed her temples and glanced at her phone. Still a few minutes before Steph's truck would swing in to view, but a wait in the fresh air would be more pleasant than remaining inside. She reached the glass exit doors, reaching out to swipe her security card across the scanner on the side to release the lock. And screamed.

A man's face slammed up against the glass. One eye was swollen nearly shut, covered in purple bruising visible through strings of blood. He beat against the door with bleeding, trembling hands and she caught sight of torn nails, ripped clothes and dirt. With a shock, she realised it was Gary from HR.

He was a stickler for rules and 'no pass, no entry' was one of his constant gripes. She held up her own pass and pointed at it, *that would show him and his creepy-assed ways.* But, guilt kicked in at the state of him — something was evidently wrong — and even as he mouthed something that looked like 'please', Hannah had swiped her card for him to stumble through the doors.

"Lock 'em" he croaked, falling forward. He peered out into the night, across the car park. "They're coming. We're not safe. Lock the doors."

"What the hell, Gary?" asked Hannah. "Have you been drinking? Drugs?"

He ripped the swipe card from her hand and passed it over the scanner, pressing the lock button. The doors clicked closed and he flinched before sinking to the floor and curling into a foetal position, moaning.

Hannah peered out across the car park letting her eyes adjust to the darkness. Illuminated by the dim light of the moon, and a couple of security lights, a couple of men appeared in the far distance. "There's just scrubland over that side of the car park. What's going on?"

She knelt beside Gary and put her hand on his knee. He jerked back, the rip in his trousers revealed his leg, bruised and bloody. His ankle and knee were swollen, and his skin was clammy to her touch. She looked more closely at his face, his unharmed eye was glassy and unfocussed and beads of sweat ran, mixed with grime and blood. "Hey," she said more gently. "What happened?"

"I left here just as it was getting dark and was climbing into my car when I thought I heard a scream," Gary said, gulping the air, his voice shrill in the void of the atrium. "So I grabbed a golf club as protection and went to see what was going on." He paused, his good eye widening, and winced. "And, oh god it was horrible!"

"Go on," said Hannah, eyes back to the still approaching men in the distance.

"I followed the noise. And... and... they'd pinned someone down and were eating him alive." Gary moaned again.

"That's ridiculous." Hannah rubbed at her face. *I'm too tired for this shit.*

"I saw it, Hannah. With my own eyes. They were eating this guy alive and he didn't stop screaming and then we locked eyes and he stopped. Just for a second. Like he accepted defeat. That's when they looked up and noticed me and I ran."

"Go on..."

Gary's voice cracked. "I turned and ran but tripped on a branch, twisting my ankle. I tried to get up, but it hurt and I fell again. One of them caught me before I could get to my feet. He, no, the thing... it ... it grabbed my foot and started pulling. I wrenched my knee trying to get out of its grasp, but whatever it was, it was too strong..." He tailed off, pushing his head between his knees. "I thought it was going to rip my leg off."

"Were they high on drugs or something? That would give someone artificial strength, perhaps?"

"It resembled a man. Deranged. Mad. But jacked up. Talking in grunts and lumbering and lurching like it'd lost most control of movement. It reminded me of playing on the X-box." He whimpered and took a deep gasp of air. "I think they're zombies."

Hannah turned away, quickly covering up her mouth as a nervous giggle left her. She'd always known Gary to be strait-laced, even if he did look a bit too long at the women in the office before averting his gaze. She looked round. He was off his rocker, but *something* had happened, and she was trapped in the office building with him.

"Nonsense," she said, aiming for a soothing tone. "Zombies don't exist. They're men. Probably high as kites on something." She shuddered at the thought before her own eyes widened. *Steph.*

She grabbed her phone and dialled. "C'mon, connect," she muttered. "Where's the ringing tone?" She redialled, pacing back and forth, picking at her lip with her thumb and forefinger. Still nothing. She hit redial, looking out to the car park, hoping she'd catch her girlfriend in time to keep her from the weird idiots who still ambled towards the bright light of the atrium. Eventually, Steph's voicemail kicked in. "Hey, babe, glad I got through. There's something really weird going on in the carpark here. Keep your doors locked and park next to the front door. Please. Um, stay safe. Oh, and we might need to take someone to the hospital." She hung up, taking a few deep breaths to calm down and then face her colleague. She realised Gary was still talking, sitting up with his knees pulled close to his chest.

"I managed to whack it with my golf club, somehow I'd kept a grasp of it. Thank god. Whatever that monster was, it didn't even flinch. I hit it again and again. But nothing, it just kept on pulling at me and grunting and didn't seem to notice. I should have broken its neck. Then it got distracted by another like it and I managed to get to my feet. Golf clubs make good crutches it seems." He giggled, high pitched and nervous. "Oh god, I got away and that poor sucker probably died. It could have been me. Oh god. What are we going to do?" Gary's voice rose in pitch and he grasped for Hannah, clinging on to her ankle, and fell silent.

Hannah looked down at him and shook her head. His shoulders heaved up and down and loud sobs filled her ears. "I'm going to get you some water," she said. "Just over at reception."

"Don't leave me." Gary clung harder. "Please. Don't abandon me to these things."

"I'll stay in view. You can see the reception desk from here." Hannah glanced back out the doors to see the men, well perhaps Gary was right, — *creatures?* — were getting closer. They did look oddly shaped and certainly couldn't move in a straight line, lurching from side to side and back and forth like toddlers learning to walk. *Think, Hannah, think...*

She bit the inside of her lip and jogged over to the desk, grabbing a couple of water bottles from the guest fridge. The security screen showed the log of the last entries and exits, her recent swipes at the top of the list. Gary was right about his timing; at least, she realised, his exit swipe visible on the log. *Think.* He had clearly been attacked, was panicking and right now seemed to be running on adrenaline. Whatever state he was in wouldn't last so perhaps it really wasn't safe to stay where they were. She looked back at Gary. He sat on the floor in front of the doors, his hands jammed into his armpits as he rocked. *Useless then...*

She picked up the front desk phone and dialled the emergency line. It rang, over and over. The company's hired security firm went through to voicemail. *Shit.*

She hurried back to Gary, unscrewed one of the bottles and passed it over. "Drink this, you'll feel a bit better." She did the same, trying to slow her breathing and remain calm. No point in panicking too.

Gary gulped the contents down, stopping to look around in fast nervous movements. When his gaze reached the car park, he stared out at the lumbering figures. "They're still coming. We need to do something."

"Whatever the fuck is happening, you don't have to tell me that." Hannah paced again, irritated by Gary's reliance on her. *Where was Steph?* She'd let Gary in because he didn't have his pass and — *that's it!*

"Gary," she said, quietly. "I think I have an idea."

"Go raid the executive suite and get absolutely rat-ass drunk?"

"Don't be stupid. I don't want to lose my job." She paused. "Nah. I'm being impractical; it involves you running. But we could wait in one of the meeting rooms till Steph gets here." Hannah's brow wrinkled. "She should be here by now though. Wonder what the hold-up is."

"Zombies..." Gary whispered, his voice so quiet, she could barely hear him.

"Okay," Hannah rolled her eyes. "So let's imagine they're zombies. Whatever they are, you said they're not very coordinated and can't move fast, right?"

"Yeah..."

"And say they got into the atrium here, they couldn't go anywhere else because everything is locked down without a pass, so they'd be trapped?"

Gary looked up at her, wincing at the light. "Okay, but if we let them in here, where the hell do we go? I don't want to be stuck in the building with them."

"What if we trap them here, barricade ourselves in the meeting room that has the emergency exit, and when Steph arrives, leave from there? I can tell her where to park up so her pickup is close to the door. And then we can get you some medical help. Yes, this could work."

"What if there's more of them?" hissed Gary. "And they're outside."

"Okay then, you stay here, and I'll go get rescue." Hannah raised her eyebrows and stared at her colleague.

"You're crazy."

"I know, but if we stay here they might get in anyway and then whatever they are, we're toast. I'd rather take my chances on the outside, thanks, where we can at least drive out of danger."

"Don't lea—"

"I know, 'don't leave you'. Come on then." Hannah knelt down and started pulling Gary upwards. His arm shook under her and he winced at every movement. "You're going to have to suck it up, I'm afraid."

Gary whimpered in return but became more pliable and with a bit more shuffling, Hannah was able to get his arm around her shoulder and semi-drag him on his feet towards the reception desks and nearby meeting rooms. Halfway across the floor she glanced back. A bloody and muddy trail followed them ending at Gary's foot. *Shit*.

Looking out the doors, she winced. The

creatures were nearly on them. Misshapen and unsteady, they continued towards the light. *Like moths to a flame.*

"Gary, where's the light switch for the atrium?" Hannah asked, hope rising.

"I don't think there is one. I was told it's automated through the security system."

Hannah's shoulders sagged in defeat but she righted herself as the shift caused Gary to slide back down towards the floor. "Oh no you don't," she said. "Let's get to the meeting rooms."

A loud crack on the glass made them both jump. Several disfigured faces pressed against the front glass, eyes glazed and vacant, as they smeared themselves along, trying to look in. Chunks of flesh hung from strips of skin, bone showing through. Teeth were missing. An arm flapped and flailed at impossible angles.

"You were right, Gary," Hannah whispered, trying not to dry heave. "They're not men. They're zombies. What the fuck?"

"And one of them is the guy they were chomping earlier." Gary emitted a high pitch laugh that didn't stop.

"Hey, Mr Useless! I need your help here."

"I'm... s... sorry..." Gary took big gulps of air. "Meeting room."

"I'm going to switch the lights on in the first one, and then we can dive into the one around the corner. The one with the back exit. I don't know if that's what they're attracted to, the bright lights. Or maybe they'll follow your tracks. It's a plan though." She exhaled. "It's a plan."

Hannah leant Gary up against the wall and let herself into the meeting room visible from the atrium. Glass panels in the door illuminated the room, as the light went on and Hannah glanced round, looking for anything that could help them. With an idea building in her head, she went back to Gary. "I think I'm going to go back and grab a few things but first, let's get you safe."

In the second meeting room, the emergency light above the exit cast a green glow creating long shadows that moved and jumped as Hannah sat Gary down. "Stay here."

"Don't lea—"

"I know, but I'll be back. We need supplies."

Back in reception, Hannah watched in horror as the metal frame of the front doors seemed to be gradually caving in under the relentless banging of the zombies. Heart racing, she turned towards the elevator and stairs. "I could hide in the cubicles til daylight," she muttered. "Or perhaps the executive suite is a good way to go. Get drunk. Pass out…" She took another step. "Oh, for fucks sake, there's still that idiot. Can't leave him."

In the first meeting room, Hannah stacked the chairs and dragged them to the hideout. Rummaging in reception proved fruitful with gaffer tape, a couple of screwdrivers, a weak torch, and more water. She ripped the tops off the bottles as quickly as possible and poured it over Gary's tracks to break up the path. A crunch from the doors sent her running back to the hideout.

"You okay?" Gary sounded concerned.

"Yeah. No. I don't know." Hannah braced back against the meeting room wall, her legs turning to jelly. "I'm scared."

"Me too."

Hannah slid down the wall, head between her knees, breathing fast, the room suddenly spinning.

"Hey, Hannah!" Gary pulled himself over the carpet to her. "Don't do this. You need to pull yourself together."

A massive splintering crash from the atrium jerked Hannah to her feet. "You're right. We need to barricade the door."

She slipped the bolt round in the lock and wedged one of the chairs under the handle. With adrenaline coursing through her body, she soon had the rest of the chairs stacked in piles across the door and frame.

"There's a projector screen in here, isn't there?"

"Of course," said Gary. "What are you going to do?"

"Cut it into pieces and stick it across the door glass. Hide any sign of us."

"Nice. Should we cover the emergency light as well?"

Not quite so useless now. Hannah breathed a big sigh of relief and started cutting the screen up. "Here," she threw a piece at him. "Cover up the light. I'll do the door."

She crept to the chairs and listened. Smashing noises came from the atrium and she imagined seating being thrown and plants being uprooted. They hadn't quite reached the reception area by what she could tell. The gaffer tape ripped from the roll, sounding impossibly loud in the stillness of the room. With each piece, Hannah held her breath and listened. Nothing changed. A couple of layers of fabric on the glass later and they were plunged into darkness.

Didn't think that one through. Can't see them coming now. She shuddered.

Using her phone screen as a guide, she and Gary settled down near the emergency exit.

"I should try Steph again," Hannah said. She unlocked the phone and turned the brightness to the minimum before dialling her girlfriend. This time, it rang. Once, twice, and then she could have cried.

"That you, Hannah? Thank fuck."

"Hey." Hannah's shoulders shuddered up and down as she tried to rein in her relief. "What's going on?"

"It's mayhem. The roads are either blocked or diverted and there's helicopters circling over the city centre. I'm nearly with you but it's taking a while. Are you okay?"

"I... We... Me and Gary, that is— We're holed up in a meeting room. The...the...zombies have got in the front door. I don't know how long we've got."

"Zombies? You are kidding me."

"I've seen them Steph. Hurry. Drive into the delivery area round the back. Let me know you're here."

"Sure." There was a pause. "Love you."

"Love you too."

They sat, silently, as the dark closed in around them. Hannah brushed her fingers over the stale-smelling carpet tiles, a distraction as she tried not to pick at her nails. There must be something she could do, rather than be a sitting duck. She needed a weapon...

Gary clutched at her arm. "Did you hear that? I think they're in the other meeting room."

Through the wall came sounds of grunts and slamming. Then silence.

"I hope your girlfriend arrives soon. I don't want to die. I always thought I'd go out in a more dignified way."

"Hey, where's your company loyalty?" Hannah's mouth twitched at the thought. "Sorry. Gallows humour, I guess."

"Do you think I should write a letter, you know, just in case we don't make it and they find us? There's delegate pens and paper on the table, I just need a bit of light."

"You could do. Hold on."

Hannah grabbed the stationery and trying to remain low and quiet, stubbed her toe on the metal table legs. "Fu—" She clamped her hand over her mouth. The pen dropped to the table top, clattering and rolling. The silence rolled on as she and Gary froze and held their breath.

A loud crunch came from the wall, plasterboard falling off in rough chunks. A chink of light appeared, and a hand thrust through. The jagged edges of the hole pulled at the skin until it peeled off like a glove; plasma and fluids dripped down exposing rippling veins and wet bone. More arm pushed through and it flopped and flapped. A fetid stench replaced the musty air in the room, like something had died weeks prior and rotted down in the dark and the damp. It stung Hannah's nostrils and made her eyes water. She swallowed hard, over and over, to prevent herself from vomiting. The hand withdrew, and the groaning noise faded.

The relative silence rolled on.

Hannah handed Gary the little torch from reception and he used the dim light to scrawl on the company headed paper in jagged, twitchy handwriting. In turn, she used the light from her phone to illuminate a workspace. She emptied a table of contents and flipped it on to its side, working in slow, exaggerated movements to remain quiet. With the screwdrivers from reception, she went to work, taking off the legs, one at a time, and laid them out next to each other.

"What are you doing?" whispered Gary.

"Weapons," she replied. "They might not do much, from what you've said, but I'm not going down without a fight."

A shuffling noise came from outside followed by a thump of something into the door. Hannah grabbed a table leg and passed on to Gary. They both leant forward in nervous anticipation at what could come.

"Should we just sneak out now?" asked Hannah, her breath shallow as she whispered.

The whole door shuddered with a bang.

"What if there are more out there?"

"Damned if we do and damned if we—"

A splintering crash sent Hannah running to the fire exit. About to press the bar, her phone rang out loud clear. The groaning and crashing increased in volume.

"I'm here, where the fuck are you?" Steph demanded.

"You alone outside?"

"Yeah."

The door frame caved in and an arm flailed into the room. Hannah tried not to dry heave at the putrid stench. The chairs clattered and jammed together. She froze.

"Hannah!" Both Steph and Gary shouted at her.

She shook her head from side to side to clear

it and leant heavily on the emergency bar. Nothing happened. "Gary, help me."

They both barged against the door. It stuck. Behind them, the chair barricade broke and the room filled with the rotten stench of death and swinging lumbering bodies heading in random directions. Unable to go far, the creatures closed in.

With a last, concerted push, the door swung open and Hannah ran out, cold night air hitting her in the face. "C'mon," she yelled, and sprinted across the hard tarmac towards Steph's truck, gulping down lungfuls of fresh air, free of the cloying decay.

A scream stopped her as she reached the vehicle. She turned to see Gary being dragged back, through the half open door, by the creatures.

"Gary!" she shouted but it was too late. Frozen to the spot, she watched in horror as the creatures feasted, blood splattering up the door, her colleague still struggling and screaming until he stopped moving.

A deafening beeping filled the air followed by a revving noise. Hannah whipped her head back round, her fingers scrabbling and unable to find purchase on the handle. With effort, she slowed her fingers down enough to get her hand working, yanked open the door and threw herself on to the seat.

"Hey," said Steph. "Tough night?"

"Yeah."

"Going to close that door so we can get out of

here?"

"Yeah." Hannah pulled the door closed and crumpled forward, sobbing. "I thought I was going to die."

Steph squeezed at her arm. "But you didn't. Focus on that right now. Let's get out of here and work out what to do next." She leant over and kissed Hannah on the forehead.

Hannah closed her eyes for a second and took in the warmth of Steph's touch. "Okay," she said more steadily. "You're right."

She opened her eyes and screamed. A zombie had lumbered to the truck, illuminated by the headlights. Its hand slammed onto the bonnet. She recognised the torn trousers and shirt of her former colleague. Gary was now unrecognisable, with bulging skin on his face, the flesh splitting off the bone. Jagged edges showed a piece of his skull missing and he dragged a leg behind him at an awkward angle. Teeth marks punctuated his flesh and he groaned. Not like she'd heard him earlier but deeper, more guttural. More primal.

"Kill it. Please. Put it out of its misery." Hannah started crying again. "That was Gary."

"I don't know what kills them, but I'll try." Steph reversed the truck. The body lurched, somehow remaining upright. The tyres screeched, and Gary's zombie body bounced off the front grill and onto the bonnet.

Hannah winced as, in seeming slow motion,

he rolled over the windscreen. His face crushed against it, smearing blood and flesh, his raw bones scratching against the glass. But he kept moving. The roof crumpled under his weight and an arm came flying off to splatter on the road next to Hannah's door. With a heavy thud that shook the truck, he landed in the pickup bed and rolled over the tailgate to lay in a crumpled heap on the ground.

Steph floored the truck again, leaving a trail of smoke and exhaust dirt over the now-unmoving body.

Hannah watched in the rear-view mirror as the distance increased. Gary, or what Gary had become, didn't move. Tearing her gaze away, she looked forward again. "Shame we can't pick up that Chinese."

Steph raised her eyebrows.

"Yeah, sorry. Gallows humour." said Hannah. "It's been a bad night at the office."

Author Bios

J. Daniel Stone

NYC born and raised J. Daniel Stone writes urban horror with a queer focus. He sold his first story when he was 22-years-old and has since written four novels (The Absence of Light, Blood Kiss, Stations of Shadow and Daubed in Darkness), as well as a short story collection (Lovebites & Razorlines) and a novella (I Can Taste The Blood). He writes under a pseudonym to keep the wolves at bay.

Visit him at **www.SolitarySpiral.com** and all socials **@SolitarySpiral**

Emma K. Leadley

Emma K. Leadley (they/she) is a UK-based speculative fiction writer and queer, creative geek. They've had over 30 pieces of flash fiction and short stories published by independent presses, including Eerie River Publishing, Bag of Bones Press and Fox Spirit Books, and their novella **Telling the Bees** will be released August 2023, from NewCon Press. Emma lives in Nottingham and regularly argues with their rescue greyhound for space on the sofa. They can be found online at autoerraticism.com.

Maxwell I. Gold

Maxwell I. Gold is a Jewish American multiple award nominated author who writes prose poetry and short stories in cosmic horror and weird fiction with half a decade of writing experience. Four time Rhysling Award nominee, and two time Pushcart Award nominee, find him at www.thewellsoftheweird.com.

Mark Allan Gunnells

Mark Allan Gunnells loves to tell stories. He has since he was a kid, penning one-page tales that were Twilight Zone knockoffs. He likes to think he has gotten a little better since then. He loves reader feedback, and above all he loves telling stories. He lives in Greer, SC, with his husband Craig A. Metcalf.

Caitlin Marceau

Caitlin Marceau is a queer author and lecturer based in Montreal. She holds a Bachelor of Arts in Creative Writing, is an Active Member of the Horror Writers Association, and has spoken about genre literature at several Canadian conventions. She spends most of her time writing horror and experimental fiction, but has also been published for poetry as well as creative non-fiction. Her work includes Palimpsest, Magnum Opus, A Blackness Absolute, and her debut novella, This Is Where We Talk Things Out. Her second novella, I'm Having Regrets, and her debut novel, It Wasn't Supposed To Go Like This, are set for publication in 2023. For more, check out CaitlinMarceau.ca or find her on social media.

Brandon Ford

Brandon Ford's published works include more than a dozen titles in the realm of horror and suspense fiction. His most recent books include The Mystery of Kelly Christopher, Progressive Entrapment, Dreams of Sharp Teeth, and Drowning in Oceans of Black. He has also contributed to a number of genre anthologies, most notably The Death Panel: Murder, Madness, and Mayhem and Stiff Things: The

Splatterporn Anthology. He also hosts a weekly horror movie commentary podcast titled The Blind Rage Podcast, which can be found on iTunes and Spotify. He currently resides in Philadelphia.

Lindz McLeod
Lindz McLeod is a queer, working-class, Scottish writer and editor who dabbles in the surreal. Her prose has been published by Apex, Catapult, Pseudopod, The Razor, and many more. Her work includes the short story collection TURDUCKEN (Bear Creek Press, 2022) and her debut novel BEAST (Brigids Gate Press, 2023). Find her on Twitter @lindzmcleod or her website www.lindzmcleod.co.uk

James Lefebure
James Lefebure is a Scottish born, Liverpool living horror author. Splitting his time between watching horror, reading horror and writing horror he can often be found arguing with people that Jason would whoop Michael. His two novels The Books of Sarah and God In The Livingroom have proven to his long suffering, fantasy reading husband that James will probably never write a story about dragons or an orphan with a destiny. He can be found on Tiktok, (jameseylefebure) Instagram (Jameseylefebure) and facebook JamesLefebureWriter. He does have a twitter but doesn't understand how it works enough to use it.

Zachary Rosenberg

Zachary Rosenberg is a Jewish horror writer living in Florida. He crafts horrifying tales by night and by day he practices law, which is even more frightening. His forthcoming debut novella will be published by Brigids Gate Press and you may find his works released or forthcoming at Air and Nothingness Press and Nosetouch Press. You may follow him on Twitter at @ZachRoseWriter

Michael R Collins

Michael R Collins was born at a very young age in the wilds of southern Idaho. After a few decades, he finally got his fill of all the sagebrush and rattlesnakes he could eat, so he struck out into the world. After slinging some bass guitar, and general shenanigans in Austin, Texas, he currently lives in Pennsylvania with his partner Mel. He is a Bi author who has most recently published Miracles For Masochists (with James G. Carlson) and Verum Malum. He has a plethora of short stories, and a few alibis. (Just in case)
He is also a co-host of the Bi+ Podcast.

James Bennett

James Bennett is a British writer raised in Sussex and South Africa. His travels have furnished him with an abiding love of diverse cultures, history and mythology. His short fiction has appeared internationally and his debut novel 'Chasing Embers' was shortlisted for Best Newcomer at the British Fantasy Awards 2017. His latest fiction can be found in the well-received 'The Book of Queer Saints', BFS Horizons and The Dark magazine. Novella 'The Dust of the Red Rose Knight' came out in March 2023 and a short story collection 'Preaching to the Perverted' is set to follow next year from esteemed publisher Lethe Press.

James lives in the South of Spain where he's currently working on a new novel.

Feel free to follow him on Twitter: @JamesBennettEsq

Callum Pearce

Callum Pearce is a Dutch storyteller, originally from Liverpool. He is a fiction writer published multiple times across a variety of platforms. A Lover of the magical as well as the macabre. He lives in a foggy, old fishing town in the Netherlands with his husband, a cat shaped sprite and a trickster god in the shape of a dog.

Featured in lots of anthologies or online with stories for adults and young people. He has also written several factual articles for LGBTQ+ lifestyle and music websites. Check his pages for things that are available now, coming soon or free to read online. He is currently working with Nordic Press and running House Of Loki. They are producing excellent and engaging work for readers and writers of all ages.

Callumpearcestoryteller.com
twitter.com/Aladdinsane79
www.facebook.com/calmpeace13
house-of-loki.com
nordicpresspublishing.com

Mark Young

Mark Young is a tropical fish from the planet

Aquaria. Only when his spaceship crash landed on Earth was he compelled to document his findings in the form of (what earthlings call) horror stories.

He now lives in a lake with his life partner - Little Red Herring Hood where they write, draw and watch too many films and watch too much TV. They also raise their adopted children: all kinds of fish and other species not indigenous to local waters.

If you find this biography mildly amusing, a little salty, completely strange or terrifying, feel free to get hooked by his discoveries located on the interplanetary database: www.markyoungofficial.com

Not forgetting social docking bays: plaicehook, apistogram but not twatter (basically he doesn't have the fishing line nor the inclination). Insert happy smiley face emoji here.

Kevin J. Kennedy

Kevin J. Kennedy is a horror author, editor, and anthologist. He is also the owner of KJK Publishing.

He lives in the heart of Scotland with his wife and his three cats, Carlito, Ariel and Luna. He can be found on Facebook most days if you want to chat with him.

He fully supports LGBTQIA+ rights.

Thank You.

I'd like to thank everyone who picked up a copy of the book. Your support means the world to all of us. You allow us to continue with our passions and it makes it all worthwhile. I hope you found some new authors to follow. I hope you enjoyed out book and if you have time, I hope you can leave us a review somewhere. We would all love to hear your thoughts.

Thank you.

Kevin J. Kennedy

Printed in Poland
by Amazon Fulfillment
Poland Sp. z o.o., Wrocław